Where Two Rivers Meet

A Novel of Minnesota's Main Street Women

Cynthia Frank-Stupnik

HERITAGE BOOKS
2023

HERITAGE BOOKS

AN IMPRINT OF HERITAGE BOOKS, INC.

Published 2023 by
HERITAGE BOOKS, INC.
Publishing Division
5810 Ruatan Street
Berwyn Heights, MD 20740

Heritage Books by the author:

Pins and Needles: A Novel of Minnesota's Main Street Women

Postcards from the Old Man and Other Correspondence from Clearwater, Minnesota

Scruples and Drams: A Novel of Minnesota's Main Street Women

Steppes to Neu Odessa: Germans from Russia Who Settled in Odessa Township, Dakota Territory, 1872–1876, 2nd edition

Where Two Rivers Meet: A Novel of Minnesota's Main Street Women

Cover art by Todd Stupnik

International Standard Book Number
Paperbound: 978-0-7884-2821-0

Athena, favored daughter of the great Zeus and goddess of wisdom, patriotic war, and weaving is daring and most capable. With an olive branch at her feet, Owl and Eagle rest on her shoulders.

Chapter 1

Spin-Off

"Stop!" Abigail pleaded. "Thomas! Please, stop."

Hanging on to her husband's forearms tightly, Abigail became dizzy and nauseated. *This man could keep going.* Thomas could keep her in circular motion forever, dragging her with him.

Abigail's heart pounded as if it could beat out of her bosom. She tried wiggling out of his arms, knowing she might fly across the room if she succeeded.

This was no slow promenade-like walk into the ballroom or the sweet waltz at the beginning of this celebration. This dance was the after-show; many of the important guests had already left. With no one to impress or cause eyebrows to flare, Clearwater friends and family could be themselves. When Abigail's brother Tarrant Robinson, the band leader, shouted to his band members to play an old-fashioned Irish jig, someone pushed Thomas to the center of the dance floor. Shocked and acting helpless, Thomas loosened his tie and started to shuffle and click his heels. Like no other person in Clearwater, Thomas, T. C. or just Tom, had learned Irish music, dance, songs, and folklore from his father in Pennsylvania where he had been born and raised. John Porter had immigrated from Dublin in the early 1800s.

When Thomas pulled Abigail onto the dance floor, she stumbled along as he led her in his famous kicks and spins to impress their guests. Then someone egged on the band to go faster and shouted, "Twirl the roof off the building."

While normally she could spin as fast as her husband, tonight, Abigail tripped and slipped. With his head turned, she tried to grab his attention long enough to show she was having problems.

She felt a long lock of her gray hair break free from where it had been tightly curled and coiled on the top of her head. Now it hung around her neck like a crooked necklace. Her corset became so tight she could not gasp for air. As she sped around the room, the rich, red wallpaper with creamy velvet flowers spun into a beautiful bright light. Her first cameo, a blue and white replica of Athena, the Greek goddess, a gift from her father for all the help she gave him on his rounds delivering babies, nursing the sick, and repairing broken bones, spun like golden threads around her neck. So dizzy and tired, Abigail felt herself cross over the river and into the light as she waited to see her Lord.

"Abigail! Abigail!"

~~~~~

When she turned to see who was calling, Abigail recognized a shock of red hair bobbing up and down behind her. She waved as George vaulted to meet her at the top of one of the trails leading to Vermont's Mount Mansfield. His voice sounded as excited as his beautiful bouncing hair looked.

"Why are you following me?" Abigail laughed as she hugged her young husband who smelled like fresh linen taken off the clothes lines.

He felt good too. They came together like two magnets. In fact, if George and she had encountered each other at home, their meeting would have ended differently.

"The letter came! The letter from my cousin in Caledonia. You know, about the trip back to the California gold fields." George grabbed his wife and swung her around.

"What?" She felt her happiness fall to the ground along with the basket she had recently woven. Put me down, George!" She wiggled to get out of his grip. "Put me down!"

"Oh, Abigail, don't be silly. We've talked about this undertaking a few months now."

"I'm not being silly, and I wouldn't include me in the 'we've talked' category," she snapped. "I thought it was just that, all talk." Abigail bit her lip before adding—*and another get-rich scheme*. "I
~~~~~

know you said you wished you had a second chance to go back to California. Yet how many times did I remind you that you nearly died from malaria on the last trip? You seemed to agree that it was all foolish thinking. I thought you were listening and really hearing me."

Anger burning in her belly, Abigail felt betrayed. The two had just set up house again after his first trip. So broke and sick with nothing to show for his gold fever trip, George had returned to live with his sister Orpha and her husband, the judge. She and Cassius had remained living with her parents.

Almost always a challenge, Hannah, Abigail's mother, nagged and bullied her furiously at times. She had a few trap doors through which she could escape taking a hike with her son Cassius, climbing into the attic to rest her mind while working on her grandmother's loom, going to the shed to weave her baskets, or accompanying her father, Doctor Joseph Robinson, her shield and protector, on his medical rounds.

Walking to the edge of a ravine, Abigail looked down and around. Too early in the season for chamomile, and she was running low. She seeped the petals in a pot of hot water to make up a soothing tea. A cup with a bit of honey relieved colicky, sour stomachs. *I could use a cup, right now.*

Bursting with yellow, dandelions carpeted the ground. Their cheeriness usually perked up Abigail's spirit. Even though she planned to add a few bouquets to her basket, her world had turned gray. Besides, the whole town was covered with them. No more medicinal use up here than down below in Stowe.

Upset, Abigail exploded, "Just once I'd like to run away on my own adventure." She waited a moment to calm down before adding, "It was hard enough the last time to raise money for your gamble. Besides, George, have you forgotten about Cassius? He's only seven and needs you here at home." She threw in some guilt to give her husband's heart a good tug.

Instead of guilt, George turned angry. Abigail recognized it early in their relationship. His neck turned splotchy-red, spreading its bloom up to his cheeks. Right now, though, she could care less.

She had a gut full herself. If he wanted a fight, she would give him a fight.

"No! I haven't forgotten about our boy—nor you. What do ya' think I'm doing this for? It's for us, all three of us. I want to earn enough to buy a farm or business of some type of our own."

Abigail refused to be bullied into acceptance of his wanderlust, his inability to stay put. She wanted to shout that he was full of big ideas but had little to build on. She thought of their meeting a few minutes before. How could such a romantic, playful moment turn into a nightmare?

Abigail stomped and kicked angrily at the dirt on her way back down the mountain. She ruminated about having to move back with her parents. With George gone, she had little money to pay for rent or food. She and Cassius had to go back, like sheep dragging their tails behind them.

Abigail fully understood why women all over the country began voicing their concerns about their rights. Many of the local men shook their heads as if someone had told them a joke about women working outside their homes. Yet, they forgot women have had to take up men's jobs when they have been to war. They planted, harvested, and plowed the fields. They raised the children while the men were away and still took care of the inside of their homes, cooking, cleaning, darning, mending, and sewing. These same women kept the family books and balanced their budgets. When the men returned from war, the women retreated to their domestic sphere, cooking, cleaning, sewing, raising their children, and some like her, being bored.

Her father, Doctor Joseph Robinson, Stowe's family doctor, never treated her less than any person because she was a woman. Instead, he expected her to do her best in school and assist him in his medical practice. He knew from when she was young that she had the intellect and compassion for it.

She had little idea how her mother felt about suffrage or other women's issues though. Abigail never welcomed enough conversation to discuss the matter at any length. They had been simply mother and daughter, not friends, not someone Abigail felt free to talk about life's mysteries. She usually only talked when she was talked to about how she should behave at an event, how she should carry out some instructions, or when she was given reminders to pick up the house, set the table, or help put her younger brothers and sisters to bed.

After being taught to be seen and not heard and other appropriate ladylike rules, Abigail played hostess often when her mother accepted afternoon callers. Abigail had never been invited to these little soirees. Often, when they exchanged local gossip, her ears perked up, though, when the dialogue turned to "Yeah, if women ran the world" matters. When Hannah asked "Abigail, please refill our cups," or "Abigail, bring more sponge," or "bring more gingerbread," she overheard how their mothers, grandmothers, and the generations of women before them had been treated by their fathers, husbands, and the legal system.

Abigail did not understand how the legal system could possibly treat women unfairly until a new neighbor, Mrs. Archer, came to visit one summer afternoon.

"My own darling, long-suffering mother who cooked and cleaned like a dog received a trifling token from my father's will." Mrs. Archer stopped talking long enough for Abigail to bend over and refill her cup, "Thank you, my dear." She took another sip and began again. ".. and that to be paid annually by my brother but discontinued if she dared marry again. I tell you, Mrs. Robinson, she did not receive the house she owned, she was born in, and lived in all her life. Mother inherited it from Grandfather when he died. It was stated in his will, yet you know as well as I do, women can own almost anything before they marry. Once they say, 'I do,' the husband becomes lord and in some cases her slave owner. She and everything she owns belong to him. That's the law." Abigail walked back into the kitchen, all the way considering what she heard. *Why have women not raised their voices? I think I'd stay unmarried.*

Mother must be really interested in the way the discussion went because she said, "Mrs. Archer, help yourself to another slice of gingerbread, won't you?"

Nathaniel, Abigail's younger brother cornered the kitchen blurting out, "Ma's company's eating all our dessert so we won't have enough after supper tonight."

Abigail put her finger over her lips and said, "Shush! Ma will skin you alive if she hears you in the dining room. You can go outside through the cellar."

Abigail sat at the kitchen table and listened until her mother's friend continued talking.

"You're a snoop, Abby, just a plain snoop."

"Go outside, Nathaniel. Quit causing problems. You'll get in trouble with Ma and then Pa if you don't go."

"Aah, you'll get in trouble more if Ma finds out you're listening in on their conversation."

Abigail shushed her brother again. Consequently, he "hmphed" a bit before he kicked a chair and headed down the steps.

Apparently, Hannah had heard no fight going on in the kitchen because Mrs. Archer began again. "My grandfather's will stated that my mother was to receive the family home, all its belongings, and ten acres surrounding it after Grandmother died as long as Mother took good care of her during her lifetime. The two of them received a yearly allotment and extra money for house repairs if needed. Grandfather left his sons plenty of property and money. Unfortunately, Father, an irritable man, resented her for owning the home in the first place. He took grandfather's goodness and generosity away from her. His will stated the very house she had been born in, cooked in, cleaned, and raised their children in to be given to my brother Andrew, the oldest and most like Father. Oh, he gave her some of her clothes, not all of them, their bed, mattress, and bedding, but not the rest of her Birdseye maple bedroom furniture."

Hannah Robinson shook her head as if she had heard the story many times before. She took up napkin and daintily blotted her lips. "I know men hold the keys to the world. The laws are the laws."

"But I ask you, Mrs. Robinson, who wrote the laws?" Here Mrs. Archer became quite dramatic when she tipped her head and raised her hand to emphasize her exasperation, "Of course, the men. They have little incentive to change them."

Abigail felt so sad about Mrs. Archer's mother. *Where was the love and respect the husband and wife had for each other when they were courting, that love between man and a woman she had read about in her novels. How could it all be turned into such ugly words written in a will? I'd surely never marry anyone who treated me so badly.*

Abigail heard uncommon optimism in her mother's voice, "To be fair, I think many men nowadays are treating their wives fairer. I won't say they all are, but in our family, our boys have been raised to respect women and treat them as equals."

Indeed, Abigail knew this to be truth, even though her younger brother sometimes pushed his luck in the respect department, "My own Joseph treats me like an equal. He often says we share and share alike. He also said half his income is mine. But I often question, so why does my half always pay the debts?"

Abigail laughed quietly. She loved her father and knew he was also a good husband and as good of a provider as he could be. As a doctor, he was sometimes paid in eggs, chickens, or pork when a hog was slaughtered. Unfortunately, ready cash came in much slower. Yet, he was a kind, tender, caring man who seldom lost his temper. Abigail knew he treated her mother respectfully.

It was usually her mother who was the taskmaster and disciplinarian in their family. She might swat a child at times if anyone was out of hand, but she handed the corporal punishment over to her husband who seldom went that far with his discipline. Instead, he tended to talk to the child, which Abigail could claim firsthand was harder on her than a-licking. His kind reasoning and guilt laying made her remember her mistakes.

So, when Abigail told the family she agreed to marry George Camp, her parents acted two ways, acceptance of what they knew had bred between the two through the years, and unsureness of George was ready for such a commitment. Her father went on with his business after George received his blessings to marry Abigail. Her mother, on the other hand, chose to point out his immaturities on every occasion with her "I told you so's."

Therefore, when Hannah got the latest news about George returning to the goldfields of California, Abigail could almost hear her say, "I told you so." She knew she would shake her finger at her too. "I told you that young man ain't sewn all his wild oats yet. Leaving you again and that little boy of his." Hannah would be right.

Nevertheless, Abigail knew her father could use her help in his medical practice. That would supply some cash. The two connected, almost like they were of one brain. When she was younger and still unmarried, he took her with him on his rounds simply to give mother and daughter a rest from each other. Abigail learned to set children's broken bones, clean up and bandage wounds, diagnose simple colds, sore throats, and more serious conditions like diphtheria.

When her father thought her ready, she was about thirteen, Abigail helped him deliver babies. Before she married George, she had quite a following of mothers who wanted only her as their midwife or caregiver before and after their labors. She knew when they should push, when they should hold back, and when she needed her father's keener experience.

"Abigail, Abigail!" She heard her name being called from far away as she felt her shoulder being massaged.

"Mother!"

Blinking hard a few times, Abigail tried to focus. Her eyes at first blurry, Abigail made out her daughter Maude, stooping and fanning to give her air. After a few moments, she realized Thomas was kneeling and cradling her head in his lap. Jared Wheelock, her brother-in-law, and the Clearwater area doctor stood over her with his stethoscope hanging around his neck. But where was George?

Waking from a painful dream, Abigail remembered with such sadness that her George died many years ago. Amazed, she could still feel the power he had over her, not only his scent but his moods. Abigail now knew this was not heaven, and she would not be meeting her maker today.

She looked at Thomas. He had pushed up his glasses to rest on top of his bald head. His eyes had narrowed, and his forehead had creases of worry. Abigail's friends, Anna Whiting, Maggie Marvin, Kate Stevens, as well as Cassius's wife Martha, her cousin Hannah, and her own sisters Annette and Mary gazed down from the tight circle they had formed around her.

"Gracious! What's all the fuss?" Abigail muttered as she tried to sit up. As she lifted her head, she reached for the back of her hair. She winced as she felt a good-sized egg growing back there. She tried to tuck in the strands that fell on her right side and found an equal sized egg growing there, both creating pulsing pain.

"Careful, Abby, careful." Thomas warned. "Take it slow and easy." He scooted up on his haunches, lifting her to stand.

"Got her, T. C.?" Jared asked as he stood to the side to give him extra support. Thomas grabbed Abigail around the waist to steady her as she stood on her feet.

Straightening, Abigail shuddered as something cold and wet fell down her back. Her hand went from her skull down to her waist. Someone had loosened her corset—greatly. As much as she hurt, Abigail felt better too—unencumbered, sloppy almost, and she could breathe like when she took off her corset at bedtime.

Maude bent over and plucked up the rag that had slid down and onto the floor.

"Maude, please grab something and cover me up so no one sees my dress hanging."

Quickly, Maude tossed her cape over her mother's shoulders as she and her father guided her through a tunnel of friends and family to the cloak room.

Abigail looked left and right as the blurry room of people clapped. Embarrassed by the attention, she realized everyone was dressed in his or her finest regalia as if they had attended a party. Then she remembered. She had joined the same event. Everyone, a pantheon of locals she loved and respected, had gathered in Clearwater's Morrison House to celebrate Thomas Porter's, her Thomas's election to the 1881 Minnesota House Legislature.

What a ruckus she had created!

"Abby, you gave me, well, all of us," Thomas said as he circled his arm indicating everyone in the ballroom, "quite a scare. .. I'm so sorry I was dancing so fast."

Taking deep breaths to calm herself, she patted his back, acknowledging his concern.

Abigail heard Thomas whisper something to Maude before he handed her off to the women. The only words she could make out were "confounded contraptions."

"You'll be fine, Ma," Maude said confidently as she guided Abigail to the cloak room. "We'll get you fixed up in no time."

After disrobing, Abigail redressed with the help of her sisters and her daughter. The bustle that Maude had talked her into wearing because, "Mother, it is so vogue" had to stay put because it was sewed into the material. Even though she had talked both the seamstress and Maude into a much lesser one, it was still there. Abigail agreed with Thomas that adding more to one's derrière was silly, but it was stylish and not as unhealthy as a real corset.

She knew women who just had to have that unnatural nineteen-inch waist. Once they became pregnant, they continued to cinch up as well. As a midwife, she had instructed them to forgo on the trappings of glamor because it was hard on them as well as their babies if they lived. How many women she had nursed when they went into labor too early, only to lose their precious cargo?

Nevertheless, Abigail had not paid attention to her own advice even if she were "thin as a rail," like Thomas often proclaimed. Besides, she told him, "I still have a few bulges I'd like to smooth out."

Maude had cinched her up to begin with. Of course, she had no idea how tight the contraption had become. Yet, Abigail knew she should have said something when she felt like she was suffocating. She wanted to look her best for Thomas's big evening.

Even though her own mother was gone now for nearly twenty years, Abigail could still see her shaking her finger while criticizing, "Vanity, vanity, thy name is woman!" She, too, though, wore the corset up to the day she died.

Abigail admired her husband. Content on farming, working to help Clearwater and Wright County grow and prosper, he had turned down many attempts over the past decade to get his name put on the state ticket. Now, as he grew older, nearing sixty, he saw that he could be useful to the state, and he went about winning the election like everything else he did from raising horses to pigs to wheat and oats—with gusto.

Re-dressed in a much-loosened corset, Abigail and the women returned to the ballroom.

"I agree," Jared said. "You need to go home now and get some rest. Remember, this isn't your first and only head injury, Abigail. You had one shortly after you arrived in Minnesota thirty years ago. I'll be over tomorrow to check on the bumps. I'm most concerned with the right bump."

Cassius and Martha came with their winter coats, making Jared's and Thomas's points even more clear. Abigail saw younger people dancing. She wanted to stay and continue to celebrate with her husband.

Abigail looked at Thomas. "Let's just stay long enough to say good night to our guests. I feel fine, really." Thomas looked at Jared for advice. Jared shrugged, obviously knowing his sister-in-law's strength of will.

Sensing a minor battle won, Abigail felt strongly that she had no intention of telling anyone about her pain. "Cassius, could you please get me a cup of punch. I'm very thirsty."

Thomas led her to their table bedecked with patriotic red, white, and blue bunting and ribbons. The decorating community had outdone itself for this big celebration.

"Imagine, Thomas!" she said, grabbing her husband's arm. "Clearwater, our river town, represented again in the Minnesota House of Representatives. This time by you."

One by one, Clearwater friends like Simon and Kate Stevens—everyone in the village called them Uncle Simon and Aunt Kate—George and Anna Boutwell, Sam and Anna Whiting, Will and Lucy Webster, the Colgroves, all of their friends and family paraded by to check on how Abigail felt and bid their good nights and good wishes. Abigail greeted almost everyone with the same apology: "I'm so sorry about all the commotion."

Nevertheless, the remaining crowd agreed it had been a grand evening celebrating the man of the hour, the Honorable T. C. Porter, her Thomas.

Jared and wife Mary, Abigail's younger sister, held up the end of the line of well-wishers. Jared said, "Don't forget to take that medicine I gave you, Abby. It will ease the pain and help you sleep tonight. When I come tomorrow, I expect to see you still in bed," he said, giving her a look that he meant business. "Concussions are serious, Abby. Maude and Martha will make everyone breakfast and help with all the company. Your head needs to heal for a few days now." Jared turned to Thomas, "Make her rest, T. C. Wrap some snow up in a towel and have her lay her head on that. It'll ease the pain and take down the swelling as well."

Abigail rolled her eyes at both men. "I'll be fine. My old noggin hurts for sure, so I'll take it easy."

As Thomas ushered her to the door with Maude, Martha, and Cassius right behind, she turned to look back at the ballroom. She and Thomas had been truly honored by their turnout. Everyone they loved and respected had shown up. Her whole family, now Thomas's family since he had no one in the world to call brother, sister, uncle, or aunt, except a stepbrother who was believed to be in Superior, Wisconsin, had attended this grand event.

Stepping out into the night, Abigail tucked her woolen cape around her and snuggled her hands further into her muff. From above came the whooing of an owl. *Who? Who? Who?* She looked to see if she could make out where the sound was coming from. Hiding right above her, she saw only its yellow eyes. The bird's lonely call escorted Thomas and Abigail as they rode down Main Street toward home. Dusty, named for the corn dust he rolled around and shook off all over them when they first met him, barked and wagged his tail as they rode up the driveway. When Thomas helped her from the carriage, Abigail saw the owl land on the bare branch hanging over the shed. "Good night, old friend," she whispered before patting their new dog's fur and heading toward the lean-to.

"Are you sure you can walk by yourself? I can help you, you know."

"Everyone is making too big of a fuss about this fall. I'm fine. You do what you have to do."

"Well, if you're sure. I'll be in after I bed down Gilda," Thomas hollered as she entered the house.

Abigail's darling grandchildren were all tucked in upstairs. She reminded herself how her life had changed since she had come to Clearwater. The woman she had been in Stowe, reliant on George and their families, and the woman she had become here in Minnesota were two separate beings. If they met in a room, they would not recognize each other.

Chapter 2

Throwing Caution to the Wind

True to their take-charge characters, Maude and Martha helped Abigail undress for bed. They were leaving as Thomas came in with a cold pack.

Abigail heard the weariness in his voice. "Good night, girls. Maude, I grabbed a few icicles that were hanging from the eves. I smashed them up and threw them in the wash tub in the lean-to. They'll stay frozen out there. Thanks for all your help." He looked at Martha and said, "It'll be a short night for you and Cassius with the youngsters waking so early. I hope you can fall asleep fast."

"We'll be fine, T. C. We had such a grand time. Cassius fell asleep as soon as his head hit the pillow. Maybe he'll be the first to wake to watch the children while I get a couple more winks. Besides, sleep is a commodity I have had to live without since having children," Martha said as she chuckled.

When Maude and Martha left, Thomas took the ice-filled cloth to his wife. She lifted her head so he could rest it behind her. "Let's see how we can get you comfortable, Abby. How about more pillows?"

Abigail shifted and turned gently, trying to relax. "I'm not sure, Thomas. I feel like I am resting on a rock." She could see how worried he was, so she tried nestling in. "Let's just blow out the lights and see if I can relax."

Thomas sat on the edge of the bed and pulled off his boots always with an "Ugh" and a pause before talking, "I know you don't like laudanum, Abby, but you took a serious thump on the head. If you just take a half-spoonful, maybe you could rest."

"No, no, no, you know I won't take the stuff. I should have made up some of my chamomile tea for myself, but I didn't want to keep the girls up any longer than I had to."

Thomas crawled in bed and pulled the covers up and over his shoulders. "Okay, Abby. Wake me if you need anything," he sighed.

Before long, her husband breathed slowly and evenly. His light snore, usually a peaceful sound, made Abigail nervous that she might wake him. As quietly as she could, she sat up and pulled open her bedside drawer. She took out her diary. Gathering up a blanket, her pillow, and the icepack, she quietly opened her door and tip-toed to the parlor. She felt her way to the divan with only the red and yellow embers of the fireplace to guide her.

After making up her bed, Abigail lay down. She slid off. Maude had said many times that the horsehair covering was too slippery for laying on. Now, she believed it. She tried to rest again, this time digging her toes into the end of the divan. Abigail felt like she had to hang on for life or slip off the divan. This would not do!

She got up and lit a lamp. Once completely moved to Thomas's wingback chair, she pushed the wicker stool close so she could rest her feet. The two of them had made this stool as one of their first team efforts when they were a newly married couple so long ago. Thomas had built the legs and frame, and she had woven some bulrushes to cover the top.

Abigail tried to relax but she still had no sleep in her. The fireplace glowed with red and yellow embers. She leaned forward and stirred it until it flared. The fire mesmerized her.

She sat back again, adjusting the cold rag. Granted, it gave her some relief from the throbbing pain, but she knew it would be dripping soon. Abigail eased into the chair and stared into the fire.

It had been a beautiful night of celebration. Picking up her diary, Abigail thought she should write a bit about the ball their Clearwater friends and supporters threw for them. As she opened the book, the pencil stub fell onto the floor. She felt so comfy in her chair with the ice wrap, she had no desire to bend down to search for the pencil. The journal's dark blue, nearly black velvet cover still gave her a soft delight when she swept her hand over it.

As a teenager, when Abigail helped her father in his medical practice, she began journalizing. Fascinated by his interesting patients and their diagnoses, Abigail knew that what she wrote had to be kept secret. Her father warned her his patients' business was just that — "their business and no one else's."

Abigail remembered as if it were yesterday when she walked to Stowe's Mill Village and to her future father-in-law's store to see if she could buy a diary. Once inside Riverius Camp's Mercantile, she noticed one of the glass counters laid out with a few pink and blue books. Yet, as she paged through each of them, she noticed most had scriptures like "I can do all things in Christ" or "Give thanks to the Lord for He is good" written in fancy fonts and scrawled on half the pages. If that were not enough, none of them had more than twenty-five pages. She wondered if the manufactures believed young women had little to say. None of these books were useful for her project.

Walking home, Abigail thought about how she could create her own diary. Her father had plenty of paper and would not complain if she borrowed some. What could she use for a cover, though? She wanted it to be soft and flexible.

Once inside the shed, Abigail looked through her materials. She had a storehouse of nettle, wisteria, willow, and honeysuckle, yet these would snag her hands. Last year, she made a basket and mats from cattail leaves for berry picking and drying. *Cattail reeds would be perfect for this project.*

Abigail began to work. Choosing only flat reeds, she dropped a bundle in a bucket of warm water to mellow and turn pliable. She found her father's leftover paper. She calculated her book should be about five inches long and six inches wide. Abigail grabbed the awl, a ruler, and large scissors from her toolbox.

After patting dry the reeds, she laid them flat on the bench. As she started working with them, one or two turned up on her. She fussed with them until they flattened out. She learned to weave from her father, Dr. Joe, who learned it from his mother, Grandma Robinson.

He often told little stories about life as he taught her to weave. He said those reeds that turned on their own could be compared to raising children. At times, one of his "little lambs" chose not to follow his rules—chose to do what he or she wanted to do. Because the couple had lost two precious babies early on in their marriage, he found it hard to punish any of them. He often preferred to "spare the rod," instead of giving a "good ole' lickin'" to a misbehaving little one like his wife Hannah occasionally urged. Begore long though, whether one of them had to be spanked or just given "a talking to," each learned to obey.

Abigail looked at her reeds and decided instead of making one long mat and folding it over onto itself, she decided to weave two shorter ones, one for the front and one for the back. She knew overtime the mat would split in half if she did not do this. She cut off the frayed reed ends before measuring so each flap went beyond the paper a quarter inch or so. As she laid out the materials, she decided to use a plain weave, merely interlacing one reed over and one reed under. Row by row, she wove each cover of her diary.

Even now, Abigail remembered her ambitions. She told everyone in her family and all her friends she wanted to be a doctor or nurse, yet she knew she had to finish school first.

Once she told her mother, Abigail saw Hannah give her eyes a roll, as if to say, "Keep dreaming." Even as a youngster, Abigail realized women were wives and mothers and held down no real money-making jobs. None of this made sense to her. Why could women not do more with their lives? Her mother and other women like her commanded their households while a baby rested on her hip. That took organization and work. Yet, few jobs were open to them and little confidence was given to them. As far as attending college, she and other women found few open the them because they were females. Even if a school would take her, she still needed money to attend. That, this family had little to give her to pay for an education she might never use, her mother often told her. In the meantime, this journal would become a tool for her own medical education with notes and comments about her observations.

While many of the rounds Abigail went on with her father became learning experiences and turned out fine, a few had sad endings, and a few were downright scary. However, from complicated colds to lancing boils to removing fingers, toes, or larger limbs, Dr. Joe demonstrated wisdom and patience.

When she went with him to help deliver babies, she came to understand her father's gifts. Of course, there were times and situations during childbirth that baffled her father. A mother could have a normal first birth and then the mother might lose every baby after that. Thankfully, only a few mothers and fathers had to deal with these tragic events. Mostly, under his tender care, a mother rarely lost a child. If she did, it was often because she should not have had any more children; she was "plumb tuckered out." When her father told Abigail, "The husband doesn't understand or care." Way back then, she had no idea what he was talking about.

As she grew older and wiser, Abigail began to understand women's reproductive processes. She wrote about the day she received her own education in a woman's monthlies. Abigail had no idea why she was eavesdropping when some of the silliest girls in her class were sitting sideways at their desks behind her sharing some frightening stories during their lunch hour.

Dinah whispered, "My mother just told me I would be becoming a woman soon."

Nancy muttered a reply, "Yeah, mine gave me the same talk a couple weeks ago, too. My older sister, Celia, confirmed it. She said she has this friend who comes every month too."

What were they talking about? A friend who comes every month and turns her into a woman?

Julianna, Abigail's close friend, said some girls cry and moan with pain and bleed from their bottoms once a month. Susanna's mother called this time of month the "flux."

Mary said, "Well, my mother told me I will have to wear something that looks like a diaper. I'll have to change it almost as often as we change the baby's diaper." Mary went on to say, "This time of the month can last up to four or six days because of all the blood."

Janey Mae asked, "My mother called it the 'curse' because Eve tempted Adam with the apple. God also told her in Genesis, because Eve had sinned, she'd also suffer in pain during childbirth."

So, apparently, this time of the month has something to do with childbirth but a curse?

Yet, when Alice claimed her father warned her never to touch anything iron because she would cause it to rust, Abigail listened with shock and skepticism.

Who can I ask about this?

Abigail only trusted her father, but she was too embarrassed to ask him.

After listening to these frightening stories from her classmates, Abigail turned around in her seat. "I've never heard about any of this. Even if there is a strand of truth to it, some of it sounds like superstition to me. Besides, wouldn't I know about it? My mother has never said a word about this, nor has Father, and he's a doctor."

Lucy Webber started to laugh at her, and a few others joined in. With a mocking voice, she said, "Ab-bee-gale! You think you know so much just 'cause you help your father fix someone's broken finger. But you know nothing about the 'birds and bees.'"

Abigail sat upright, turned around, and stared at the chalky blackboard straight in front of her. Her eyes stung with tears, and she wanted no one to see her cry. *Oh, that Lucy can be so mean*! *Yet some of the girls follow her around as if she is a queen.*

Could what they are saying be the truth, though? Why had Ma not told me about this awful ordeal? Who else can I talk to about it?

She was close to her Grandma Robinson, her father's mother, but lately she had taken to her bed. First, she came down with *La Grippe*, and lately, she suffered from dropsy. Her father told her she might pull out of this, or she might not. Always a strong woman, she was aging and lacking the strength to keep herself busy, which brought on some melancholia. Abigail surely did not want to bother her now with this.

Maybe Aunt Mary, her father's sister, would tell her the truth. She lived in Morristown, nine miles away. She did not have the time to walk that far, and her father needed the horses in case he was called out in an emergency. Besides, she doubted her mother would let her go. There was always something to do around the house after school like watching her younger sisters, ironing, taking the wash off the line, gathering wood for the stove, or helping with supper. She would have to wait until the family got together, and that might not be for a while.

After she got home from school, she went straight to her father's office and grabbed *The Medical Companion* for information to help her understand something that would help her understand what the other girls were talking about.

"One of the principal constitutional characters of the female is menstruation or the monthly evacuations peculiar to her sex. This ... generally takes place about the age of twelve or thirteen."

Oh, goodness. Is this what her classmates were talking about? I'm thirteen. Thank goodness none of this has happened to me yet.

Abigail read on: "Some are inclined to sickness, headache, and pains in the back and loins during this periodical evacuation." She immediately became scared. Now she had no reason to ask her mother or anyone else about this upcoming time in her life.

Abigail felt her head being moved slightly and a cold pack being replaced.

"Shhhhh, Mother. I'm sorry, but Uncle Jared told me to change your old packs every couple hours. I thought I could be gentle enough so as not to wake you."

"That's okay." Abigail felt her words forming like brick blocks in her mouth." Groggily, she asked, "Are you up already, Maude?"

"No, no!" Maude whispered. "I heard Dusty barking. I didn't want him to wake everyone yet, so I let him out. How are you feeling? Can I get you some of that medicine Uncle Jared gave for pain?"

"No, but could you make me a cup of willow bark tea? The jar is on the top shelf in the pantry by the other roots and herbs."

"Of course. Sorry you're feeling so rough. Uncle Jared warned us of this. He said you could get a bad headache for a while, become confused and even dizzy."

Abigail waved her hand. "Oh, I'll be fine. He worries too much. Sorry I'm causing so much trouble for everyone."

"Mother! Stop it. You're never a problem. I'll be right back with your tea."

Abigail tried to relax, wrapping the blanket around her feet and legs. She felt tempted to go back to bed, but she did not want her restlessness to wake Thomas. Morning would break soon, and he would be up doing his chores. She leaned back, adjusting her head so the ice hit the right spot.

Before long, Maude came back with a steaming cup of tea. "I hope you can go back to sleep, Mother. Please, let me know if you start hurting more. I may just have to force the laudanum down you anyway, at least until Uncle Jared gets here in the morning."

"Don't worry. I'm sure this will calm me. Thank you for the cold pack too. Now, try to rest."

Maude retreated quietly. As the Porter fireplace flames turned to flickers, Abigail covered her soft diary with her hand, remembering why she sewed a velvet cover for it.

~~~

So many years ago, when just a teenager, Abigail fell in love with some material her mother had used to make a dress for a neighbor.

"Momma, I've never felt anything so soft and lovely. Whose dress will this be?"

"Mrs. Pratt's. She spares a penny to pay the pound. Didn't want to give me what I usually charge for my labor. Didn't even provide me with the thread."

Abigail knew the Pratts; she knew Mrs. Pratt. Abigail took care of her two little girls last summer when she took the stage to Waterbury to help her sister after she had a baby. She paid her the salary she had earned but often gave her a little more. She said, "I know you will hand over your pay to your mother, but I want you to keep this extra for yourself, Abigail."

Abigail questioned whether Mrs. Pratt had really tried to bargain with her mother about the cost of making the dress. It might have been one of the many times she had recognized that her mother exaggerated a situation or two. She felt disloyal at times for feeling
~~~

this way, but her mother got upset easily over trifles. Abigail liked Mrs. Pratt and suspected she had simply forgotten about the thread.

In truth, Hannah Robinson watched the pennies in her household. Abigail turned over everything she earned to her mother, except for what people like Louella Pratt gave her to keep for herself. From caring for other children, cleaning someone's house, or helping in the kitchen during canning season, Abigail made a few dollars to help with the family coffers. Even if she were a busy wife and mother, Hannah made it her duty to help supplement the household income when she could because her husband's patients seldom paid their bills in a timely fashion.

Abigail overheard her mother's lament. "Joseph, you must demand to be paid. Here you go out to deliver Holman's new baby, and they haven't paid for the last one yet. How do they expect us to live?"

"Yes, dear. I know," Dr. Joe replied. "They got behind on their rent, and now with another mouth to feed, they're struggling."

"You've sympathy for others and little for me, "Hannah started to sob. "How can you expect me to feed and clothe this family on the little bit we've got coming in?"

Before her father went out the door, Abigail heard a deep sigh as he patted his wife on the shoulder and said, "I'll remind the husband today, dear."

Hannah Robinson added to the family income in little ways, and of course, Abigail learned her methods by helping her. Many of the town women bought eggs from her only from her because she had a talent for raising chickens that laid brown eggs with double yokes. She knew which egg-laying pullets to buy and how long it took for the little momma to lay an egg for selling. Her unusual patience and tenderness amazed Abigail even when she was a child.

Her mother's reputation for churning creamy, sweet butter, could not be topped anywhere around Stowe. Hannah had a steady and growing clientele. Sometimes she was so busy she had to pull the molded yellow square off her supper table to satisfy a needy customer.

However, Hannah excelled the most as a seamstress. Often called on by friends, relatives, and neighbors, Hannah had a talent with needle and thread just like her own mother, Abigail's Grandma Perkins. Of course, Abigail, too, sewed well. Her grandmother told her it was an inherited virtue, a gift, passed down to the women in their family for generations.

Consequently, when Abigail felt the luxuriously soft fabric of Mrs. Pratt's material, she knew she wanted some to cover the diary.

Hannah offered her daughter a deal. "If you come right home from school each day, help with your sisters and brothers and with supper while I sew, I'll make sure I save some material for your little book."

The two of them worked hard to carry out their obligations. Abigail did not feel like her mother was nagging her to help with the little ones or making supper. Hannah seemed to be at peace sewing. She hummed happy tunes as she concentrated on her stitches. Abigail wondered if that was what her mother was about. With all the cooking, cleaning, child rearing, chicken raising, and butter making, she did not always have the time to do what she enjoyed, her craft, sewing, which made her feel fulfilled.

When she had time in between her duties for her mother, going on house calls with her father, and attending school, Abigail worked on the blue velvet covers. She decided to make one long sleeve that she would slip over the front and back. She measured her book in its wide-open position. By tucking and folding as if wrapping a present, Abigail sewed it together with strong, but stretchy catch stitches. She opened and closed the rich velvet cover many times. With no pull or tug, she knew it would last a long time. She found a long black satin ribbon to add some privacy to her journal.

Indeed, Abigail had reason to believe she needed to have a secret knot. Someone, her mother, or sisters, had been peeking into her diary. She never dog-eared any of her pages, and the book had had its page corners turned for sure.

If she had to accuse, and she knew she needed proof, she wondered if it were her younger sister. Mary had such curiosity, forever asking questions, always asking why. With black thread, Abigail sewed the ribbon taut onto the velvet on the back flap. Then she adhered a four-holed, black button onto the edge of the front flap. Up and down through the layers of woven reed and velvet, Abigail pushed the needle until she had created an X. She wrapped the ribbon around the button and tied it off with a surgeon's knot. She and her father were the only ones who knew such a knot. If at any time her diary were not tied right, she would know *someon*e had snooped.

Abigail heard herself moaning. She had one of her wrap-around headaches, and her belly and legs hurt as well.

"Momma!" she called. "Why? Why?" She heard herself asking her mother why she had not told her about the pain and sickness she would feel every month.

She bent forward and fearfully, prepared to purge. Gagging brought up nothing, but she hated dry heaves as much as the real thing.

Again, Abigail felt like throwing up. *Oh! Not here! I've no bucket.*

Nothing came, but her stomach convulsed into tight cramps.

"Momma! Help me. I'm so sick."

Bending over again, the diary fell from Abigail's lap. Frantically, she tried catching it, but in reaching, she felt excruciating pain.

"No! No!" *My diary. Tie it and hide it.*

She heard talking. She heard urgency in loud and fast footsteps.

"Abigail! Try to sit up. Can you talk to me?"

She felt herself being unfolded and set up again with her head resting on the back of the chair.

"My head! Oh, my head!" Waves of pain travelled down her neck and into both shoulders.

Abigail struggled to holler, but she heard herself mutter, "Help! Help!" as if her mouth were packed with cotton.

"Ma, we're here," Maude said as she wrapped the cold rag around her head. "Pa, she is burning up. She must take some of Uncle Jared's laudanum. Just a spoonful, please, Mother."

"The cold pack should help. I'll ride over and get Jared. Maudie, can you take care of your mother alone for a few minutes?"

"I'm here, too, Pa, Cassius announced, thumping down the steps. "I'll run and get Uncle Jared. You two stay and see after Ma."

Cassius? Why is he running for Jared? Abigail heard all the noise around her. She wished everyone would be quiet so she could rest. She coughed as she felt the bitter heat moving from her tongue to her throat. She gagged, then shuddered. *What am I drinking?*

As if someone forgot to close the front door, cool air poured down Abigail's forehead over her face to her shoulders, arms, and legs. Calmness arrested the fight in her body like it often did the few times she climbed Mount Mansfield to an overlook of Stowe.

From up there, Abigail was Athena looking down from her Olympus. Her eyes circled her scenic kingdom, her beloved village filled with her loved ones. The lakes looked like silvery coins. The Waterbury River snaked through the evergreen, oak, maple, and ash forests, which surrounded the peaks and valleys of the Green Mountains. Pain and distress released their hold on her.

Chapter 3

The Quality of Mercy

A headful of pounding pain woke Abigail. Her pillow turned to cement.

"Maude, Maude!" Abigail heard whispers coming from her dry mouth.

"Abby, I'm here." Thomas said, grabbing her hand.

"Let me in there, T. C." Jared pushed past him and placed the cold stethoscope on Abigail's chest. "Her heart is racing," he said, as he grabbed Abigail's wrist. "So is her pulse. I think she needs another dose of laudanum."

Abigail tried to shake her head left and right, but it hurt too much. She tried saying "No," but it came out a whisper and a whine.

"Yes, Abigail," Jared said sternly. "You must get this down. It'll help you rest. I promise. I won't over do it."

Obediently, Abigail sipped the bitter medicine again, gagging as the nasty stuff slithered over her tongue, down her throat, and into her stomach. Soon, she relaxed and felt herself entering a different world.

~~~~~

Abigail tried to recall how long she had been in Clearwater. She remembered arriving on the shores of the Mississippi and Clearwater Rivers to become housekeeper for the townsite hotel.

She could not believe what the men called a hotel. A small log cabin and an equally small add-on sat below the dam of the Clearwater River. The original cabin had a cooking and dining area with a long table and benches taking up much of the room. A tiny room was separated by a door. Inside the room, which became her bedroom, a hand-built log bedstead stood next to the wall and under
~~~~~

a window. Another add-on room with only a curtain for privacy held two beds for boarders. A ladder pointed to a large empty opening in the ceiling, apparently so more boarders could sleep up there.

Tents were strung up around the hotel. The workers and newcomers, used to living outside, slept and ate out there. She was the first and only woman to arrive and live in the area for a while. The year was 1855.

Her brother-in-law Jared had gotten her the job. He was one of the first from Stowe to head west to check out the opportunities of Minnesota Territory. He wrote to Abigail's sister Mary, his wife, and told her to share the letter with her and anyone else interested in hearing about his trip. Abigail had read his message over so many times; she knew much of it by heart.

He told about the "excitement in the air around St. Anthony and Fort Snelling." Yet, when he heard about some "hullabaloo north, around a region some referred to as El Dorado, he hopped a steamboat to check out a site near the shores of two rivers—the Clearwater flowing into the Mississippi."

The captain, "a big talker who had been making the round trip from St. Anthony to St. Cloud and further north to Little Falls," told Jared a few tales "as he meandered his steamboat between the sand bars, strong currents, and away from the shallow shorelines."

What the captain went on to say became legend in Clearwater for many years afterward, and Abigail knew it well. Apparently, a year or so back, chaos broke out between two parties who claimed they had been the first to settle this location. All were peaceable men, and no one was severely hurt. They shook hands before one group left and took up land across the river on the east side.

The remaining settlers discussed long and hard about what to name the new town. The men explored the definitions of El Dorado and Clear Water. To many, they contended El Dorado because of the all the "golden opportunities" of the white pine forests surrounding them. Others argued the richness could only be attained from the power of the clean, clear water provided where the two rivers meet. Thus, they staked their claims on "Clear Water," eventually written as one word, Clearwater, after the same-named river that flowed into the Mississippi.

The letter and Abigail's memory of her own experiences intermingled with what Jared described; she no longer knew who experienced what. After crossing the river on the ferry, Jared stepped onto the town's shoreline. He immediately became drawn into the business of the village, a burgeoning district of ordered chaos. Jared relayed what he saw, heard, and experienced so well that she felt as though she were with him now.

Fresh cut pine and sawdust perfumed the air. A horse-drawn dray had backed down the slight incline to load up crates of merchandise brought up by the steamboat and ferried over for delivery. Horse-pulled wagons carrying stacks of lumber raced up and down the streets. Men carrying logs on their shoulders crisscrossed in front of him and others as they proceeded in a hexagon of directions. Whining saws, grinding wheels, and loud shouts joined in concert with the roar of water bursting over the dam.

Jared decided to find the hotel so he could drop off his baggage. As he took the planked bridge across the Clearwater River, he saw the townsite hotel beyond a low-hanging oak branch. He walked around a few tents to enter through the open door. Midafternoon, copper-like dust from the sawmill suspended in a shaft of sunbeam pointed to a corner table. He set down his bags.

Assuming no one to be around, Jared said he had time to look over the room. The kitchen had a stone fireplace and a cast iron cookstove with pipe leading to and exiting the north wall. A worktable stood near the wood box and an enamel bowl and pitcher on a stand. Another small table held a stack of tin plates with scraps of bread and what looked like beans needing to be scraped and washed. The black enamel coffee pot had been pushed to the back of the stove.

Jared wrote, "Abigail, you might be interested in knowing that I met one of the hotel owners. Simon Stevens, who followed me into the hotel a short time later. After I arranged a bed for a night or two, he and I got to talking."

Yet, what came next was a surprise to both Abigail and Mary.

"Stevens said the owners are looking for a housekeeper as none of them had time to keep up with the place, cooking, cleaning, and other stuff. Both your cousin Francis Morrison who is here building a fancy hotel and I couldn't help thinking of you, Abby."

As Abigail continued to read Jared's letter, she could not help but wonder *why me.*

"Abby, you know how you've told everyone, including me, you and Cassius needed a fresh start? This could be it. The job isn't glorious, but I know your ability to cook almost anything that comes out of our lakes and rivers and your housekeeping skills are up to the challenge as well. You'll find lots of men to feed and clean up after. If you are worried about being outnumbered, I'll be around for your protection. The owners are a good lot too. And if we both like the area, I plan on sending for Mary and little Mary later."

With her mouth hanging open, Mary said, "I knew Jared was frustrated around here trying to pick up his medical practice, hoping some patients would give him a chance. But almost everyone in Stowe puts such stock in Pa as their doctor. I thought he'd be finished with his meandering out west and coming back home soon."

Absentmindedly, Abigail patted her sister's back. *Travel to Minnesota Territory and cook for a bunch of men? Outlandish! What would people say? Then again, what are people still saying now? It's been nearly two years since George's attempted suicide in San Francisco and then his death up in Marysville. But Minnesota Territory is so far away. How would I get there? Nonsense, just nonsense!*

So, caught up in the battle of her own thoughts, Abigail did not notice that Mary had been crying.

"Oh, Mary! I'm sorry. I know how you miss Jared."

In fact, when Jared decided to go west to explore new country, he knew Mary would be forlorn and afraid of staying alone. He asked Abigail if she and Cassius would come stay with her and Little Mary until he returned.

"Even with you here, the house is so empty. Little Mary misses her Pa so much too. She worries that he'll die like Uncle

George. I promise her every night when she says her prayers that he'll return soon."

Abigail felt a punch in her stomach. "Tell me, seriously, the child doesn't worry like that?"

Abigail's shock achieved the look of total dismay on Mary's face. "I'm so sorry, Abby," Mary sobbed. "I promised myself I'd never tell you." She pulled her hanky from her sleeve and dabbed at her eyes.

Abigail pulled up the hem of her white apron and wiped the tears that had formed in her own eyes. *You are not going to bawl*, she told herself.

How long after the news arrived from the California goldfields that George had died had she woken to hear Cassius crying in his sleep for his Pa? She would wake and go to his room only to find her father, Doctor Joe, soothing him. The two, Grandpa and her son, had become so close. Abigail felt thankful for that and her family's support even if George's death left her feeling empty, alone, and lost. At the same time, she had no idea her loss had such an effect on her family.

"What will you do, Abby?"

Abigail stared past Mary. She could not help but think of her parents and others on which she had become so reliant since George left the second time for California. First, word in the springtime of 1853 from the *Vermont Watchman*, which came out of a San Francisco newspaper that he had slit his throat, "under the influence of want and privation."

Her gut-feeling had been right; George's strength would not hold out on another trip to California. Abigail had little satisfaction in that. When she read the short articles, she wanted to race to California—to find him, to feed him, to help him realize it would all be okay if he would just come home with her to Vermont. Of course, she could not go anywhere without money, and the trip could take weeks or even months.

Abigail had never felt so helpless. Her stomach hurt every day. She felt tears burning so she tried blinking them back. True sleep came hard pressed. She tossed and turned every night, fighting with her pillow for more comfort. Sometimes, she slipped out of the house and walked around town, trying to figure out what she could do to help him. She knew she had to let go and let fate take its course. The family tried to keep her spirits up, even her mother. Finally, a month later, she received a letter from George.

> Abby, I know how you're worrying. Sorry you had to read the nasty news in the papers. I can imagine the gossip hounds taking my ordeal hither and yon. I know you've little satisfaction knowing you were right that my health couldn't stand up to the trip. The heat got me by the Isthmus. Came down with malaria again. The men stood by me for a while after we got to San Francisco. Told 'em I'd be all right and to just take off. Every day away from the goldfields was a day lost from making some money. Promised I'd follow when I got better. They left me with a few dollars, but I had little to pay for medicine, food, and a place to stay. I came to my wit's end though. Had to spend the last couple dollars seeing the doctor. I had no money so couldn't eat.
>
> I'm on the mend now. San Francisco City Hospital fed me well. Got a letter from the rest of the party. They read about my problems in San Francisco after they arrived in Marysville.

George's letter went on to say they sent him enough to pay his bills and travel to meet up with them. He promised her he would write to her in a week or so.

Ironically, over the next few months, every time Abigail started to worry about her husband, she received a letter from him. His words tried to lift her spirits, but she could read between the lines. While not sick or starving, the heat and humidity sounded awful, making it hard to be comfortable and work with gusto. Sometime locations were "dry or panned out." He reassured her he had been making pocket cash by helping a few others who had staked their claims so he could pay for room, board, and his medicine. "I don't want you worrying again."

Yet, near Christmas of the same year, when Abigail had heard nothing from George, she became worried again. Every so often she had a gut feeling, expecting to see him walk in the door and holler, "Surprise!"

When the area newspapers announced his death near Christmas that same year, Abigail felt her life fall apart. It was not enough that the community knew her business about his attempted suicide, now they knew her sorrow. One by one, friends and relatives from around Stowe stopped by to "share her grief," or offer her a plate of cookies, a cake, a pie, "and some spiritual advice." She felt some of their words that were meant for comfort made her feel judged and found guilty.

And like George and Jared had written, there were gossipmongers a-plenty in Stowe, for one, Lucy Webber, now Koerner, her old nemesis from their school days. She had married well; her husband, son of the president of the Waterbury Bank, held the position of vice president. She had moved away, over ten years before, but that did not mean she still did not have good connections left in Stowe. In fact, she came home often to visit her family and friends like Janey Mae Hudson and Alice Krommers who had kept in close contact with her.

Word got back to Abigail that Lucy was "so happy" she had not married George Camp, when they were dating. "What a failure of a man, and even more as a provider for his family!" she announced. "Not like my James, who is a wonderful provider. I had so many beaus to choose from. I'm so happy I chose my James," she bragged.

Dating and marriage? A couple of years before Abigail and George married, they went through a two-week period of doubt and frustration. During this time, George admitted to her he saw Lucy a couple times. Abigail was hurt and disappointed. *Of all people, Lucy Webber*! But as far as she knew that was the only time Lucy and George had seen each other.

One afternoon last summer, as Abigail crossed the street, she saw the friendly little trio standing in a semi-circle talking and staring into the window of Mrs. Warren's Hat and Purse Shop. Although all three were dressed in their finest and the latest styles, Lucy had worn the more elaborate—a brown-silk dress with black trim, matching lace, and satin ribbon day cap. Even a few hundred feet from her, Abigail heard Lucy's loud voice, leading her friends into laughter. She wore so many under garments, she swayed as she moved and made the most swishing sounds of the three. *In this heat! All the weight each is carrying around today. Dressed as if they are fashion plates for Godey's Lady's Book.*

Each carried the newest styles of silk and bead reticules to hold their hankies, money, and name cards. Of course, even from down the street, Abigail saw Lucy's more ornate bag—mauve silk, pink, blue, and yellow embroidery and beads and lace trimmings. She probably designed and made it herself. *Making a statement, that's Lucy's motive. I must admit, though, she's always had a flair with color and all kinds of needlecraft.*

Years before, along with two others, Abigail and Lucy competed in a weaving contest for the Turning of the Leaves Festival. Abigail had won, but only by outsmarting Lucy. The contest rules had to be followed to the letter. First, each artist was to state in which category his or her entry would be competing. In addition, each applicant had to provide a copy of the original pattern for the project. Finally, at the time of judging, the project had to be finished and ready for use.

The day after she took her entry to the contest chair, Abigail went down to Camp's *Mercantile*. Learning Greek mythology and Homer's *Iliad* from the new teacher, Mr. Frangopoulos, or "call me Mr. Frank" because his name was so difficult to pronounce, Abigail wanted to weave a French-inspired reticule bag. She wanted to design symbols of the goddess Athena with a shield and owl. She looked through all her threads and skeins of yarn. Nothing really inspired her. She wanted a special color and a special touch, something rich and flashy to catch the eyes of the judges.

Once she opened the store door, Abigail smelled the mélange of pipe tobacco, smoked sausage, coffee, sweet spices like cloves and cinnamon mingled with kerosene, and other types of household and agriculture smells. She walked between the old stove and the checkers' table and chairs with the checkerboard sitting on top. As she made her way to the bins filled with bolts of fabric and many-colored stacks of yarn, she saw Lucy standing with her back to her.

Raised to be New England "nice," the two greeted each other with mediocrity. Abigail heard Lucy's lack of love for Abigail in her voice when she said, "Oh, hello, Abigail." She recognized her mocking emphasis as she pronounced her name like she did when they were children: "Ab-E-gale," with lots of emphasis on the e and a bit of hip swing as she said it.

Abigail raised the benchmark and hoped Lucy could not hear her disappointment in seeing her here with a whispered, "Hello." Neither talked about their projects nor asked what the other was creating. Abigail knew though, as did Lucy, their best handwork projects were completed on the loom.

Abigail spotted the yarn she wanted. Copper-orange, one sandwiched between two black bundles of yarn. She grabbed for it as Lucy rested her hand on Abigail's. Abigail pinched her fingers into the weave so as not to lose hold. She looked at Lucy's blue eyes; Lucy glared at Abigail's grays. Abigail grimaced while digging her fingernails into the yarn and holding fast as she pulled out the hank. With Abigail's other hand she slapped away Lucy's grip.

Lucy smirked, held back the lower part of her dress as she backed away and made her way to the counter.

"Mr. Camp, Mr. Camp?" Lucy was nearly shrieking. "Abigail Robinson took your last skein of copper yarn."

She's tattling? She's tattling on me?

"Hello, Miss Webber, what are you looking for?"

"Mr. Camp, I need some of your copper-colored yarn, and Abigail took the last one."

Riverius Camp walked to the yarn table and looked around. His red hair had streaks of white shining through, what his son George's would look like someday. He stood about the same height as Abigail's father, maybe five-foot-five or so, but at that moment he looked so much taller.

As the store owner moved twists of black, gray, brown, and red yarn around, he shook his head as if in disbelief that he had only the one Abigail had taken.

"Miss Lucy, I won't get my next order until sometime next week. I'll save one for you, if you'd like."

At that moment, as Abigail gripped the prize-winning, glorious soft copper yarn, her hand glowed with guilt and selfishness. She knew she should offer Lucy half.

"I just don't think it's fair that Abigail Robinson gets the whole skein. I think she should give me half."

Give, did she say? Give? I have stood on as much 'high ground' as I can handle.

Abigail tried to ignore Lucy's demand. She stood as tall as her five-foot frame could hold her. She saw Mr. Camp's pleading stare at her. She gave in. With a less than hearty "Fine," Abigail laid the yarn on the counter.

The damned peacock, so pleased and proud and prancing around the counter like she had already won the contest.

Abigail could strangle someone, surely not Mr. Camp, her, maybe, future father-in-law. But she wished he would have given her more support.

Not wanting to be glared at by Miss Hoity-toity, Abigail said, "I must run another errand. I'll be back to pick up my half in a little bit."

"It will be here, Abigail. Don't forget, I'll save out whatever comes in for you and Miss Webber here. On Monday, if I'm not here when you arrive Abby, Miss Webber," Riverius Camp said as he nodded to each young woman, "just tell Mr. Jonas or Mrs. Camp that I'm holding yarn for you."

Abigail nodded back at him. "Thank you, Mr. Camp," with as much fake sweetness she could bring up from the gall in her stomach. She did not say farewell to Lucy, but as she left, she closed the door with a slam. The bell's ring was loud enough to be heard outside.

When she got home and went through her stock of yarn and threads, she fine-tuned her design for her reticule. *The base of the bag will be black.* She would create the owl from brown and white strands, but Abigail wanted to create a shield and the owl by weaving the copper into the form of an oval shield. Even with only one half of the skein of yarn, she figured she had enough for the bag.

Concentrating on her project, Abigail had decided to use the table loom. *Easier to handle, and by taking it into my bedroom, I can weave quietly as late as I want.*

Would it be enough for the judges to recognize these as symbols associated with Athena, or did she need to weave the goddess and daughter of Zeus into her design? She pondered and stressed about her bag all afternoon.

The more she thought of Lucy Webber's weaseling and conniving behavior earlier in the morning, the more Abigail realized the two were in warfare. She decided she would weave Athena into her design, even if the judges had no clue who she was, what she represented, or how she turned Arachne into a spider. She determined to create a scene so beautiful, with goddess, shield, owl, spider and web, the judges would be impressed even if they did not understand her mythological creation.

Yet, knowing how shipments sometimes do not arrive on time or at all in their small community, Abigail wondered what she would do if she failed to get another half skein.

She came up with an ally—George, the storekeeper's son. The two were committed to their relationship. As soon as they finished school, they planned on marrying. Abigail told him about her incident the day before at his father's store.

George told her she could count on him to somehow "fix" the problem. She asked not to know about his plans. She wanted to be innocent of any charges, even if Abigail knew her own slate was not clean.

Come Monday afternoon, George showed up at the Robinson house.

"Pa told me to inventory the load of yarn that just came in. I took the only copper-orange yarn I could find. He said nothing about holding out anything for you or Lucy, so he must have forgotten."

Abigail looked at the yarn and hid it under her arm in case her mother or father walked in. Since the color was not a complete match with what she already had, she could blend it together, creating a variegated orangish-rust scheme. Maybe Abigail felt elated, maybe she felt shame, but she also felt it time to diminish Lucy's feelings of superiority.

The day before the festival entries were due, Abigail decided to show her father her handiwork.

With the back of Doctor Robinson's hand, he gently brushed upward. "Very soft! Such a smooth texture. Neither Grandma nor I could have done as well, Abby. The orange and copper on black have created such energy. The shield shines with glory. Oh, and the brown and white owl with its coppery eyes is a powerful display of wisdom."

"Thank you, Pa." Abigail knew her father only handed out compliments when he believed them to be true. For him to praise her as much as he had now, she knew he felt she had reached a pinnacle. "I worked hard to finish on time. You are my harshest critic. Yet, the judges may not have a complete knowledge of mythology. I'm still a bit uneasy about this, and, of course, I am in competition with Lucy Webber."

Abigail felt some guilt about her motives to beat Lucy in this contest, but she had no plans to tell her father how she did it either.

Doctor Robinson picked up his medical bag. It shuffled and clanked a bit, breaking Abigail's concentration on her final stitches. It was okay. Except for packing it up for display, Abigail knew she had finished her handiwork. It was ready to be dropped off at the festival center booth at the town hall.

The day of the Turning of the Leaves Festival came. Abigail and her father stepped over mud puddles as they walked to the event. Her mother would go when they returned home so someone would be with the younger children.

A hard frost the night before brought a clear morning.

Abigail remarked, "I'm glad I wore this cloak. It's chilly."

The cloak—one with a brown background with green flecks—Grandma Robinson had woven many years before she died. Even though it was warm and comfy, Abigail felt chilled when she and her father entered the hall.

Doctor Joe stood near the doorway looking over the open room. The main meeting area held all the food and textile entries and smelled good with crusty loaves of bread, flaky apple pies, and yellow pound cakes lined up on the tables. Abigail held no interest in anything else but the embroidery and weaving exhibits that lined a table in the back. Abigail held her breath as she walked toward the tables.

The first entries were lovely pillow covers: one an eye-catching, cream colored with pink flowers. The other entry, a yellow case, had been embroidered with brown, red, and green leaves floating around. Abigail admired the work these women had done, although they earned only white ribbons.

Abigail stood in front of Lucy's light blue reticule with the same-colored, drawstring. She had outlined the Green Mountains in light gray. For the front of Stowe's very own backdrop, Mount Mansfield, Lucy wove dark grays, and she paid particular attention to its face—the Adam's apple, chin, and nose. Then she melded greens, browns, golds, and yellow yarns to show the changing autumn leaves, the exact theme of the festival. Her taut weave and color designs blended beautifully. Abigail could not locate the ribbon. She picked up the bag and looked under. The pattern looked broken, unfinished. Lucy's entry form stated she had been "DISQUALIFIED! Project not completed according to FESTIVAL rules."

For a few seconds, Abigail felt a pang of remorse. She mused over the implication until she found her own bag. It lay upside down on the table. The judging form had fallen, or more than likely, had been thrown to the floor and had a footprint ground into it. As she bent to pick it up, she saw a beautiful purple ribbon under the table with the same footprint of mud smeared all over it.

Picking up the judging form and the ribbon, Abigail tried to read the judges' statements, but mud had blotted out some of the words of the comments. "Excellent color scheme/well-blended/completed—yes. Excellent, original theme—Athena/Greek mythology—." The score sheet indicated Abigail had earned 50/50.

Doctor Joe had been stopped by a few friends and patients. He quickly caught up to Abigail and read the results over her shoulder.

"Nothing I didn't expect, daughter. You should be proud," he patted her shoulder. "I'm sure you can use the five dollars, too."

I am proud of my work, but not my actions. "Father, of course, I am happy with the results. But I feel badly for those who did not do so well." Abigail did feel bad for the two who lost in the pillow category, but she felt guilty for deceiving Lucy, who was, truly, the better weaver. Abigail had learned her lesson: *Might never makes right.*

〰〰〰〰〰

Waking from her long ago and harsh daydream, Abigail realized she had been staring out the window for quite a while. *Even when I have picked up some cash helping a few women with their births or helping Father in his practice, I've hardly made enough for Cassius and me to live independently—much less pay for a trip west. I have become a burden, not only to the folks but to others in the family.*

"It's nonsense, Mary. Isn't it?" Mostly, she was thinking out loud and asking the air to answer her. "I'm sorry, Mary. I was really talking to myself. But it is nearly impossible to take such a trip. How would I get to Clearwater? How much would it cost? How long would it take? I can't imagine going alone. It's not just a hop, skip, and a jump to get there, you know."

I need to think seriously about this. It would be a break from everything. If I could get there, I could last long enough to make enough to come back if I don't like it. Besides, George and other men like him aren't the only ones wanting adventure! Oh, the gossip that I'd leave behind, running off to help run a hotel for men.

Chapter 4

A Time of Grace

On Monday morning, like every other school morning, Cassius stopped to say good morning to Abigail at Aunt Mary's. She gave him a big hug when she stood up to greet him.

"Oh, oh, oh," Abigail said as she squeezed him tight. *He is the love of my life.*

But as she rustled his hair, noticing how he was losing some of its blondness. Abigail also realized he was growing up too fast. He was nearly as tall as she was.

"Oh, Ma," Cassius said as he brushed her hand away.

George, if you could only see our son now. He's no longer a little boy.

Trying to ignore her son's impatience with her, Abigail pulled him away from her and said, "I want to have a little talk with you when you stop on your way home from school."

"What about?"

"Oh, don't worry about it now. You're going to be late for class." Abigail handed him his gray metal lunch box. "Besides, Aunt Mary made apple pie. She gave you a large piece for lunch."

"WOW! Thanks, Auntie!"

Mary gave the boy a firm hug, "You bet. We gotta keep you growing."

"Now, off you go. We'll talk tonight." Abigail said, giving Cassius a little shove. "Be smart and be good."

After washing up the morning dishes, Abigail walked to her parents' house to talk with them about the possibility of her going west.

"Don't forget, Abby, Francis and Hannah Morrison are already in Minnesota," Doctor Joe told his daughter. "All her letters tell how much she and Francis like the area and the new adventure they're having."

"If you like starting all over again," Abigail's mother Hannah remarked, shaking her head. "I love that girl, she's my namesake, but even when she was little, she was a rough and tumble. Never satisfied sitting and embroidering or sewing, out climbing trees, helping her brother build a fort, getting dirty. If she hadn't had a dress on, you'd think she were a boy so caked in mud and dirt. But smart? She led her class in grades. She could have gone further in school...*humph,* if there would have been a closer school to attend."

Sounds like me when I was younger. Oh, how I hated all that falderal and fluff we girls had to endure. I wanted dirt, scratchy branches, and adventure.

Abigail set down her teacup, dabbed at her mouth with the napkin, and thought a second before saying, "I know it all sounds so exciting. I know it would be a chance for a new start away from Stowe and all the gossip, and of course, the concerns you've had for Cassius and my welfare. As far as I'm concerned though, I can't even start to imagine going until I've solved my money issues. To be honest, you know my situation better than anyone."

The look her parents shared burdened Abigail with defeat. She knew they had no extra cash just lying around for frivolous things like her borrowing some to take off into the unknown on a whim. She felt relieved she had not dwelt on the matter any longer than she had. Going west to be housekeeper for a townsite hotel in a remote part of Minnesota Territory, some place called Clearwater, was out of the question.

Abigail placed her napkin neatly beside her cup and started to stand up when her father cleared his throat and said, "Hold on, Daughter. Your mother and I heard about Jared's letter when Mary came with Little Mary yesterday afternoon. We talked it over all night."

Hannah cleared her throat as she diverted her eyes from her husband to Abigail. "I know all this has been hard on you, Girly, mourning George and living with all the gossip concerning his suicide attempts." Hannah cleared her throat again. "I agree with your pa. You're never homeless because you have us and others to help you. Yet, this opportunity might get you on your feet and be as independent as you've always wanted to be."

Incredulous! Mother hadn't called me Girly for a long time. Did Father have to plead with Ma for some sympathy? Amazed, Abigail felt an inkling of hope.

"I talked with Riverius yesterday as well." *Goodness! Am I hearing this right? Father and my father-in-law Riverius haven't talked to each other in over a year after their words about George.* "He gave me this hundred-dollar bill for your travel expenses."

Not quite hearing her father right away, Abigail stared at the green offering and then looked back at him until it really registered.

"Abby, wish we could match it, but unfortunately, all we can afford is this right now," her father said as he cleared his throat, grabbed the bills under the cookie plate, and handed them to her.

Slowly, she took the money and looked to her mother for assurance. "What in the world? I don't believe it. How did everyone get to know about Jared's letter?"

"After the two Marys left for home, I rode over to talk with him and Wilhelmina. Seriously, they would have to know anyway if you were leaving and taking Cassius with you. I wasn't going to tell you, but I felt. .. no, I still feel ... he has a responsibility to George to take care of you as much as we do."

Again, Abigail looked at the money and then at her parents. "I just don't know what to say."

Yet, it was out in the open now. *I have to be taken care of.*

"But, Pa, I assumed they didn't care about us anymore now that George is gone. Maybe, they blamed me for his death somehow. Everyone knows I tried to get him to stay behind. He wouldn't listen." Abigail talked back her tears, biting her lips as well. "I'm grateful though. I want to get to the point where I can take care of Cassius and me."

"Pride, it was Riverius's stubborn pride that caused him to stay away. According to Wilhelmina, she said she threatened him a few times that either he make amends with you or she'd do it. But he said he'd do it soon. She waited and waited for him to make an accounting of himself and her."

Slight acknowledgement. My mother-in-law could have tried to see us anytime.

Doctor Joe continued, "He pulled out a wad of bills from his pocket and unfolded them in front of me. He has enough, so don't you worry," her father said with a glint in his eye. "He told me he wanted you to have the money now so as you can rest easy and do what you need to do to survive."

"After George's memorial service over a year ago, I seldom saw his folks or heard from them. They hadn't seen Cassius in a few weeks, and then one morning stopped by to take him on a picnic. Didn't talk to me much. I always figured they blamed me for George's death, and you know how Cassius looks like his Pa. I assumed he was a sad reminder."

"Just so you know, this time, we didn't talk or holler about George like we had before. I think Riverius has come to terms with it and takes some of the responsibility. He tried to push him to go west again. I blamed him for not stopping his son from going and leaving you and his child behind. But maybe now we'll both try some forgiving."

Life has not been kind to the Robinsons and Camps since George left, became so sick in San Francisco, and died before Christmas almost two years ago. I hope we can now move on. I want to try.

"Now, I won't take no for an answer," her mother said, interrupting her husband's and daughter's discussion. "You have nothing to wear for your travels. We need to go to Harrington's Dry Goods for some fabric to make a couple of dresses for you. If you want some of your older clothes taken in, I will help you with that."

Never once had Abigail thought of traveling clothes, much less having anything she owned fit her for such an endeavor.

"Oh, Mother! Thank you. I totally forgot about clothes, but then again, I had no idea how I could manage to follow Jared to Minnesota Territory until now."

"Not sure when you want to leave, Abby, but I'd think we'd need to get to work on organizing as soon as possible."

Hannah stood up and grabbed the teapot. As she refilled their cups, Abigail looked up and thanked her. First, she heard a sniff, and then she recognized tears in her mother's eyes.

~~~~~

After Abigail and Hannah found some lovely material for dresses, the two got busy. Abigail could not believe how fast her mother worked.

"Mother, I've been struggling with something since I decided to go west. I don't think it is fair to disrupt Cassius's education on my chance that all will work out. But I also don't think it is fair to leave him. As far as I know, Clearwater hasn't a school yet, no youngsters he can play with, and no one he'll know except me and Uncle Jared."

Hannah pulled the pins out of her mouth and poked them into the pink, crocheted cushion before replying, "Turn a bit to your left." As she stuck and re-stuck pins, she asked, "Your father and I were discussing just that. Don't you think you should hold off on taking him with you just now? What if you don't like it? Once you decide what you are going to do, stay or leave to come home, you can send for him."

Abigail slid her slippered feet on the stool. She looked down at her mother who, kneeling and concentrating, looked left and right, analyzing whether the hem was straight.

"I'm glad you feel this way too. You and Pa can back me up when I try to tell him tonight after supper."

She turned around one last time for her mother's approval before stepping down from the stool. This dress, or skirt, would be for her travels and for other more formal affairs once she got to her new location. Abigail wanted to stay as fresh as possible on her trip. Hannah even made her an extra bodice to change into when she needed freshening up.

"You'll need two—one washed and drying, and the other ready to wear," Hannah proclaimed. "You'll be fighting dust and coal dust between the stage and train."
~~~~~

One bodice or blouse was out of the same green plaid material as the skirt, had narrowed sleeves, and when worn together, the complete outfit looked like a dress. The other, white silk with bell sleeves to keep her cool in the summer, coordinated perfectly with a belt of the same fabric as the skirt, which had lots of room for petticoats. Abigail felt in style for the first time in a long time.

After supper at her sister Mary's with her parents, Cassius, and little Mary, Abigail excused herself from the table and told her son she wanted to go for a "walk and talk." She grabbed a shawl because the temperature had dropped and the wind had picked up.

"How was school today?"

"Ah, boring. I don't know why we had school this summer anyway."

"Of course, you know why. The farmers have agreed to let their children get some schooling in now before harvest. This is a short period. You'll survive."

"But Ma, we're leaving in less than two weeks. What's the point?"

Well! If that doesn't lead right into this sensitive conversation.

"That's sort of what I want to talk to you about," Abigail said as she grabbed his hand and squeezed it. She bit her tongue so she would not break down and bawl. "I think it would be best if you stay here with Grandma and Grandpa for now."

"No! I'm not staying back. You promised. It's not right. Why should I stay here and you have all the fun?"

Fun! I wish I could just walk across the street and be there. I wish it would be that easy.

"Cassius, I need you to understand something right now. I would love to take you with me. I could use your help with all the challenges I'll face, but I can't be selfish. I must think about what is best for you. I don't know what this "fun," as you call it, is going to be like, where I'll be living, and if I will be happy with this opportunity. Meantime, you're going to be in a warm and loving house, going to church, and attending school."

"It ain't right; it just ain't right."

"That's just it, Cass. It is the right thing to do. I promise I'll try to decide as fast as I can. Maybe you could come with Aunt Mary if Uncle Jared writes her to come because he is interested in staying in Minnesota Territory as well. She will need a big strong man like you to help her with Little Mary and all the luggage."

Cassius struggled when she pulled him to her and hugged him. Eventually, he put his arms around her as she started crying, hot tears of anger, frustration, sorrow, and love falling on the crown of his head that felt and looked like George's.

≈≈≈≈≈

The stagecoach rocked gently as Abigail grabbed her father's hand to climb in and took the seat. No longer, totally dark, early morning gray gave way to a light fog as the sun began to rise. An elderly, but sophisticatedly-dressed man, silver hair, black waist coat, white shirt, and black tie, had already boarded. He nodded to her as she sat down.

Abigail and her father had left everyone still sleeping when they took off from Stowe to Moscow. Somewhere out beyond the stage house, an owl hooted its goodbye to her.

Doctor Joe stood in the door and talked with her, "Now, Abby, you need to send us a note when you get off the train and before you grab the steamboat at Dunleith, Illinois, on the Mississippi. Don't forget to drop us a line saying you made it safe to St. Anthony Falls. Last we heard, Hannah and Francis will be meeting you there."

"Pa, please don't worry. I'll be fine. I've got to admit, I'm a little nervous, but I'll take one phase of the journey at a time. Thank you and Mother for everything. I know I thanked her so many times. Without the Camps and you and Ma, this trip wouldn't be possible."

"And the grace of the good Lord," her father admitted.

"You're right, Pa. The timing of all this is remarkable."

"I forgot," he said as he handed her a book. "Your mother sent this to give to you. She told me it will be good reading material on your way to Minnesota Territory."

Excited, yet so nervous, Abigail 's eyes burned. She could weep at any moment. She took the book from her father, but still dark, she could not read the title clearly. *I need to be strong. I cannot stay here and be taken care of anymore.* She patted her father's hand before letting go.

When she heard: "Last call," Abigail felt relieved She wanted to get moving. *The longer I talk about this trip and the new job, the more tense I become. Will I make all my connections? Am I going to be overwhelmed being the only woman in a village of men?*

Joe Robinson backed away from the stagecoach. Abigail hollered out the side window, "Bye! Take good care of my boy."

She fought back the tears she wanted to release. She knew now she had to shoulder what she was leaving behind. She settled in and looked down at the book her mother sent, trying to balance it on her lap. Old and musty smelling, the book's green cover read *Celebrated Women of Every Age and Country* and the copyright read 1804. Abigail wondered where her mother had kept it because she had never seen it in her parents' house. She browsed through it and found biographies of many women she had heard and read about like Joan of Arc, Queen Elizabetha, daughter of Henry VIII, and Sir Thomas More's daughter Margaret who was strengthen to her captured and imprisoned father. Abigail knew she had lots of women's stories to read to help her be inspired for her path ahead.

Nearly at the last second, a man climbed in, causing the coach to jolt and rock. He tripped and nearly sank into her lap when he stepped over her to sit down.

"I'm sorry," he said, collapsing onto the seat. "Good morning."

Feeling annoyed because of the man's clumsiness, and a bit shy of his juxtaposition on the bench, Abigail took the book and sliced it between the two to keep their space. Nodding a greeting, she brushed out wrinkles and dust from her new dress. She looked at dirt on his beige pants and his scuffed brown boots. When she finally turned to greet the man, she blinked in surprise as she recognized her younger cousin Ellet Perkins smiling at her.

"What? Ellet! My goodness!" she exclaimed, turning sideways to see him better.

"Hello, Abby. Surprised?"

"Why, yes, but why are you here, and where're you going?" She had to admit, her cousin looked like he had the world by its tail.

"I don't know, Abby. Maybe, like you, I'll go to Minnesota."

Abigail stared in disbelief. "I just saw you last Saturday night at the Judge's and Orpha's. You never said a thing." Amazed her own sister-in-law, Orpha Camp now who lived in back of the Robinson family had kept.

"Everyone in the family wanted it to be a surprise. Thanks to Hannah and Francis and my folks for the help with the fare. No one really wanted you to have to go it alone on the long trip to Minnesota Territory, and I thought this was a suitable time for me to see what is happening out west."

"I can't believe it. What a surprise!"

Abigail looked out the small side window. There was her own Doctor Joe with the widest grin he could have on his face. She couldn't help but think, *there he goes again thinking I need to be taken care of. I admit, though, this time I don't care. I could have asked for a better companion.*

As she waved goodbye to her father, the stage bolted off on the first leg of Abigail's odyssey.

Chapter 5

Unknown Territory

The stagecoach swayed Abigail to sleep like she had once rocked her baby boy, Cassius. Despite an occasional bump on the road, she relaxed, moaning quietly.

Abigail woke. Dark inside and out, she could not see where she was. She straightened up, finding herself propped up with a circle of soft, white pillows. *How did I get into bed?* My mouth feels like I've been chewing on my flannel pillowcases. Outside, she heard the familiar sound of an owl, always asking *Who, Who?* Abigail raised her arms and stretched. When she yawned, her head hurt.

Where am I?

She looked around. *Oh, of course, Ellet and I stayed the night in Rutland before we took the train to continue our trip to Minnesota. The train leaves before dawn—must be time to get up and get ready.*

Abigail flung the covers off the bed. Slowly, she sat all the way up and tried to swing her legs to the side of the bed. *I can't believe how tired I am. My legs feel like stumps.* She fell back, sideways, onto the pillows.

A male voice asked, "What? What's going on?"

Startled, Abigail realized someone lay on the other side of her bed. She lay back, as quiet and still as possible. She hardly breathed as she felt bed movement, shoe shuffling, clattering - and then flick, the sound of a match lighting.

"Abby, Abigail?" A man walked closer to her and shone the lamp in her face.

Who is he? Abigail shivered, more from fear than cold.

"Are you awake? You aren't trying to get up?" his soft voice asked. The man slid the lamp onto the side table. Staring at her in what looked to be his long, white underwear, he tried to touch her arm. Aghast, Abigail pulled it away.

"What's wrong, Abby? You aren't afraid of me? I'm your husband."

George? I thought he was dead.

A female voice held another lamp and called out in the dark. "Pa, what's going on?" It came closer and asked, "How's Mother doing?"

Mother? Whose Mother? When the woman set down the lantern, the light helped Abigail see her face. She looked familiar, like someone she knew a long time ago.

"Water," Abigail whispered.

The man handed the young woman a glass from the table. Abigail took it and guzzled. *Where am I?*

"Pa, Ma's trembling. She looks frightened."

Why did she call me Ma and the man Pa?

Excitedly, the man said, "Jared should be here. After a week in a coma, Abigail's finally awake."

Jared? I have a brother-in-law named Jared.

"Want me to run for him, Pa?"

"No, for some reason she is comfortable with you, Maudie. I'll go."

Abigail turned in bed so she had her back against the pillows and was sitting up. She knew she was awake. She heard the man say she had been in a coma. *When did this happen? I fell asleep on the stagecoach, somewhere in Vermont. How did I get here?*

The man gathered up his boots from the floor and his pants and shirt from the small rocking chair. He walked out of the bedroom to get dressed.

The kerosene lantern lit up the room on her side of the bed. *That chair looks familiar. Mother's rocker for hemming and other needlework? Why am I in my parents' bedroom?*

"Ma, how are you feeling?"

I don't know how to answer her, but she is so worried. Abigail looked around the room. Still dark outside, yet there on the side table rested her silver hairbrush with the engraved *A*.

"Thank you for asking. I have a little headache," she said, wincing with pain.

"I know," Maude said sympathetically. "Pa went to get Uncle Jared. Ma, don't you remember falling and hitting your head at Pa's ball at the Morrison House?"

Who are Pa and Uncle Jared? After clearing her throat, Abigail said, "I don't remember anything. I'm sorry." Abigail searched the young woman's face for some type of awareness but could see only sadness on her face. "What's this Morrison House?"

Alarmed, Maude's eyes opened wide as she exclaimed, "Oh! Uncle Jared warned us you might have some forgetfulness."

"You keep mentioning a Jared. Who is he?"

"Well, he's my uncle, your brother-in-law, and our village doctor."

"I know him, but why is he here? He went to Clearwater. I was supposed to meet him there to become a housekeeper for the hotel."

"Let's wait until Pa comes back with him. Maybe all of us can help you remember. Don't you at least remember me, your daughter Maude? You've been in a coma for over a week now, and the man you refer to is your husband, Thomas."

Outside, a dog barked. Soon, a door slammed followed by quick, heavy footsteps.

"Maude, good morning," the man whispered. When he came closer, Abigail recognized her brother-in-law, Jared Wheelock, but he was so gray, and his eyes looked troubled. "And how are you, young lady?" he asked as he looked down at her.

Abigail tried not to look at the other man Maude said was her husband. He stood behind her holding onto the back of her chair.

"Jared, Jared," Abigail said as she grabbed his arm. "I'm so glad to see someone I know." She looked at Maude and this Thomas. She saw worry on their faces. "Where are we, and what am I doing here?"

"Well, Abby, we both made it to Clearwater many years ago. About a week ago, you fell and hit your head again. You just woke up, but you have a concussion." Jared patted her hand. "You'll be fine, unfortunately, your memory isn't quite where it ought to be."

He leaned over and placed the stethoscope on her heart, "Now, Abby. Answer my question. How're you feeling?"

"My head hurts some, and I admit, I'm a bit afraid."

"Your heart is good. You don't seem to have pneumonia from lying here so long. Can I get you to sit up a bit?" He took her arm and helped her to sit up. "Ah, uh ... huh," he said as he gently felt the lumps.

"What do you think, Uncle Jared? Ma doesn't know Pa nor me."

"The swelling has gone way down, and the largest lump is much smaller. Unfortunately, I'm more concerned with the right side," he answered, helping Abigail to lay back in bed. "As I told you, Maude and T. C., and now Abby," he nodded to Abigail to add her into the consultation, "Memory loss is a common side-effect after a concussion. I'd suggest we just talk as much as possible and be honest with her. As soon as Mary wakes, Abby, I'll send her over. She has been quite tired and so worried. She'll be so relieved you have woken up."

"Mary is here, too?" How did she get here?" Abigail looked at Jared, then Maude, and finally Thomas, or T. C. as Jared called him. "Little Mary is here, too?"

"Abigail," Jared stated. "Mary followed you about a month after you left Vermont and brought Cassius and Little Mary, or Isabella as she wants to be called now, with her."

"Cassius is here in Minnesota Territory? Oh, I want to see my boy," Abigail shook her head. Close to tears, she flinched in pain.

"Ma, I'll write him today. Minnesota became a state in 1858, though. It's 1881." Maude said as she smiled. "Cassius had to go back to work up in Perham, you know, Otter Tail County, with his wife and children."

Married? Perham? This is way too much to remember.

"Well, I'm happy with how you're doing, Abby. Before I leave, though, I want you to take a small sip of laudanum." Jared picked up the spoon from the table and opened his satchel.

"Jared! You know that I refuse to take that stuff. It's addictive. Some mothers have killed their babies by trying to relieve their symptoms of colic. It calms them down alright. They find them dead when they think they are merely napping." Although her rant seemed familiar to her, she saw the surprise in everyone's eyes.

Maude laughed out loud. "Oh, Ma. We didn't plan to deceive you, but you were so sick and in pain. We had to give you some. Uncle Jared said it might be the only thing we could do to calm the stress on your brain."

Thomas nodded. "She's right, Abby. We did it for your own good. We didn't want to lose you."

Jared raised his hand to stop the commotion. "Put the blame on me, Abby. I made the final decision. Normally, I try not to mask the pain of a skull trauma, but your case was severe, and the second you've had. Besides, you thrashed around so much, I worried you'd cause more problems to yourself."

"I don't remember hitting my head either time." With dawn approaching, Abigail could see the concern and fear in everyone's eyes. "I'm sorry. I just don't remember," she whispered, trying to calm herself while soothing their feelings. "Okay, okay," she said, raising her hand to stop them talking. "But I've had enough! If that stuff put me into a coma, I won't take another spoonful. I'll have willow bark tea to take away the pain if I need it. Remember, I brought plenty with me when I left Stowe."

She looked at this man Thomas. Through his thick spectacles, she read sadness when their eyes met and something very familiar as well. Abigail wished she could give him some reassurance she recognized him. He grabbed his coat from the back of Maude's chair.

Jared patted her arm. "We'll let Abby rest now. It may take time but talking may joggle your memory. I think seeing the two Marys will help a lot, but no other visitors today."

Carefully, she laid her head back on the pillows. It was all too much. She knew she could trust Jared though. She must have married again, stayed living in Clearwater, and became mother to Maude. She tried to remember how she hurt her head.

Maybe when I wake up again and the sun comes up, I will recognize everyone. Closing her eyes, Abigail let the exhaustion take over. She heard Jared's soothing voice and no longer felt afraid or irritated. She also heard Thomas's voice speak in low, slow syllables, "I'll be right back."

~~~~~

Abigail felt herself drifting away. She found herself standing above a riverbank with its waters moseying south in front of her. Swathed by a dark forest of oak, maple, elm, and tall cedars soldiering above protecting her; now she knew where she was and why she had come.

She recalled arriving in St. Paul with her cousin Ellet. She remembered going by all the classic scenes from Iowa to Minnesota she had learned about and waited to see. Abigail visualized where she had worn this impressive dress and soon knew where Thomas was going. She pictured herself sitting around a large round table with her whole family at Clearwater's Morrison House. Red, white, and blue bunting added to the chair molding circling the large dining and dancing hall. Like stalwart soldiers, two flags stood on each side of the stage between the band members. On the left, the United States flag stood with its thirty-eight white stars on red backdrop and thirteen red and white stripes for its original colonies. The Minnesota Regimental dark blue flag displayed its thirty-four stars and an eagle carrying a banner with the saying, "E Pluribus Unum," meaning out of many, one.

In this area, Zebulon Pike had been commissioned by the federal government to search for appropriate areas to set up military posts.

As they continued northward, Abigail grabbed hold of Ellet's arm every time an eagle swooped from the cliffs. She watched ducks and geese coast along the shoreline and dive for breakfast. At dusk, slowly and warily, deer, moose, and even an occasional bear emerged to drink from their old water source. From Winona to St. Paul, Abigail was mesmerized by the beautiful landscape.

What Abigail had seen in pictures and read about in newspapers and magazines came to life. The great panoramas, artists' renditions some three and four miles long, of what they had
~~~~~

seen on their cruises on the Upper Mississippi from Missouri to Fort Snelling, had caused a following for the well-to-do from the east coast to all around the world. Adventurers took trains, steamboats, and stagecoaches to join others on the "The Fashionable Tour."

"Grandeur surpassed," Abigail whispered to Ellet as they looked over the railing of the steamer. The way he stared and nodded in agreement made her realize he was in awe as well.

Their eyes travelled from the high bluffs to the shorelines where a myriad of wildlife—shore birds, beaver, otter—met peacefully to rest and refresh. Most of the time, calm waters reflected the sky, providing never-ending artistic displays.

As they drew closer to St. Paul, a frequent traveler, a Mr. Sledge pointed out some of the area's landmarks.

"Once we get around this bend, you'll see Fort Snelling," he said as he pointed slightly left to where Ellet and Abigail would see Fort Snelling.

It was true. As soon as the steamboat aimed left, she saw the golden fortress aloft a white mount. Mr. Sledge also pointed to where the Minnesota River merged with the Mississippi. As the boat aimed right, they drew closer to the fort. The slopes, so steep and bare, looked nothing like the Vermont hills she had left behind. The fort's walls built thick for protection from the Indians reminded Abigail of pictures she had seen of the large palaces in Greece.

"Look over there, below the fort. Can you see all the different communities of Indians and fur traders? Look over there on the islands and shores too."

How can anyone live in such small, wooded shacks? Not understanding why, she became unfamiliarly uncomfortable when she recognized teepees and saw a few canoes being paddled by real Indians. She knew Minnesota Territory had several tribes, and many of them did not get along with one another. She had only seen a few in Vermont because they had all but had been driven away decades before she was born. When she brought up her trip west, Abigail could read fear in her friends' eyes due to the knowledge all Easterners had about the frontier. Regrettably, she now could understand their fear. However, the pageantry before her was more spectacular than any of the panoramas had exhibited. This was one of the journeys both she and George talked about taking before they were married.

George, you were always leaving to go somewhere without me—buyer-merchant for your father to large eastern cities, on long, weekend fishing trips with your brothers, trips to the gold fields of California. Now, you'll never come back.

The newsworthy gentleman then pointed to the cave that once belonged to Pierre Parrant known to many as Pig's Eye for a black patch over one eye and a nose like a pig's snout. The commander at Fort Snelling had him removed many times from the area because of the bootleg booze he sold to settlers, Indians, and soldiers. Then he moved again to the cave alongside the riverbank. Inside the cavern, the old European fur trader had set up his cabin and tavern and continued his business for a while. Parrant, booted out for good, left the cave. Many of the area's residents referred to the site as Pig's Eye Landing, which soon would be renamed St. Paul.

Sometimes, oddities like this landing and Smugglers' Notch back home, create a density of beauty. Many times, she had hiked the few miles up into the mountains from Stowe. Avalanches of rock created the Notch thousands of years before. The rugged terrains provided caves and other fissures as hiding spaces for the goods bootlegged from Canada due to President Jefferson's embargo against Britain way back before the War of 1812. Yet, Vermont and New Hampshire, along with other border states relied on this trade for a living, and thus, many continued to do it illegally.

Abigail also knew firsthand that many in Vermont were abolitionists, and part of the Underground Railroad, pirating southern slaves to freedom. Smugglers' Notch was vitally important for hiding these people in the caves. Somewhat warmer than outside, these caverns provided refuge for run-aways until someone came to lead them north to Canada. While these huge boulders as large as houses and barns provided a safe-haven for many, a few became necessary hiding places for a few vulnerable women who trusted dangerous midwifery. Dark and menacing-looking, just like the caves, some midwives promised alternatives to women who needed to make changes in their lives. Unfortunately, only a few women made it out of the caverns alive.

As the steamboat drew closer to St. Paul, its beautiful white bluffs welcomed everyone on board to their destination. Abigail had only two days left before she reached her destination, Clearwater.

Waving from the dock was Hannah Robinson Morrison, Ellet's sister and Abigail's cousin. After they were told they could exit, Abigail raced down the plank to meet her while Ellet retrieved their bags.

"We made it! Hannah, it's so good to see you."

Hannah, plump and cuddly, squeezed her hard. Abigail felt her over-warmth secreting from her heavy clothing. Women wore heavy clothes and tried to pretend they were comfortable. Yet, as thin as she was, Abigail felt the heat through her lighter clothes as well. The early afternoon warmth onshore had replaced the coolness of the morning travels on the boat. Seldom did she experience such heat in Stowe, Vermont.

"Welcome! Welcome," Hannah said giving her brother a loud kiss on his cheek. "You are so grown up now, Ellet. How good it is to see you both." She turned around to grab Abigail's arm, assuming Ellet would follow. "My carriage is right over here. Francis is in Clearwater, Abigail. He will be welcoming you from up there tomorrow afternoon. Along with Jared, you'll be happy to have the two looking after you."

Abigail nodded in agreement. Usually, she resented the thought of being looked after, but now, in all this strangeness that made her stomach twirl, she welcomed the idea of familiarity. She was getting closer to her new job and new life. She had thought so much about her future duties she had not thought much about her bodily safety until she looked around her. It was all too new and unknown. Likewise, until now, she had not admitted even to herself, she was uncomfortable with the thought of seeing an Indian.

Ellet loaded the bags in the back of the carriage and helped the women board. "I'll drive Hannah. You two women just chat. You'll have to give me directions though."

"Oh, don't be silly, Ellet. We will bend your ear, too," his sister said, laughing and waving her fan.

Ellet took up the reins and steered his way to exit the unloading dock. Drays and buggies carting boxes, crates, and people came to a standstill as each took its turn moving away from the river.

Hannah said, "Once you get to the street, turn right, and go about twelve blocks before turning left and traveling straight north. Then you'll be going many, many blocks. I'll keep my eye on the road too."

Watching traffic entering Lower Landing, Hannah said, "Abigail, it might be a while before you're down here again, but once Ellet gets close to turning right, look left. You will see the school Harriet Bishop from Vermont started up for some of the first children in the area—way back in 1847. You know, after growing up in Panton, she left for New York to attend school and teach. She learned under the famous woman educator Catherine Beecher. We've visited with her on a number of occasions."

Abigail started looking between the wagons and carriages. She saw the rugged cabin, but it was so far away, she could not see much. "I've read about her." Marveling over her cousin's ability to handle the Minneapolis streets, she asked, "Hannah, you drove through all this congestion by yourself this morning to pick us up?"

Like a picture moving in front of her, Abigail observed more of this part of St. Paul. In between small brownish hovels and a few teepees sitting closer to the water, beautiful brick homes stood like warriors. This new city truly had everything and everyone thrown together.

"That's nothing, Abby. Francis has always had me running all over for his business. Unpaid help, you know," she said with a laugh. "Whether we lived in Vermont, New York, Indiana, or here in Minnesota, I had to learn my way around quickly to order the materials or deliver important papers he needed for his sawmills, bridges, and now, a hotel up in Clearwater."

"Well, I'm impressed, but who takes care of your boys when you are working?"

"We've always had a live-in girl or woman. Francis doesn't trust anyone else to help him with his business but me. I keep his books, too."

Abigail's folks always said Hannah was a smart girl and could have gone on to college to become anything she wanted. Yet women in Stowe never went on for education because few colleges accepted women. Even fewer of the women and mothers worked out of the home like Hannah either. Francis Morrison, her husband, obviously valued his wife's intelligence.

She stared at the busyness on the passing streets—men carrying lumber on their shoulders, horse-pulled drays loaded with wood and blocking the roads, people running in all directions, a fruit and vegetable market taking up nearly half a block with vendors shouting in all different languages. Abigail tried to fathom living in such a city.

It took nearly an hour to reach the new suspension bridge that crossed the Mississippi River over to St. Anthony.

"And we're almost there. This is the bridge Francis and the crew of the best engineers from his Mississippi Bridge Company built. I had the opportunity to be the first to cross it after it was built earlier this year, you know."

"I'm quite impressed, Sister. Francis does a good job with almost everything he touches. I'm glad he gives you some credit for being his backbone and helper."

"I am too, Hannah." Abigail looked at the Mississippi as it made its way south. As they drove up close to the Falls, she heard crashing water and felt the force of the rapids pouring to an unknown abode below. She remembered as she boarded the steamboat at Dunleith, Illinois, she felt its power underneath her feet as well, even as the boat sat quietly near shore.

"Don't worry, he does," Hannah said distractedly. "Ellet, you'll be turning soon. Go right to cross the bridge. Go slowly though. I hope the good breeze today will help us feel its sway."

Sway? Mother was right. Hannah loved challenges and excitement. Abigail tightened her grip on the side of the carriage.

"Abby don't be afraid. The bridge is safe and according to Francis, it needs that bit of sway. We'll be fine," Hannah started to tell her brother to turn, but Ellet started to make his way to the Toll Booth. She grabbed out the necessary ten cents and passed it to her brother.

As the horses trotted with quick clicks on the wooden platform, Abigail caught her breath as she sensed some movement when they met other rigs. She looked down at the river that seemed just a few feet below. Abigail had to admit she had a slight but almost spiritual awareness of the mighty river's power.

The rest of the trip went quickly. They took a right and rode north on a well-worn wagon path for a bit. She saw an occasional farmstead here and there before pulling up to a large but modest house and farm.

"We're here," Hannah announced as Ellet pulled up to the driveway. "Just pull in on the side of the house, Ellet. I'll have one of the boys come out and take care of the horses and carriage."

"How much land do you and Francis have, Hannah?" Ellet asked as he helped the women down from the carriage.

"That'll be something Francis can tell you, but I know from here, it is nearly as far as your eye can see.

Abigail surveyed the broad landscape. *The Land!* It stretched green with corn, gold with wheat and oats, and more green with rows and rows of various garden crops like cabbages, cucumbers, squash, and beans. A dozen or so Rhode Island Reds clucked their way around the yard. *Paradise! Their friends and relatives in Stowe would be so jealous.*

"It is just lovely here, Hannah."

"You may be amazed at our scarcity in the house. We have so much unfinished. Francis is so busy right now, but when he finishes building the sawmill and hotel up in Clearwater, he promises he'll finish inside."

The house was a simple, two-story, wood-framed structure, with a wrap-around porch, and large front windows. The barn and two outer buildings stood behind with a large area fenced in for the few horses and a couple cows.

Abigail wondered how they could have done so well as they had for being here just a couple years. Brown Jerseys grazed in the pasture by the barn while another four other horses, in addition to the two that drove them home from the steamboat, nibbled in the pasture. Of course, Francis had always been successful with everything he did. Although he said he was a farmer in heart, he had begun his bridge building in Vermont and New York, as well as working on railroads out east as well. He had a lot to offer this new country, which was obvious from the bridge they went over today. He now had taken on duties of hotel building as well as lumbering up north.

Oscar and Henry ran from the house to greet their uncle, Abigail, and their mother. Towheaded like her own son Cassius, six-year-old Oscar ran into his uncle's arms. His older brother Henry wrapped his arms around him. Soon there was shouting and giggling, as the brothers and uncle started wrestling around.

After a few minutes, Hannah good-naturedly, laughed and hollered to get them to hear her, "Boys, boys, and you, too, Ellet, let's settle down a bit." It took a couple moments before everyone was brushing back their hair, tucking in their shirts, and swiping off dust from their pants. "Do you remember, Cousin Abigail, boys?"

Henry put out his hand to Abigail to shake it, while Oscar stood back a moment. "Yes'm Abigail. I remember you. Your son Cassius and I got in trouble when we forgot to ask before we took off fishing."

"I haven't forgotten, Henry," Abigail answered. Although it was a few years ago, she remembered how frightened she was when she couldn't find the boys. She smiled to show she had no hard feelings and added, "But you're both big and strong now and when he gets here in a month or two, you'll have to come visit and see what other trouble you can get into."

Then copying his older brother, Oscar shook her hand as well. "I bet you don't know me, Abigail. I'm six and not as old as Henry."

All three of the adults laughed. Abigail answered, "But I do remember you. I held you when you were baptized, Oscar. I'm your godmother."

Oscar looked at his mother, "What's a godmother?"

"I'll explain later," Hannah answered, brushing his hair back. "Right now, I want you to help Uncle Ellet bring in the bags and take care of the horses. We need to eat an early supper because Abigail must catch the boat to Clearwater early tomorrow morning."

"Can't we go too? We can come back right away, but we could see Pa," Oscar begged.

"Unfortunately, not this time, Oscar. Your pa is coming home later this week after he helps get Abigail settled in. He needs to help you with the farm work around here. Now, shoo, go, help out."

"Let's go in and have some tea or coffee, Abigail. Seems you won't be resting much before we have to get you back to the boat so you can finish your journey." Hannah, round, short and self-confident, led the way up the steps. *Whack!* "Oh! I forgot," she announced loudly, reaching for her chest. "Abigail, watch that step. I can fix lots of things, but that needs something only Francis can repair."

"Hildie, meet my cousin Mrs. Camp. Abby, my right hand-woman, Hildie," Hannah stated. "I couldn't do anything without her, Abby, and that includes her husband, Charlie."

Hildie grabbed up her apron and pulled the cast-iron pan off the stove. "Glad to meet you, Mrs. Camp. I'm frying up some chicken for your supper. Mrs. Morrison wants you to have a good meal tonight because of your long trip. My husband butchered a couple chickens before leaving for our farm for a couple days. He'll be sad he missed you."

"Thank you, Hildie, but please, call me Abigail or Abby."

"She won't. I've tried since she came to call me Hannah, but she won't. We have gone around and around about this." Abigail laughed, and Hildie shared in on their understanding. "I don't like being hoity-toity, but Hildie doesn't see it as that. She calls it 'respect' for her employer." Hannah wiped her eyes and went and patted Hildie's shoulder. "I guess we both get what we want out of this relationship."

Abigail admitted to herself she was glad she had not had to solve this fight. She could tell how committed they were to each other.

"Abigail," she said with a wink, "while you wait for your bags, would you like a cup of coffee or tea?"

"I don't want to put you out but I could use a quick pick-me-up."

"Mrs. Morrison and I decided you need this as well to begin your job in Clearwater."

Hildie handed Abigail a small cloth covered crock. Abigail recognized what it was immediately and gasped, "Oh, one of my worst fears is not having a starter for baking some loaves of bread for the men I'll cook for. How considerate! Thank you, both of you," Abigail said, looking at both women and holding the starter as if it were a baby.

Soon the three sat around the table, sipping on coffee. Hannah carried the conversation for a while, but when she took a breath and a sip of coffee, Abigail asked Hildie about where she came from before she and Charlie came to Minnesota.

"We both come from Tennessee. We got married there in the thirties. A little later, we moved up to Illinois, but our land weren't no good there. We put a lot of money in the place but got little out. We sold out for what we could get to start over again a couple years ago. We live a couple miles from here."

"You'll find, Abby, many families are in the same situation. Left existing homes to come west because land was getting played out, then the next stop wasn't much better. Minnesota Territory is giving them new chances. But Hildie didn't tell you the rest," Hannah said, nodding to her housekeeper.

"I don't wanna bother anyone about my problems, and it's too late for help now, but we lived so far out of town, I could never get a doctor on time to help me with ..." Hildie struggled to talk.

Hannah realized this was a difficult discussion for her friend so she filled in. "Hildie and Charlie lost six babies."

"Oh, dear. I'm so sorry, Hildie. Did you ever know what happened?" Abigail asked as she patted the woman's hand.

Hannah refilled their cups. "Hildie, remember, I told you Abby is nearly a doctor. She learned from her father, Doctor Robinson."

"Posh, Hannah! I'm far from a doctor, but I've had lots of experience delivering and taking care of babies. I think I've seen and dealt with it all."

Hildie sipped her coffee. Staring at the large black stove as though it released her secrets, she began to talk.

"Jimmy was our first child. I had a smooth confinement, and he delivered easily. He had the blackest hair. Let me tell you. He were a good baby. Seemed like he started crawling earlier than other babies I knew, and oh, he was so strong. We'd gone into Quincy to get supplies. My first trip off the farm since Jimmy was born. We had to camp out one night going and one night coming back. We had a nice couple of days. The weather was good. The nights were cool enough we didn't battle the 'squitoes. Jimmy loved the wagon trip. He kept saying "giddy yup." It was on our way back home, he started crying something fierce and bending his little body. Then he gagged and puked something awful. Then he come down with the diarrhea."

Hannah filled in the rest. "It's okay, Hildie. It's okay. I'd have told her what I knew if I'd have known it'd exhaust you." Hannah wrapped her arm around her housekeeper and friend's shoulder, giving her a hug every once in a while. "Her baby died out there on the Illinois prairie," she whispered. "She and Charlie were helpless."

Abigail had helped her father with a few of these types of cases. She asked, "Hildie, are you saying your baby wasn't sick before you went into town? Did you feed him anything from the village, you know, candy, soda crackers, water, from the general store?"

"I think we did. Yes, I know Charlie bought a can of beans for supper and the shopkeeper threw in a bag of crackers. Oh, I remember I got him a cup 'a water from the barrel in the store as well. But we never opened the can of beans. He were too sick for us to stop and eat. I did give him the water and a soda cracker earlier though."

"Interesting. When was this? I mean what year?"

As though it was hard for Hildie to remember, she said slowly, "Johnny was born in August 1848 and died July of 1849. He were over eleven months old."

"1849, hmm. You're saying he had no symptoms before? Did you or Charlie drink any of the water or eat the crackers?"

"Not that I remember. We picked up our supplies, flour, sugar, coffee, and some fabric, and left. Charlie figured we could get back home to help the hired man with the chores. So, we left for home almost right away."

"Did anyone in town tell you to stay out? Were there any warnings about cholera?"

Hannah blew out her breath and then sighed deeply. "Well, it sure could have been that that killed the baby."

"Cholera?" Hildie gasped. "No one warned us of cholera. The storekeeper was happy to see us. He knew Charlie from another trip he took. He even held Johnny and greeted me with great excitement. I hadn't been there before."

"I know I had to help Pa with the cholera. We were both fearful of getting it. Lots of people all over Vermont died."

"I remember the panic, too, Abigail." Hildie said as she looked into Abigail's eyes with what looked like understanding. "We had read in a Springfield newspaper that Quincy had numerous cases of the cholera. It seemed like it started early spring. I remember when we planned our trip though it was later summer, long enough for the sickness to be long gone. We wanted to go to Quincy because we'd get the best price for our hog. We needed the money to make out for the upcoming winter and we needed to pick up supplies. After we got back and buried Johnny, we heard others around us dying of *la grippe*. Neither Charlie nor I got it though. Just figured he were too precious for us to keep. God wanted him back."

Abigail had a hard time believing God took away loved ones. Her beliefs had been formed early on by her family and her faith she embraced and learned from the Stowe Unitarian Church. *God does not create sickness, nor does He take babies away. He set up the universe and let the natural world work itself out. We have the responsibility to find answers to our problems.* "We have to set our purpose then follow in our tasks," her mother Hannah often said. Abigail always wanted to ask her mother, "So what is my task?" She knew what her mother would say. "To be a good daughter to your parents, to take care of your children, and to be a partner with your husband."

Sipping her coffee, Abigail mulled over Hildie's spiritual beliefs. Many in Stowe shared her thoughts. Some even insinuated

Abigail's lack of faith had been the cause of George's bad luck and death in California. Abigail began to question her faith. What was it all about?

Had God taken George from me because I had not been strong enough to keep him at home? Or could it have been that my husband had not used the common sense he was endowed with, took the risk, and paid for it with his life? If this is true, Cassius and I simply got in the way of George's downfall, and his misfortune became ours.

No! God is not punishing me. Women often get the back side of the spoon. We can emerge if we learn how to play the game. God is still in heaven and in us. We women need to grab hold of His strength, emerge, and show others we can be strong.

Chapter 6

Re-birth

The *Governor Ramsey*'s Captain Young, a walking and talking history book of the upper Mississippi River, gave Abigail and two male travelers a tour of the river as the steamboat pulled away from the shore.

"I know we're technically not part of the Fashionable Tour of the upper Mississippi, but we're still going further north. We have plenty of beautiful sites to taken in yet. So, I always give my tourists information about where we are and where we're going. If I get called away on some business matter, I'll continue where I left off."

As the small group walked toward the stern, the captain's hand on her arm gently guided Abigail as everyone followed. Pointing to the St. Anthony Falls, he said, "It were formed thousands of years ago. Its power gives power to all around it. See the sawmills and the grist mills lining the banks," he added, pointing to both sides of the river. "There are those, like John Stevens and Franklin Steele, big men in the territory, who predict their river becoming known all over the world for its production of flour and wood."

Again, Abigail felt the power of the Mississippi River underfoot. Until the last few days, she had only read about this grand old river. She had marveled about its Fashionable Tours as well and could almost feel the glory others felt as Captain Young led the small party to the port side of the boat.

Here she could see not only buildings lining its bank, but the misty waterfalls. *I could stare into its cascade forever.* As Abigail focused on its movement, she felt beckoned to join the water. *It feels so natural and so easy to just fall in.*

The captain's voice interrupted her trance. "They're putting on quite a show for you, Mrs. Camp. I haven't seen so many bald eagles soaring above the river falls. Must be dozens of them this morning."

Abigail felt peace like she hadn't felt in years. "Captain, the Falls, the eagles, the peace, it is all so hypnotic. I have to admit, I could stay here forever."

"You aren't alone, Ma'am. The Dakota people revere this area, especially below the falls, as their spiritual place. They come here to celebrate and pray to their Holy One."

As the steamboat turned, they could see the island below the falls. Captain Young pointed out the many nests in the cedars trees that female eagles return to year after year. He called this small rocky area Spirit Island, which is sacred to the Dakota.

"Many of the tribes fear and respect Great Water, and they know his powers are dangerous if you aren't prepared to follow his rules."

As Abigail looked around the area, the captain continued explaining how the Dakota sent their holiest of holy men to plead with the evil spirits of the river for safe passage before their braves went on their buffalo hunts. "Great Waters provides them with fish and turtle for nourishment as well as beaver and mink for warmth. Close to the river's shores, they dig for clay not only to make their peace pipes but to recover their baskets and canoes. After they are finished, the Indians say they're reborn or made new."

Abigail identified with what Captain Young was saying. Standing here, not knowing her future, but trying to erase the pain from her past, she felt clean and remade.

Holding onto the rail and staring back at the plunging water, the captain said, "I want to tell you a little tale about a Dakota wife and mother. She killed herself and children right there." He pointed at the cataract of plunging waters. "After a hunting trip, her husband, an Indian warrior and powerful man, came home with many trophies for winning the contest on who would kill the most buffalo. Some of his winnings included horses, beaver, buffalo, and bear skins, which made him a rich man. But one prize brought about his downfall. Another tribe gave him the trophy of a beautiful young woman to be his bride."

As the steamboat finished its turn, the captain stared into the western sky as he continued his story, "His current wife, Ampato Sapa, believed their marriage to be good and strong. In addition, the Great Spirit had blessed them with two children, a son and a daughter."

Abigail could not help but believe the good captain had recited this tale a few times before. It seemed to roll off his tongue smoothly.

"But she had no desire to share her mate with a younger woman," he went on to say. "With much hollering and stomping of feet, Ampato let him know her anger. Her husband tried persuading her to believe that she would always be his first love. He tried convincing her that the new wife could help her around their tent.

So angry, Ampato Sapa gathered her children, grabbed a canoe, and stomped toward the falls. Here, while her tribe watched, she pushed her crying children into the canoe before her and into the water. She fought against her husband's strength while he held onto the back of the canoe. The violent currents were too much for him, and he lost his grip. The canoe and family spun in circles for a while. The children started screaming as they and their mother twirled toward the edge of the falls, plunging downward, never to be seen again."

Abigail, so caught up with the telling of the legend, looked back as if she could still see the falls where the woman had fallen with her children. She could not fathom Ampato Sapa's decision nor the choice she felt forced to take.

One of the gentlemen on this tour asked the captain questions about maintaining his ship.

"Ah, good question, Sir. I'm glad you asked. We hire only skilled men to work and navigate the waters," he said. "We take long trips up to St. Cloud and back."

Somewhat bored with the conversation, Abigail pulled herself to attention to listen, nodding absentmindedly as she looked around the second floor of the steamboat. It was a working boat, for sure. The cargo area held wooden barrels labeled crackers, pickles, nails, and even whiskey. Some were only stamped where the container was coming from and going to. Bulging burlap bags of potatoes piled high against the inner wall, long wooden boxes labeled Winchester, and small crates marked canned peaches and pears. From someplace below in main cargo, she could hear the clucking of chickens in cages.

Abigail also saw tools of the boatsmen's trade displayed on the walls. Gray ropes spiraled around black hooks. White ladders hung sideways, and long poles stood waiting to be used to measure the depth of water or to push tree snags away.

Every few miles, the captain pointed to either a beaver or muskrat lodge and said, "Building for a hard winter." She nodded because she had heard that tale several times in her life. Yet, as the pilot above and his boat steered around rocks, and maneuvered around sandbars, he told her how to tell the difference between the two.

"Beaver build their homes higher and wider than the muskrat. Look over there along the bank ahead of us," the captain said pointing. "They're put together from all sorts of things—branches, sticks, even rocks. Can ya' imagine the creature lifting rocks? Then 'e muds it all up. Muskrats build a smaller version outta' plants, roots, and some cattails. Ahahh! We humans think we're the smart ones."

Moving slowly around bends and strong currents, the steamboat created new pictures at every turn. Abigail opened her journal to describe her trip. She felt poetic as she tried capturing the movement of the tall, green, and golden grasses waving prairie to riverbank. Here and there, a red-winged black bird took flight, landed on a green stem, balancing despite the breeze.

Spindle-legged, gray sandhill cranes stepped gracefully through marshes and bogs. When they reached the gravelly shore, with their long, pointed beaks, they poked the sand for seeds, grasses, and even a few snails to snack on. In flight, their red foreheads pointed straight while their bodies stretched long and arrow-like, with their skinny legs trailing behind.

Abigail loved to see the white-plumed egrets slink their way from the tall grasses to stand like statues on the river's sandy shore. A few flexed their wings, flitted off to rest and eat around the golden slough. Two started fighting, pecking at each other's necks and heads.

Abigail leaned against the steamboat's railing, amazed at the power struggle. *I wonder who is the strongest, the one who kept his territory or the one who walked away.*

The loner flew off and landed on a fallen tree bleached from the sun. With a backdrop of green prairie, the still life created a mood Abigail wished she could capture with paints she left at home.

Morning chill gave way to warm afternoon breezes. The captain had left her side to talk with his pilot. She watched as the steamboat approached another island. Ducks, geese, and even a few pelicans shared warm sunny spots on the small piece of earth and trees. A few stray logs came floating in their direction. One of the crewmen took a long pole and pushed the wood away from them.

Because she asked the captain to tell her an hour or so before they stopped in Clearwater, he did but said, "Even though I think you look fine." She went to a storage room to clean up and change her clothes.

Abigail decided to wear the white blouse with the plaid skirt. Fastening her collar together, she wore a wedding present from George, an oval, pink and white cameo broach, "Really portrays you," her new husband told her as he hung it around her neck. Along with the bag she weaved, and the cameo necklace her father gave her, this would be the third acquisition of Athena.

In fact, the small, raised carving looked just like her, and it also captured her hair. Every morning, she brushed her blonde curly hair back and wound it into a bun at the nape of her neck. No matter how much she brushed, her thick hair never laid down nicely. She looked as though she had plopped a helmet down over it. The pink in the cameo picked up on this, but fortunately, it also highlighted her facial curves and her natural complexion. Whenever she wore this charm, not lately because she had little to wear with it, she felt powerful, alert, and confident. This was exactly what she needed today as she started a new job, meeting her relatives, employers, and many men for the first time.

Abigail came out of the small room and made her way to the bow. She felt the boat paddles slowing their constant slap, slap, slap against the river water. As the boat pulled closer to the shore, the scene before her charmed her at once. The thick green trees lining the bluffs, the curve of the river, and a lovely island dividing the water into a Y made her marvel at the river's majesty. *Nature is the artist.*

As they drew closer, Abigail thanked the captain for the great tour before he left to organize this stop and to take on new passengers and goods. She tugged at her white gloves to make sure they were snug and pulled open her parasol, readying to disembark.

"Please, wait until my passenger, her luggage, and supplies are off the boat until you try to board," Captain Young hollered to the new travelers.

Abigail lifted up her skirt and stepped down the plank and onto the damp, muddy bank of the Mississippi River. It was a warm mid-afternoon. Jared, followed by two other men, pushed their way through the crowd. After a quick bear hug from Jared, the other two each picked up a bag from the steamboat landing.

"Abby," he hollered above the noise, it's good to see you. These two characters are your employers. "Simon Stevens and Horace Webster meet Mrs. Camp."

Simon Stevens and Horace Webster took turns shaking Abigail's hands. Stevens said, "Welcome to Clearwater, Mrs. Camp. Let's talk more when we get to the hotel. It's so noisy, I can't even think."

Horace Webster shook her hand and then nodded in agreement as he cupped his right ear. He picked up one of Abigail's bags and started heading up the incline. Stevens followed suit.

"Abigail! Abigail!"

Looking in all directions, Abigail could not tell the direction of the person who was calling her name. She saw no one at the top of the hill they were climbing. Really, no one from the boat would be calling her by her first name, but she looked backwards anyway. The left side of the hill didn't have enough room for anyone to stand, much less holler her name. But lo and behold, on top of the hill beside a small building, Abigail recognized her cousin's husband, Francis Morrison—the one who had built the first bridge in Minneapolis. He was waving his arms and had his hands cupped around his mouth to shout one more time when she recognized him.

"There's Francis!" she shouted excitedly to Jared before she returned her wave and shouted, "Francis!"

"He's pointing for us to gather at the top of the path."

"Francis told me he was coming down to meet you sometime today. He is busy building his hotel." Jared bent down to pick up the last, but larger bag. "Abby, how was your trip?" he asked as he set down the bag a moment as the climb got a bit steeper. "Gracious, what do you have in the bags, rocks?"

"Sorry, Brother-in-law. Books, some boxes of various herbs, bottles of tinctures. You told me to come prepared to help you in your practice as well as keeping house for the hotel."

They trailed over a beaten grassy path that rose upwards from a small bluff. An archway of green leaves from the overhanging trees led to the opening street of the village. Finally, at the top, they met Francis Morrison.

"Abigail! How nice to see you. You too, Doc."

The three stood in the pathway, Abigail patting Francis on the back as he half -hugged, half-patted her in an-opposite-sex-type of cousins' greeting, which was never a full, frontal embrace

"I saw your wife and children yesterday. Did you know Ellet accompanied me to St. Paul? He's staying over with Hannah until you get there."

"It will be good to see him again. I like the idea of him hanging around. You know Charlie's not that young anymore. Nor is Hildie. It's good to have some new life helping out down there so I don't worry so much when I'm away."

Abigail recalled the boys and Ellet wrestling around and wondered who he should be worried about.

"Ellet can help for sure. I met Hildie. Charlie was on an errand."

"I see. Well, listen, Abigail. I left my builders up there," he pointed to new construction on the top of the hill. "I told them I'd be gone a minute or two. They're at a crucial spot so I best be going. I'll come down and see you soon. Maybe I'll make one of your famous suppers tonight."

Just like Jared had written, the town sang with busyness. Saws ringing, water purging, men hollering, horses neighing and clopping. They moved out of the way of a dray filled with barrels and boxes just unloaded from the boat backing up from the side of the street. Abigail realized a group of men were staring at them or her. *Probably not used to seeing a woman up here.*

The look of male ego and determination on Jared's face made Abigail realize he would do the carrying. "We haven't far to go," he said as he nodded recognition to the huddle of men. "We can go right down here and take the walking bridge across the Clearwater River to the other side," he said, leading the way through a small worn path of tall grasses.

Abigail stopped to smell fresh sawed pine mixed with the clean, clear water. The young, bustling village had picked an appropriate name for itself.

As they reached the narrow foot bridge, Abigail smelled smoke. She could not detect where it came from, but she assumed it was close to her new place of business. She walked slowly across the rickety wooden plank, looking right and left for the hotel. She saw nothing, but she followed close behind Jared as he stepped off the bridge. He pushed his way through a long, overhanging branch that had blocked Abigail's vision. He held up the opening for her. Like a curtain rising, Abigail saw tents, smoldering campfires, and a wooden structure standing above it, all with gray puffs of smoke fluming out of it.

Hiking up the bottom of her skirt but not watching where she stepped, she tripped over two or three slippery ground roots, reaching toward the river. Quickly, she closed her parasol, using it for a cane to help pick her trail.

"You alright, Abby?" Jared asked, turning around and looking at her. "I meant to warn you about the rugged path."

Hmm! That's something to think about. Should I take 'rugged path' literally or figuratively? "I'm fine. It is dark down here, but I'll try to watch where I am going," Abigail hollered.

The two weaved their way through a few tents set up in a camping area. As Abigail found herself in front of a small, log cabin, she looked around, seeing even more tents set up on the other side. She waited for Jared to continue their hike when he set down her bags pushing the door which had already been opened by Stevens and Webster.

Abigail looked at Jared and asked, "Where are we?" Then as she looked around for another building larger and suitable for a hotel.

"Your new home," he answered as he opened the door and waited for her to enter.

"What? This little building is a hotel?" Abigail looked at Jared for guidance, but she saw only a smile. Ascending a wobbly-log step, Abigail pushed the door further. The contrast between the darkness of the outside and the lightness of the inside surprised her as if she had entered a fairyland. Speckled sawdust streamed through two windows, illuminating the room, with the smell of fresh cut lumber inside and out.

"Well, here we are, Mrs. Camp. Welcome!" Jared announced. Both Stevens and Webster put down their baggage a few feet in front of her.

As the door opened wide, Abigail walked in far enough to draw in her new surroundings and allow Jared to step up behind her. She scanned her new kitchen, her new workplace. On her left, she saw a stone fireplace. Next to the side of the fireplace, a wooden box sat filled with chopped wood. The cast iron cookstove had two round burners on top of the oven with a black stove pipe exiting the wall above it. Straight in front of her a small table stood with a wooden dough bowl and rolling pin lying on top.

"We worked hard to get it all fixed up for you, Mrs. Camp, to ease some of your labor. Feeding the men and cleaning up after them around here isn't easy. We've tried. Let me tell you. Wheelock, here, sets great faith in your ability to do this on your own, but we've decided to take turns helping as well, at least for a while. But chucking wood will not be your responsibility, nor will gathering water." Stevens, who Abigail seemed to be the spokesman for everyone and maybe the one in charge, looked at the three other men who shook their heads.

"Thank you, Mr. Stevens. I know I'll appreciate every bit of help I can get," Abigail said as she continued to assess the whole building. She assumed the door across from her exited outside. A large cupboard hung on the wall on the other side of the door, holding a few plates and cups and a can filled with forks and knives. A rough looking stool held a white enamel wash bowl. A bar of soap sat next to it, while a pitcher sat on the floor. Against the far-right wall, a table with two benches sat empty but waiting for supper. Everything looked clean—suspiciously clean—as if the whole room were scrubbed from top to bottom for her inspection.

"It seems to be very nice and well-equipped. But may I ask, where do all the men sleep?"

Mr. Stevens answered, "Most of our guests sleep in the loft. See the ladder over there on the right?"

Looking at her brother-in-law, Abigail asked, "My gracious, Jared. You climb that every night just to go to bed?"

Jared nodded his head. "You bet, Abby. I have a very comfortable pallet up there."

Mr. Stevens nodded at Jared and then handed her a reddish ledger, "You can keep track of the guests in this." Pointing to the page, he added, "Write their names under this column and list the date they stay. We charge three bits a night, which includes the evening meal. By the week, we charge three dollars and fifty cents, and that includes two meals."

"I pay by the week, Abby," Jared offered.

"Right," her new boss said, glancing at Abigail's brother-in-law. "Now, a few other duties you'll be responsible for besides cooking two meals a day and cleaning up around here, Mrs. Camp, are keeping account of and collecting the room and board money. Also keep a tally of the foods we have on hand in the back of the book," he said as he flipped the pages to the middle of the book. "I made a list of the food back here of our non-perishables so you just need to keep track and fill as you see fit. Oh, and add what you think we need."

Abigail took the book from her new employer. *Whew! This seems easy enough.*

"Most of the workers will sleep outdoors in their tents until late fall. By then, we hope to have another building up for them to stay in while others moved to warmer places."

Abigail nodded to let Mr. Simon know she understood. As she looked around, she saw no obvious place for her to make up her bed. Suddenly, she became concerned about her own nighttime situation. Hesitantly, she asked, "And will I sleep either upstairs or outdoors?"

Webster, who was not much of a talking man, asked Jared, "Well, you gonna put down her baggage and show her, or do I have to"?

Abigail looked at them and Jared who did as he was told. He walked to the closed door she thought led outdoors. He pulled up on the wooden latch and opened the door. Intrigued, Abigail followed closely behind him. She peeked in over his shoulders. The room looked like it had just been added on and spread across the back side of the hotel. Inside the door to her right was a bed had been pushed up to the end of the wall. Two rough shelves hung from the end wall. A small wooden rocking chair sat somewhat centered in the room. Behind the door, a window had been opened to let in cool air from the rushing water flowing over the dam. On this hot afternoon, Abigail realized this might be the coolest room in the whole building. The floor had been sanded down and looked smooth, free of slivers.

"It's so fresh and new and beautiful."

"We hoped you'd appreciate it all, Mrs. Camp," Mr. Webster said.

Mr. Stevens added his two cents, "Wheelock here said we'd be working with a real lady, so we knew you'd appreciate having your own room."

Abigail walked into the small but refreshing room, so simple yet so quaint. The whole building spoke to her of the care that had been taken to make her comfortable. In this primitive community, she had received the kind of help she appreciated, respect and the need for privacy.

"Hello, everyone, sorry I'm late."

Jared and Abigail turned around fast, startled that they had new company.

"John," Jared greeted a dark-haired man with a full beard. "It's so good to see you again. You did a good job on Abby's bedroom. Abby, this is John Farwell, one of the town's first citizens, an owner of the hotel, and our handy craftsman."

"Farwell, glad you made a showing. We can leave the rest up to you now," Simon Stevens said. "Mrs. Camp we'll be back when it's time to get supper ready."

Supper! I have so much to do in such a short time, unpack, become acquainted with my kitchen, and set up the room how I think it needs to be set up.

Mr. Stevens must have seen the shock on Abigail's face. Reassuringly, he said, "Don't worry, Mrs. Camp. We'll all be chippin' in to feed our crew tonight. We've plenty of grub. It shouldn't take too long to get supper ready." But first, we'll let you unpack a bit."

Mr. Webster nodded and shuffled out the door behind Simon Stevens.

In awe and wonder, Abigail was glad Jared was still here to talk to this man with her. "Mr. Farwell. Glad to meet you." Abigail said as she held out her gloved hand to greet the man. "You did all this for me?" *No one except my father, not even George, had tried to impress me this much.*

"Yes, Ma'am. We didn't want you to put up in a tent," he chuckled. "We need your help so we want you to be comfortable. Plus, well," he added, jutting his thumb backwards, "having a woman around will settle these wild cats around here."

Abigail felt comfortable with the man. His dark eyes sparked kindness. *He's a handsome man in a rugged sort of way.* "Thank you for all your hard work. The room is very nice and comfortable, and the rocking chair," she added stroking the arms with her gloved hands.

"Well, I can't take credit for that. Another of our pioneers brought that for you."

"It's beautiful. I want to thank him for this too."

"You'll get to meet most of everyone tonight at suppertime."

Jared backed toward the door. "Make sure you lock up all around. I noticed the bedroom door has a big hook," Jared said, showing her the iron hook on the side of her door.

"Yes, good idea, Mrs. Camp," Mr. Farwell assured her. "Our workers seem to be a good lot, but just to be safe, lock up. See you later."

Abigail walked behind the men as they left and pushed the latch to lock it. She rested her head against the door. She had made it—her travels by train from Stowe to Illinois, on a steamboat up to Minnesota Territory, and finally to Clearwater. And the river—the grand old Mississippi with its power, strength, and magic brought her to this job. She felt grateful to Jared Wheelock for thinking of her and helping her so she could take care of herself and her son Cassius.

Still standing with her back to the door, Abigail surveyed her new home. It was clean, fresh, and aglow with the late afternoon sun. As she walked to her room, a flume of golden specks poured in front of her.

For the first time in my life, I'm alone. Yes, Jared's close by, but I'm primarily alone and responsible for myself.

Abigail unpacked some of her bags, looking for a work dress and apron. Filling in the drawers would take the rest of the day, and she simply could not spare the time. She had to finish unpacking later. Once she hung up her traveling clothes, she pulled out an older dress her mother had altered for her from her travel case. She shook it a few times, trying to release the wrinkles. Ironing her clothes would have to be on her agenda soon too.

She pulled the gray dress over her head, smoothing it as she buttoned up the bodice. *Wait! I've never had a white lace collar on this dress.* Abigail grabbed a looking glass from her bag and looked at the surprise her mother had intended for her to see. *Oh! Ma. We came so close to having a relationship before I left Stowe. Obviously, you're trying to make up for our lost time together. I wonder what other little surprises you have for me in my bags. I owe everyone a thank you for getting me here.*

George, I wish we could have traveled together. However, your wanderlust and quest for adventure never seemed to include me and Cassius. I suppose it was the money. It took everything out of us for you to go it alone. Maybe, if you had thought on smaller terms, we could have explored together. Unfortunately, your get-quick-rich schemes brought you down and took me and Cassius with you. You left me with prying eyes and lots of back talk on the streets in Stowe.

Abigail pulled the white apron over her head, tied it around her waist, and brushed out some of the wrinkles. *I must do a good job here. I must prove I can make it so I can send for Cassius or go back home with some cash.*

When Abigail stepped into the golden dust pouring through her window, she felt a kiss on her cheek. Like a portent, she heard George whisper a line from Shakespeare, "All that glisters is not gold," which is something he had to learn the hard way.

Chapter 7

Finding Her Way

As Abigail woke, she recognized her sister Mary sitting beside her quietly as if she were praying or sleeping. As Abigail tried to sit up and adjust her pillows, Mary lifted her head. She had changed so much from when they lived together while Jared had taken off for Minnesota Territory.

"Mary," Abigail whispered, patting her sister's hand resting on her lap. "How long has it been?"

As if she, too, woke and struggled to remember where she was, Mary blinked twice, squeezed Abigail's hand, and said, "I've been here almost every day to give Tom and Maude a rest."

"Then it's true, dear sister, I've been unconscious for a while? I hope you have come to help me remember where I am and explain who these strangers are to me." Abigail stared out the bedroom door as she pondered her predicament—a whole new life, husband, and daughter. Ever since Mary was little and swore she had not read her diary, Abigail believed her. She realized then and now her sister would not nor could not deceive her.

Mary sobbed into her hands. "I'm so sorry you are suffering so."

"Mary, Mary, don't be so sad. Jared said I am doing fine."

Between sobs, she answered, "I know. He reassured me as well. I just worried so much. And now, all the good times, and even the bad you have forgotten like they never happened or aren't worth remembering."

"Come on now. I remember Stowe and our friends and relatives, aunts, uncles, cousins," she broke off saying before she thought *and George.* "I tell you what. I need you to be my brain. Help me remember everything I don't. Tell me the good and the bad.

Try to bring it all back to me, okay?" Abigail patted her little sister's hand again.

Sitting up and finally looking into her sister's eyes, Abigail recognized something tired, something aged for sure, but something far away in them. Mary was older, so much older than she had remembered. *Is she sad or is there something else going on?*

"Mary, how are you now? How's our Little Mary?"

Mary laughed as she wiped her eyes. "Big sister, I'm fine, but very tired. I don't know but the stress of worrying about you, and I've been plagued with stomach problems since the new year and can't seem to shake is wearing me down. I came as soon as I could get cleaned up and ready, but that was well around ten before I arrived. I know we have lots to get caught up on, especially, our Little Mary," Mary emphasized and chuckled, "now wants to be called by her given name Isabelle and just turned thirty-three years old. She is a big sister to her sister Fannie who toddled behind her cousin Maude for a long time."

Abigail rested back on the pillow. "My gracious." Imagining all she would learn and relearn, she told Mary, "Well, the story must go on soon. I just now awoke from a dream of arriving in Clearwater. I'll have lots of questions to ask."

"And I must go as soon as Maude finishes coddling an egg for you. I promised Jared I'd stay only five minutes. I'll bring the girls tomorrow to visit. Now you rest." Mary squeezed Abigail's hand. "I'm so glad you're on the mend, and we'll talk soon."

With that, like an open invitation, Maude walked in carrying a tray.

≈≈≈≈≈

"Ma, you devoured that meal like a starving animal. Do you want more?" Maude asked before grabbing the tray from Abigail's lap.

"No, no more, but I was hungry for sure," Abigail answered, dabbing her lips with her napkin. "Thank you so much, Maude." Abigail pulled up her top sheet and whisked away a few toast crumbs. "Maude, could we talk? I know Jared told me to relax, but maybe we could talk for a few minutes."

"Of course, Mother. Would you like me to refresh your tea? I know I'd appreciate another cup of coffee."

"That would be welcomed. And afterward, if I have the strength, I'd like to get washed up."

It took a few moments before Maude returned. Setting the cups on her mother's side table, she pulled the small rocker close to her bedside.

"You know, Maude, that rocker was your grandmother Hannah's."

Handing her mother her favorite teacup and picking up her own, she said, "Actually, Ma, the one you always had by your bedside is now out in Pa's Corner. That was Grandma Hannah's. He said it was too fragile for just anyone to sit on when they visited you. The rocker that was always close to your bed is now sitting by Pa's Corner, where he repairs and cleans shoes and saddles. Pa exchanged the rockers when Uncle Jared started caring for you. This one's a bit steadier and lots bigger. You always told me someone left it for you in the hotel when you came to Clearwater to be the housekeeper for the hotel."

"The room confused me at first. The layout is a lot like my parents'," Abigail said before retracting, "but I suppose a square room with lots of furniture has only a few ways to be decorated."

"Let's see. When Grandpa Robinson came to visit so long ago after Grandma died, he brought the little chest he said that held your treasures when you were little and that sits there at the end of your bed. And, oh, this little table here by your side came from one of your grandmothers," Maude added.

Gently stroking her hand over the table, Abigail recognized the coolness of the marble top. Then like a match flamed in the dark, Abigail remembered the little drawer in the front held something private. *I wish I could remember what.*

"Pa built you this bed, your dresser, and his wardrobe out of the white oak driftwood he pulled out of the river. He carved a branch with leaves into both sides at the top of headboard."

Abigail looked up and saw the leaves briefly before she felt pain at the back of her head. She raised her teacup to sip some tea. The cup felt so familiar—the way she slid her pointer finger through the handle, how it felt like a trigger to a pistol. As she brought it to her lips, she looked through the delicate cup and saw a cameo on the other side. As she turned it left and right, dainty gold swirls swam in the tea.

"Ma, do you recognize your cup and saucer?"

"I think you bought it for me when you were a child."

Maude blinked a surprise back at her mother and laughed. "Good going, Ma. I bought it when Grandpa Joe and I went with Pa to St. Cloud. They both gave me some money to buy you a gift. We boarded the morning steamboat and were gone all day. While Pa went to his meetings, Grandpa and I walked up Fifth Avenue and all over St. Germain Street to see all the changes taking place. We had lunch at the Excelsior Restaurant. I remember, I had never had such fancy food before."

"I suppose it was quite an experience for your grandpa too," Abigail said sarcastically before smiling. "Somehow I recall him coming home and doctoring himself to ease the burn in his stomach, but then he often ate what he shouldn't even though he told his patients to watch certain foods." *I know you're gone, Pa. Yet, I can feel you in this young woman, your granddaughter, sitting next to me. She's someone I know deep down inside. She's so comfortable to talk to, just like you.*

Maude coughed after sipping her coffee. "Ma, you knew Grandpa's ways more than anyone I know. Your memory is coming back."

"I bet a large boulder would have to roll on top of my head to forget my father," Abigail said, visualizing one of the huge rocks in the dark and scary hideaway north of Stowe locals called Smuggler's Notch falling and hitting her. "We were so much alike. He could fill in our sentences for each other. I suppose it's because of all the time we spent with one another doctoring back in Stowe and around Clearwater."

"I suppose. You two were a lot alike. Anyway, before I bought the cup, I walked around Mrs. Ottensmeyer's Millinery

Shoppe on St. Germain Street. I suppose all that material, silk, fur, feathers, buttons—oh, so many fancy buttons, made me think about becoming a milliner just like her. Unfortunately, I also remember being overwhelmed with everything and couldn't decide what to spend my pittance on."

"I can still picture early St. Germain. What a wonderful street with so much potential. Back then, there was little for women to buy except staples, coffee, tea, flour, sugar, and an occasional dry goods store with plain material. When Mrs. Ottensmeyer opened her store, we women who had settled the area and had a bit of cash, could find trinkets and treasures to make us feel like we had overcome. I know some of the other stores started to compete and finally provided more to choose from."

"I'm glad you remember Ma. So you know where I am talking about. As Grandpa and I continued to tramp around, we became frustrated because we couldn't find anything special for you. I nearly gave up and bought you strawberry plants, which were on sale at Limperich's. Just as we were passing the store, we almost knocked over Mrs. Farwell or Mrs. Allen as she wanted to be called coming out of the door of her new store." Maude looked at Abigail as she gently fixed the pillow on her bed. "Do you remember your old friend, Ma?"

Abigail's scanned the room. *Mrs. Allen, Mrs. Farwell.* She closed her eyes for a few moments, trying to bring the name into character.

"Don't your remember? She was a very creative photographer, an, an … I can't remember the word."

"Are you talking about the type of photographs she took? Mrs. Allen who married John Farwell? Hmmmm." Abigail tried to think. She remembered the names, especially Farwell. But Mrs. Allen? She could not think of what she looked like, but her name conjured up a feeling of comfort and love for her friend. She remembered her name was Nancy and she had a brief marriage to John Farwell, the same man Abigail met the same day she started at the hotel. He and others had worked hard to prepare the hotel for her. Tall, handsome, and rugged, Abigail liked him immediately. *I knew John. He had something about him that reminded me of George.*

"Oh, can't you remember, Ma, they separated? She took her children and moved off their farm in Maine Prairie and back to her house in St. Cloud. Later, John sold his farm and for the second time joined Captain Fisk's regiment to Montana. I remember thinking at the time their love story was a prequel to General Custer and his wife Elizabeth."

Picking up her cup, Abigail had a nagging feeling of remembrance, like a deep calling unto deep. She tried hard before she begged God to open her heart and head to think clearly. "This numbness, this lack of memory, is paralyzing me," she said.

When she took a sip, she saw Athena clearly rising out of her tea. *General Custer?* Like a parade of images, Abigail could see the newspaper articles about John joining Captain Fisk's Exhibition, mounting his horse, bending to kiss his woman before donning his military hat, and galloping west to Dakota Territory and beyond to Montana. Such romance, such devotion for the one left behind, such sacrifice each would make away from each other—yes, like Custer and his Libby also did when he too went off to fight the Sioux in Montana!

"Ah, yes. I can picture John, but I can't picture this woman. I know she is someone important in my life, influential even."

"Well, after Grandpa greeted her and they caught up on old times, I blurted we were looking for a present for you. She said she had just the thing. We followed her back to her house in the south end in Lower Town, which was on our way back to the boat landing. I remember all she talked about to Grandpa was you. How she missed having your visits, how she missed your homemade sausage and bread and butter pickles."

As Abigail sipped from her cup, she saw Athena rising in front of her. The helmet-like hair and the golden curls bursting from under the rim, along with the tea, energized her body and mind.

She took another sip and said, "Such a lovely woman. She would know just the right present to give me." Abigail settled back against her pillow and massaged the cup as if it were a lantern that could conjure up anything she wished to have.

"You remember her now, Mother? Do you remember how she hauled all her photograph supplies around everywhere? Ma, you're small, but standing next to her made you look large. Mrs. Allen's waist was tiny even after having a few babies."

"I do, I really remember her. Despite her size, Nancy had the strength of an Amazon as she hauled those picture-taking supplies around as if they were mere trinkets."

Maude took her mother's teacup from her hands. "Did you say Nancy? That was her name. I'd forgotten it too. You two were good friends. She stayed with us a few times when she had pictures to take down here. Remember, how she loved our lower closet? She said it was perfect, the size and the darkness, to develop her artwork."

Abigail closed her eyes. She tried to see her friend. Soon she heard the cups and saucers rattle to the rhythm of Maude's step as she retreated with the tray.

Funny, I don't feel sleepy, yet I can't seem to keep my eyes open. Nancy, dear friend, my heart hurts. Abigail felt tears well up in her eyes and began to understand why. She missed her friend even though she could not picture her.

With her head resting on the soft and cool pillow, Abigail recollected the first time she and Nancy met. One blizzardy late morning a long time ago, Abigail rode into Clearwater to meet others for a potluck at the Benson home. The village had invited Jane Swisshelm, the editor of the *St. Cloud Democrat*, to come lecture on abolition in the first of her Aristotle-like lessons on abolition. She knew no out-of-town guests could possibly make it to the monthly event, even if they had been invited. Abigail wondered if their lunch and Lyceum would be canceled for the afternoon because of the weather, but she decided to go anyway just in case it was still on.

She remembered some of the village locals arrived at George Benson's bringing pots of mashed turnip, large pans of roast venison and pheasant, and bowls of potatoes for a potluck. Abigail had brought two jars of homemade pickles and sliced smoked sausage. Although they requested everyone to be there at noon sharp, Mr. Benson announced they would wait an hour just in case others were coming. But at one o'clock, the guests took up plates and utensils and began their food line.

A knock came upon the door. When Mr. Benson answered it, three bundles blew into the house, followed by swirling gales of snow.

As she and Mrs. Benson raced to unwrap the women, Mr. Benson helped the tallest of the trio unburden himself or herself. Abigail grabbed the fur muff from the first woman who walked in the door before unwinding a rough, icy, wet, and smelly horse blanket and a very thick wool blanket. Finally, after removing her brown and black wool hat, a thick brown cloak with a red fox fur over her shoulders, Abigail discovered a woman with hair color set in ringlets to match her furs. Now in stocking feet, as she had already flipped off her over boots, she stood about four foot ten, shorter than Abigail's five foot one.

Mrs. Benson proclaimed, "My goodness! We sure didn't expect anyone else to arrive in this weather."

Once she felt strong enough to breathe in warm air, the leader of the group, gasped forgiveness for their lateness and introduced the three. "Good afternoon. We're sorry to be so late, but we made it through the whirling tempest from St. Cloud. I'm Jane Swisshelm, the editor of the St. Cloud Democrat and beside me," she said, nodding and patting her friend's arm," is Mrs. Nancy Allen, St. Cloud's new photo artist. She lives and works right across from me and the Democrat."

As if she had a paintbrush in hand, Abigail recreated her friend from a scene from their first meeting. Abigail concentrated hard. She took it stroke by stroke. She started at the top, from her curly red-brown hair down to her dress, a blue, green, and yellow plaid with white collar set off her dainty waist. Even though Abigail could not focus on her friend's face, she remembered Nancy smiled a lot and spoke little. When she did, she became as animated as Jane Swisshelm, nodding and agreeing with nearly everything she knew about St. Cloud's problem with certain individuals who stood staunchly against abolition.

≈≈≈≈≈

"Abby," are you sleeping? Maude told me you were resting, but she wasn't sure if you were sleeping."

"Oh," Abigail said as she opened her eyes and blinked hard to see who was calling her. "Thomas!" She stumbled over his name. "I wasn't really sleeping."

"Good!" I think we've gotta talk."

"Well, sure." She nodded for him to take the chair by her.

He cleared his throat, then coughed, and finally blurted out, "I'm sorry to ask you this, but don't you remember me at all?"

Abigail looked at this sprightly looking man with the bald head. He seemed kind. He seemed worried, his eyes squinting through his spectacles. What could she tell him?

"I still don't remember faces. I knew Mary when she came this morning, but she is my sister. I'm open to be reminded a bit though. When did we get married?"

This man who claimed to be her husband stood up and walked to the window. "It's snowing hard out again."

Abigail asked, "How long have I been out of it, Thomas?"

"Many, many days, a few weeks, I guess," he said, shaking his head. Walking back to the chair, Thomas stubbed his foot on the end of the bed. "Damn, Abby," Thomas hollered, hopping on one foot and holding onto the other. "I always wanted to fix this bedstead so I wouldn't keep stumbling over it with bare feet at night. I'm sorry. I shouldn't have shouted like that. It's just. ..."

Abigail sat straight up in bed. She remembered the voice, the eruption, the stubbing of his toes at the end of the bed.

"What is it, Abby? What's the matter?" Tom Porter said as he slid his way closer to her side, lowered his arm around her back as if to protect her neck and head. "Come on now, lie back down," he pled.

"Thomas, I suddenly remembered you kicking the end of this bed before."

"Abby! That's good news." Shoving his glasses back up on top of his head, he blotted his eyes with the sheet.

"Bits and pieces only," she said lowering into the pillow again.

"And you remember my cussing first?" Tom asked as he chuckled and sat down. "This's a good sign. I built the bed to fit in our first house, across the way. The bedroom was small and we needed to tuck in the cradle so everything would fit. When we built this house in 1871, I wanted to buy you a new bedstead. You refused because of your sentimentality."

"Was the cradle for Maude?"

Tom Porter facial expression froze. He stared at his wife.

Looking at her husband, Abigail asked, "What is it? What's wrong?"

Slowly, stumbling, Thomas said, "I don't know what to say. You don't remember our baby boy?"

Baby boy? Cassius?

"Tarrant, our son, Abby."

Thomas pulled himself up from the chair and looked across the bed, staring at nothing. Abigail thought she heard a sniffle. He putzed with the dresser, hammering with his hand to see how steady it was, straightened the mirror, imagining it crooked, and kicked the carpet like it was fluffed up.

"I don't know what to say. Why don't you come back and sit down. Please, tell me about him?" Abigail patted the chair beside the bed.

Seemingly, reluctant and hurt, Tom came back, this time walking out of the way not to catch his leg on the end of the bed and sat down. Maude came in carrying a tray with three coffee cups.

"I thought you two needed some refreshment. Pa, you haven't eaten a thing since you went out to do chores, and that was way early."

"What have we here?" Thomas asked, grabbing his cup as he looked at saucers of sliced cinnamon breakfast cake.

"Take the largest slice," Maude added with a nod.

"How thoughtful," Abigail blew and sipped at the steaming brew. "Just leave mine though. I'm not quite ready to eat anything yet. The coffee tastes good though."

"So what are you two talking about?" Maude set the tray on the floor, placing the cake on her mother's side table.

Thommas looked at Abigail and she looked back, their eyes catching each other's thoughts. Abigail recognized something, something deep in his soul.

"We were talking about our baby boy, Maudie," her father said, still looking at his wife.

"Ah, little Tarrant, named after Uncle Tarrant, your brother, Ma," Maude said patting her arm. "By the way, Ma, Unc will be coming to see you tomorrow. He's been stuck on an indoor painting job at the Whittemore house. Their wrapping up today."

"That'll be nice," Abigail answered, although deep in thought. *Baby Tarrant, baby Tarrant.* She had another baby besides Cassius and Maude?

"Your breakfast cake's delicious, Maudie," Thomas said, scraping the saucer with his fork.

"Would you like more, Pa? We won't be eating dinner for a couple hours."

"Maybe later. It's good though." He handed her the plate and fork. Patting his pocket, he found what he wanted and pulled out his pipe and tobacco. After tapping in his tobacco, he lit up, puffing and smacking his lips until it caught into a small flame before settling down.

"I love your tobacco blend, Pa. I feel so relaxed after you light up."

Taking a last sip from her cup, Abigail saw Athena rising again and her helmet holding down her curly hair. She touched her own locks and wondered how matted her hair was since she had not combed for a while. As soon as Jared would let her sit by the wood stove, she'd get Maude to help her wash it. Her mind churned. She wanted to remember all she had forgotten.

"I'm sorry. I'm lost in thought. I've a brother named Tarrant, too. I'm right about that aren't I?"

"You are, Abby-girl. He was born about a year after we married," Thomas puffed a bit, holding his pipe between his teeth while he patted his wife's hand. "He was a fat baby, bald like his papa. He giggled as I danced him around the room. He jigged around the divan, around the table legs, anything he could hold onto long before he walked." He was a healthy and happy baby."

Thomas's eyes turned red. Abigail recognized her husband's type of grief. He again rubbed his face, stirred a bit to get more comfortable if he sat or stood, and took a long puff from his pipe.

Child of my soul, why don't I remember you?

"Jared told us it was the diphtheria when he looked into his poor little throat," Thomas said sadly, shaking his head.

Maude patted his leg and raised her head as if she sniffed for thinner air to breathe.

The family of three sat quietly for a few minutes.

Abigail's pain came rushing back as if her baby had just died. Slowly, she started to talk, and her words came faster than the tears. She was thankful that she remembered something.

"He didn't have a chance. We thought he had a few sniffles. Then he had a fever by late morning. Jared came. He made Little Tarrant gag when he swiped his throat with alcohol to try to prevent that leathery sheathe from growing over the membranes of the throat." Abigail closed her eyes again. "Then he was gone. You got Thomas Tollington who built furniture to build our baby a coffin because you had no heart for it."

Abigail let felt Thomas's rough hand soothing her soft one. She tried sounding upbeat and remarked, "Later, I promise I'll remember more. I think I'm getting tired now."

"Of course, Abby. We'll let you rest. Don't worry. It'll come back, all of it," Tom said. "I'll come back and eat dinner with you, okay?"

Abigail nodded. Puffs of cherry smoke, the softness of his touch, and his gentle habits—even his cussing, felt so familiar. What else would she learn about this man she was to call Husband?

~~~~~

Her mother, Hannah, had invited her, Cassius, and the two Marys to come for Christmas Eve dinner. Her father had butchered a cow.

Abigail had lost her appetite after George took off for California. Now, probably from lack of food in her stomach, she felt sort of sick at times. However, her mother crafted best in the kitchen.
~~~~~

The whole family would be there for once, including Abigail's brother Nathan, his wife Fannie and little Ella, her sisters Mary with Little Mary and Annette, her younger brother Tarrant, as well as she and Cassius. The feast included roasted beef, potatoes and carrots, and homemade bread to sop up the rich, brown gravy. Her stomach growled. Maybe she was hungry after all. For sure, the family would do Hannah proud for all the work she would put in.

Mild outside, Abigail and Mary carried their coats. Cassius ran all the way to his grandparents' house, skidding in slippery snow, circling a group of carolers, and nearly falling when a stray dog ran in front of him.

"Cassius, slow down! You're not going to eat any sooner by getting their faster," Abigail shouted as her son ran around a corner and out of sight.

Mary laughed. "He is a true boy, Abby. He can't slow down, especially when he thinks of food."

Little Mary skipped and pulled her mother as well, wanting to see her grandmother who always had little sugary treats for her.

A few outdoor lanterns lit their way. Stores, like Mower's General Mercantile, displayed light from the gas lamps hanging near their doors. Snow covered bushes, trees, the surrounding mountains, and the ground.

From the heady bouquet of herbs and spices, along with sliced onion covering the beef roast to the orange and apple pomanders stuffed with cloves sitting in the wooden bowl in the entryway, her parents' house smelled divine. After they all slid into their places around the large dining table and Cassius squeezed in beside her, they prayed:

For each new morning with its light,
For rest and shelter of the night,
For health and food, for love and friends,
For everything your goodness sends,
Thank you!

The meal began with her father carving the roast and sliding a juicy slice onto each plate handed to him. Serving bowls heaped with golden potatoes and orange carrots passed from left to right. The Perkins', her mother's family name, white, porcelain gravy boat, handed down from one generation to her mother, overflowed with rich, brown gravy.

This mixture of fat and rich juices held together with sprinkles of flour and stirred until it became a brown sauce rounded the table toward Abigail. She watched as Cassius covered his food in gravy. As he poured, Abigail saw a fine circle of yellow grease circling around his plate.

Doctor Joe laughed and said, "It is so good to see a growing boy eat."

Abigail nearly pushed Cassius onto the floor as she gagged, pulling up her napkin to cover her mouth. She ran out the back door to the clothesline and hung on with all her might.

Her father came outside and brought her coat with him, which he shoved under his armpit. Putting one hand on her back and one her forehead, he said, "Shush, shush. Try to take a good clean breath, Child."

Crying, throwing up, and moaning, Abigail tried to do as she was told. She gagged again, only to start heaving again. *What in the world have I caught now? I hate this part of sickness. Never much help for Pa when I'm supposed to be a bedside helper. I've claimed before I'm a sympathy gagger.*

"Try to calm yourself again. Take a few more good breaths. You haven't got much in your stomach. I'm sure of that. Your clothes are hanging off you."

After breathing steadily for a few minutes, Abigail stood upright. She scanned the backyard. Her mother's garden, no longer alive with green sprouts and leafy lettuces, smelled like hearty earth. It had settled her stomach and calmed her queasiness But hunger had not returned.

"Pa, I don't think I can go back and sit at the table. Will you tell Mary and Cassius I'm going home to clean up and rest? Tell Ma I'm sorry too. Thanks for comforting me."

"Of course. Your Ma will feel bad. She made the meal mostly for you 'cause we're all concerned about you. You've lost so much weight. She'll understand though about your being sick.

Tomorrow, I want to take a good look at you. Whatever this is has gone on too long."

Abigail walked up the street to her sister and brother-in-law's house. Mary locked the front door, but she always kept the back one open, a habit she started when Jared was doctoring in and around Stowe. Dusk had darkened the house so she lit a few lamps. She washed her face in the blue and white basin in the kitchen and brushed her teeth with soda. Although refreshed, Abigail still had no appetite. She pulled her diary from the drawer by her bed.

Too early to change into her nightclothes, Abigail curled up on the parlor's settee, pushing a pillow up to the arm to rest her head. Laying there a few moments, she nearly fell asleep. *Not good! I might not sleep later tonight.* She opened her diary to where her bookmark, her first woven project, a brown and white owl on an olive branch, marked where she had last written:

> December 18, 1852
>
> Geo's gone three weeks now. Every morning I wake up sicker than the day before. By noon, I can keep down only a cup of weak tea. Before he left, Geo told Cass he needed to be the man of the house until he returned. That's a horrible responsibility for a child who still needs his pa. I saw Cass crying by the side of the barn when I went out to hang clothes on the line. He'd be shamed if I tried to comfort him, but I've got to make it easier some way. It's only him and me now. I can't be responsible for no one else.
>
> *Now six days later, nausea seems to seal my fate. Even last week, I had a nagging fear I was in the family way. I'm so tired. I feel like I'm dragging my feet. Lord! Help me! I can't handle any more. I wring my hands over George all day. I don't even know what to worry about. But he's on a ship to kingdom come—somewhere in the Atlantic down to South America and onto California in the Pacific. Oh, God! It's all too wide, too deep, and too unknown for me. Except for our dear boy, I don't know how I keep plugging away. But*

without hunger, I can't eat. Now, even with hunger, I can't stand the sight and smell of food.

Before she wrote another entry, Abigail grabbed her midwifery book. She looked out the window into the black night. She wanted privacy. No need to let Mary know what she was worrying about.

She turned to the table of contents and found "Signs and Symptoms of Pregnancy":

> The exquisite sympathy existing between the uterus and stomach is manifested in the great irritability of the latter, as in morning sickness. Most usually, though not always, this takes place before rising from bed in the morning, from which circumstance it gets its name. It may commence immediately after conception—more generally it begins about the fourth week. Among the first symptoms besides nausea and vomiting are absence of menstruation. If it is absent for two successive periods, she deems it almost conclusive as to her condition.

Well! I know that. This isn't my first go-around. I've also nursed many women with the same symptoms.

> Anorexia is sometimes present, and may be accompanied by perversion of appetite. ...

That's been my problem, but I thought I was stressed and feeling sorry for myself because George is gone. First, I lose my appetite, and now, I'm hungry but can't stand the smell of food.

We see nothing in the uterus before the seventh day to indicate the existence of a new being ... At the twenty-first day, the embryo appears in the form of a large ant ... the size of a grain of wheat. ...

So, if I am with child, I could be in my 26th or 27 day or even longer. But I may not be. I could be just sick and heartbroken over George.

Abigail browsed further and found the medical truths she could believe in:

> The only certain diagnostic signs of pregnancy are the detection of the active movements of the child; positively feeling the fetus in utero; and the discovery of the pulsation of the fetal heart by auscultation.

As for now, Abigail had no absolute proof she was with child. Her monthlies seldom showed up on time. If she remembered when she carried Cassius, she felt the quickening in about her fourth month, but because of her irregular schedule, she was never positive. Three more months would be a long time to wait to end her curiosity. Abigail felt an inner choke, like an anvil dropped on her chest. She bent over and tried not to moan or cry.

I'm alone ... so alone. Oh, how happy we'd be if George were here to share with me the joys of having another child. We faced so many difficulties before, the false alarms, the bleeding in the first months, leading to one more loss. Yet, we are so happy and thankful for our Cassius.

She heard the screech of the door, and the quiet whisper, "Abigail?" "Abigail?"

She recognized her mother's softer side when she became afraid. Yet, Abigail returned no answer nor a greeting. She choked again and fell onto the divan. She had held her fears in for so long; she lost her tight grip on herself and started to bawl loudly. She heard her mother walk delicately into the darkened house feeling for objects to hold onto before she finally reached her daughter.

"Abigail, it's all right." Hannah Robinson safely sat down next to her daughter. She patted her head, which now laid in her lap. "It's not all that bad. We'll see you through this."

As if she were a tiny child, Abigail felt Hannah rocking her. She said nothing, as she rocked and rocked.

"I'm here for the night, child. Little Mary and Cassius are already in bed, anxiously waiting for tomorrow morning after Santa Claus has come. Mary will sleep with Annette. I brought you some leftovers, bread and butter like you love."

After a few moments of shared sympathy, Abigail sat up and leaned against the back of the divan. She heard no shame from her mother because of her husband's leaving; she heard no snicker of disapproval. Like she totally understood her daughter, Hannah circled her arms around her daughter as they melded together in suffering womanhood.

"How many times I've been down this road before, Ma, only for my term to end abruptly. All of our hopes thrown at our feet. Maybe, if I could have kept one more child, George wouldn't have left me so eagerly. He could still be here."

Another round of spasms erupted from her gut. Abigail had cried before, but what she was now experiencing, was more guttural and physical as she pounded the divan with her fist, more from the deep aloneness of her soul.

After a few minutes, Hannah spoke. "Abby, you're not to blame. Why're women blaming themselves for what men are also responsible for? Your pa believes that there could be something wrong with the man as well—not just the woman. How many times you've been down this road before, always with regret when your cycle returns. Makes Cassius that much more precious."

"So, you're saying I should be more appreciative of its timing? Ma, I can't take on more responsibility," she cried in panic. "I owe you and Pa so much, Mary so much. I have no way of taking care of another human being when I can't even take care of Cass and me."

"Time will tell."

"But that may be too late. I feel strongly about this. Right now, I can't take on another responsibility."

Hannah Robinson slowly unwrapped her around her daughter. The two sat quietly for a few moments. Abigail wondered what her mother thought of her final comments, but she appreciated the silence and the ability to calm after releasing her concerns to someone, even if it were her disapproving mother.

Abigail had helped a few women in what might be now her predicament. Like she instructed them to do, she would simply drink a cup of tea of what she had concocted before going to bed. Not many people in the area knew how she could help, not even her father, nor did the patients know what they were imbibing. Insisting they be no later with their monthlies than two months, she let them put their faith in her to take care of them.

"I have a recipe if you wish to go that route, Abigail."

Abigail heard her mother speak but only heard the word "recipe." *What a time to talk about cooking!* Then she really heard what her mother was referring to.

"Mother! What are you saying?" she asked, underscoring you.

"You know you aren't the first in the family to know how to take care of others."

"What do you mean?"

"I have my mother's herbal recipe box. You know she helped other women like you do. I've never used the one or two you might need, but I know they're in the box."

"I knew she was a midwife, but I didn't know anything else, well, except for the fact you and Pa always compared me to her and Grandma Robinson."

"Most women are to some extent. I've helped, but I never wanted the job at the end of the bed. I've supported those who were in dire need by holding their hands, praying with them, and giving them the confidence to do what they were doing. My mother had the craft. You get it naturally from her, your pa, and Grandma Robinson."

I knew that both grandmothers were well respected midwives and herbalists. You had no interest, Ma? And why haven't you showed me the recipe box?"

"I suppose I relied on my mother's natural instincts. I loved to sew the most." Hannah stood up and grabbed the fireplace poker to stir up the flames. She poked around until she had a good spark and then added a log. Quietly, she said, "I was never quite sure if you had Grandma Abigail, your namesake's, skill or not. I know you helped your father on his rounds, and I know you had a few of our town women who relied on you with their deliveries, but I was never sure if you had concocted your own remedies or not. Besides, I've never hidden the brown box, I've kept it Abby. It was always right there in the kitchen. I used it for bug bites and stomachaches, always with your pa's approval though. He has the craft and knows his business."

"Of course! I know which box you are referring to but thought it was simply recipes. I'd love to look through it some time. I've practiced with herbs, roots, and plants some. I have a tea recipe that is so safe, sometimes, my patients need to take two cups instead of one to cure themselves and restore their menses. I've learned from Pa's old medical books too. I know where my recipe goes so it doesn't hurt the mother later on, no lasting health problems, and" Abigail emphasized, "there is no opium in it or anything else that is habit-forming and harmful for the baby."

"You sound like my mother, Abigail. She thought I had the craft so she talked with me nearly every day when I was growing up about her midwifery. She felt the same about opium. Although, I think she used laudanum occasionally on women who were in great pain."

"I suppose, when Grandpa and Grandma Perkins came to Vermont from Massachusetts back in the late 1700's, Grandma was about the only midwife for quite a while."

"There were few people in the area at first, but soon many towns grew up fast, and Grandma Perkins rode a horse to them and around the countryside often to help a woman in labor. She often nursed the sick and set bones as well because areas in Vermont didn't get a doctor until the early 1800's when Doctor Downer arrived. He was the first, and like others who arrived here, he had to survive like the rest of the beginners, building a home, feeding his family, and beginning a business. Most women were used to women helping them with their private business—still are. But soon other doctors arrived, your pa becoming one of the respected. They handled everything but childbearing."

Abigail became quiet again. She thought about her predicament. Grandma Perkins has been gone for nearly five years. *I might have talked to her as I am talking to my mother now. I wish I had known Mother would been so understanding.*

"I wish we'd have discussed this sooner, Mother. I always have had a bit of guilt about the controversial side of my small affairs." Abigail struggled to say what she felt she should say.

"Maybe ... I needed your approval or needed to feel your acceptance and understanding."

Hannah became quiet. She got up and added a log to the fire. She poked and prodded until it finally caught hold. Golden flames roared, spitting ashes on her. She brushed off and put down the poker.

"I can only say, after we lost your older sister when she was just two-years old, I had little to give. When you were born just a few months later, I was still grieving. I know you needed more than I could give. You and your pa became fast friends. Then I got so busy with your brothers and sisters, and all the work I had to do. It just got harder to give what I was too tired to give to you and everyone." Hannah's shoulders sunk as she sat back down on the divan. "I know I became crabby. Sewing made me escape. I loved every detail. The more difficult, the more challenging, the more lost in my world I'd become."

Abigail thought a bit before asking, "Ma, did you ever want to take a break from child-bearing?"

"I had a few miscarriages, not as many as you. I mourned those losses, but not as much as the deaths of Lucretia and little Charlie a while later when he too reached two years old. Maybe if I had been given full birth to those who I had become tendered with, I might've thought about slowing myself down, but I didn't. Your father and I truly wanted each and every one of you. But I know sometimes, women are overburdened with way too many births, not enough money to raise them right, and little support from the husband. Besides, each time I became with child gave me a break from my painful monthlies."

Now long past her "painful monthlies," Hannah had those occasional flushes, tiredness, and extra weight around the stomach like most older women had. Abigail, remembering how her mother used to take to her bed because she was so uncomfortable, could identify with her. When she had her sick times, she too spent time in bed, helped a bit by willow bark tea Hannah prepared for her.

"I never once thought of doing this before, Ma. You know that. George and I wanted more children, yet it didn't happen. Now, I can't carry this baby, even if it is the last of him I'll ever have."

Abigail took a deep breath without sighing. "I can say that without wanting to cry. Cassius and I will try to go it alone soon—to take care of ourselves."

Hannah patted her daughter's arm. "Do you think you can sleep now? I'm about tuckered out."

"You cooked all day, Mother. You should be tired. I might have a piece of your bread and butter. I finally feel like I can eat something. Thanks for the good talks and the understanding, Ma. I've got to say I feel better. Tomorrow's Christmas, and hopefully, I will have no need to worry anymore about my own version of a manger."

Chapter 8

The Reawakening

Scraping and clanking of a cast-iron plate on the cook stove, floorboards squeaking, "shushing"—all these sounds broke through Abigail's snooze.

"Oh, you're awake!" Thomas said as he looked in the bedroom door.

I guess I am. Abigail pulled herself up to a sitting position and began to lean back before Thomas moved fast to plump and slide the pillow up for her comfort.

"I woke from a dream about living back home—in Stowe. The time I spent with my mother Hannah."

"I bet your brother Tarrant would love to hear about this too," he said. "Tarrant, Tarrant?" Thomas said in a loud voice, not quite shouting.

With his copper hair aglow, her younger brother Tarrant walked in through the door after Thomas announced him.

"Tarrant, little brother, how nice to see you," Abigail stretched out her arms, inviting her brother to come hug her. "Where have you been keeping yourself? How are the children and Sarah?"

After squeezing his sister, he said, "Abigail, I shouldn't have hugged you so hard. How're you doing?"

"Posh," Abigail whisked her hand like a small broom and she was sweeping his silly talk away. Sitting up even closer to where Tarrant sat, she crossed her legs underneath like she had done when she was a child. "What brings you up here, Tarrant?"

"What brings me up here? Are you joking, Abby? I came to see how you were doing. The last I heard about your concussion was that you hadn't recovered consciousness."

"Thomas, what you have been telling people to worry them so?" Abigail looked at her husband and smiled, but she saw he had a shocked expression plastered on his face." She said, "I'm fine," trying to reassure them both. She recognized the looks of doubt the men shared.

"Our sister Mary wrote almost every day. She only resaid what Jared had diagnosed, dear sister. So don't go blaming your husband here. The man has been running ragged, getting a head start on early spring chores, heading into the state capitol for important meetings and voting on issues, taking either the slow steamer or the train back and forth from St. Paul to Clearwater to check on you. He's a big and an important man now. You have to give him some respect."

Abigail lowered her head. She felt so embarrassed. She thought Thomas knew she was teasing, now both misread her message and Thomas seemed to have hurt feelings.

"Thomas," she started to say, as she looked up at him, "I was just having fun with you. I'm sorry you misunderstood."

Her husband came closer and patted her leg, "No offense taken. I need to learn or relearn your lighter side."

"Well, I started it because I thought you were complaining. I hadn't realized you were as well as you said you were and were able to tease. I'm sorry too." Tarrant said, squeezing his sister's hand.

"I woke up like this. I feel peppy, you guys. I'm going to sit up for a while in the parlor. Maybe steal your chair again."

Thomas winced. "Don't you think you should wait until Jared says it's okay?"

"I feel quite spunky. Maybe I'll sit for five minutes or two hours. I've gotta try though. How else will I start getting stronger?" Abigail could read hope in her husband's smile yet doubt in his eyes. Determined, she said, "I want to get freshened up though. When Maude comes in, I'll have you men get some coffee or something so she can help me. I may need your help to get me out in Thomas's chair so don't go too far away."

"Well, while we wait, let me tell you about the kids. Lulu, well, Lulu is a beautiful and smart young woman. You know she is nine now, Abby. She plays the piano as well and never has to be reminded to practice. Her reddish blond hair curls to her waistline.

Freddie finished school early. He will help me with some painting for the next year or so but will soon start taking courses at the Hospital College to become a physician like his Grandpa Joe."

"How could they be so old already?" As a matter of fact, Abigail hated to admit it, but she could not remember her brother's children's faces. How she wanted her forgetfulness to fade away and her memories to light up.

Just like that, Tarrant pulled a package out of his coat. He unwrapped the portrait he had been hiding. Abigail saw a well-dressed little girl with ruffles and blonde ringlets. The young man stood holding onto the back of the girl's chair. He, too, was dressed to the nines in his new-style suit, light pants and vest, long dark jacket, and light, probably white, shirt and dark ascot. He also had light hair.

"You can't tell me your children are this old, Brother!"

Thomas took the photograph and held it in his hand. "My niece and nephew do me proud, Tarrant. They are both quite handsome."

Again, Abigail floundered in the black emptiness of her mind. *What incentive will goad my old noggin to start thinking clearly? I will not tell Tarrant I don't even remember him having two children!*

"Well, T. C., the way they eat, I can tell you they are growing. Freddy stands taller than me, and our sweet Lulu stretches up beyond her mother."

"Maude, come see Freddie and Lulu," her father insisted as his daughter walked back into the bedroom. "Aren't they looking just fine?"

"Unc, you've got lots to be proud of right here. They've grown like Pa's corn in late summer."

"Your uncle told us," Abigail stumbled because she forgot her nephew's name for a moment, "ah, um, Freddie's taking some courses to be a doctor."

"Like Gramps? Isn't that wonderful?" Maude said, handing the picture back to Tarrant. "By the way, I came in to ask if anyone wanted some coffee, or if I could make some nice hot tea too. Uncle Tarrant, you will stay for a later mid-day meal, won't you? I made some good hearty beef soup. Potatoes and carrots aren't getting done so it might be a while yet. Oh, I should've asked if you're staying here or with Aunt Mary and Uncle Jared."

"I brought my overnight bag. I can sleep anywhere. If I'm in the way, I'm sure I can stay at the Morrison House or Mary and Jared might take me in."

"Good grief. You always know you're welcome here. You know that," Abigail said. "Maude, your father and your uncle are going to help me sit up in the parlor for a while. I need to clean up though. Have some hot water to pour in my bowl? Maybe soda for my teeth as well."

"Ma, as I said before you're a pip. Uncle Jared might not agree, but I think if you sit up a bit every day, soon you'll be stronger. I'll be right back."

"We'll get out of your way," Thomas said as Tarrant stood up to move. "We'll get Tarrant settled upstairs and be back to help you, Abby," he said, squeezing her toes before he left.

"The carrots are a bit more tender, so it won't be long now," Maude winked as she carried the large silver tea kettle and washcloth over the towel, she laid over her arm. After setting everything down, she closed the door, and said, "Ma and I'll be finished in here in no time."

Abigail felt physically revived, scrubbed from toes to face, brushed her teeth for an extra-long time, and, with Maude's help, slipped into a clean night gown. She sat on the edge of the bed after getting her dressing gown and slippers on waiting for Thomas and Tarrant to return to help her to the parlor. Abigail's legs felt like wiggly worms and her head hurt, but she needed a new atmosphere. Before she forgot, she quickly grabbed her journal and a pen and slid it into her pocket.

Maude opened the parlor door and picked up the dirty clothes and tea kettle. "Pa and Unc," a term Maude, alone, used on her favored uncle, "you can come help Ma now. When I'm finished with lunch, I'm going to make up your bed."

"Maude, I'm sorry to cause you so much work."

"Look at you, the woman who raised, fed, and clothed me, worrying that I'm overworking for her," Maude said. "I'm here on earth to help you and Pa, and any and all of our relatives, if they need me."

Abigail stood up with the men's help. Her legs bent and wobbled. She half walked and the men half carried her, but she made it to Thomas's chair. With a pillow behind her back, a stool below her feet, and a blanket to cover and warm her, Abigail slid right down into the large chair. The log spat golden sparks before bursting into flames. Her new surroundings, no matter how long she stayed, glowed with promise.

~~~~~

After everyone but Abigail had second helpings, Tarrant grabbed the tray and picked up the bowls.

"Uncle Tarrant, you're a guest."

"I'll work for my keep, thank you very much, and do up these dishes."

"Mother, did you eat enough?"

"Maude, your soup tasted delicious. One cup filled me up. I'd love another cup of coffee, though."

"I wasn't fishing for a compliment, Ma, but thank you. I'll get that," Maude answered.

"Nope, Maude, you worked hard enough. I'll bring in the pot once I've dropped off the dirty dishes," Tarrant said.

"Abby," Thomas interrupted, "are you tired? We can get you back in bed if you are."

"No, not yet. I'm feeling strong. Coffee will help me become a bit more alert. Good soup, good company, good fire. I'm very comfortable."

"Ma, I used your recipe for the bread. I know Uncle Tarrant says he's the best bread baker," Maude said loudly so her uncle could hear. "Did you learn how to bake bread from Grandma Hannah?"

"Shortly after I arrived in the village to become the townsite housekeeper, I had to concoct some type of bread. I couldn't follow Grandma's recipe at first. I had to use a bit of lard to make the dough
~~~~~

because we had no butter at the time. I also threw in boiled potatoes and some of its water. The men raved about the bread."

"When I arrived to help your ma until our sister Mary came, I made soda bread. I learned how to make it when I helped down in St. Anthony after I arrived in 1855 before I came up here. The trick I learned from the cook down there is not kneading the dough beyond mixing it up. So much more tender." Tarrant added, "Your ma, though, she's hard to compete with when it comes to regular cooking. She could cook up large and tasty portions of fried potatoes and side pork. She had the knack."

"Apparently, Simon Stevens, the self-appointed cook, either undercooked the salt pork or over-baked the bread. He knew how to boil potatoes, but that was it. When I took over, even with a few of the crew helping, I had rave reviews from those who were paying for a good meal. I don't think I had to do much to be better than Simon," Abigail snickered while she covered her mouth.

Thomas added, "For what it's worth, Abby could turn rocks into soup. We didn't give her much time to get acquainted with anyone or get settled in because she got busy almost as soon as she met Simon, John Farwell, and the rest of us, to make that first meal. So many of the workers turned out on time just to see the first woman to arrive in the tiny village and to eat her fairs, we had to divide the men into shifts."

"I remember that. My goodness, they ate. And those frying pans! I'd never seen any as large as that. I want to say seventeen or more inches around. I laughed when Simon showed it to me. Then I realized why he needed one so large. At first, I couldn't lift it. Simon did all the hefting."

"Ma, didn't you tell me your friend took your door down to use for a table outdoors to set all the food?" Maude giggled, but she knew how heart sick Abigail had been because she was so proud of her private room and so shocked when she saw John Farwell tear down his work.

"I have to admit, I was overwhelmed that first night. All those men, all that food we had to prepare, yes, in shifts, like Thomas said. Helpers dragged the few small tables from the hotel dining room, but they didn't provide enough room for the food. John ran and took down my door and someone grabbed a couple sawhorses, and we had another table to set up supper."

"By the time I got up to Clearwater to help your ma at the townsite hotel, Maude, she was an old hand at cooking. She could manhandle that frying pan and the soup and stew pots like an old cowhand," Tarrant said."

"Don't let him fool you, Maude. I may have built up my strength to use that frying pan, but I was so busy trying to get all the work done, including washing clothes and ironing for some of the workers, I hardly slept, much less had more than a few minutes break. He was needed, and I valued his help."

"I think we worked well together. You cooked more inside then, and I took over some of working with the heavier Dutch ovens outside. Can't remember how much oatmeal or mush we made in the morning and soups and stews at night. We took turns baking up bread, remember?"

"Morning, night, summer, fall, winter, and spring, we had to keep those fires burning…cooking, baking." Abigail leaned back, resting her head against the back of the chair and said, "Oh, and frying, all day it seemed to keep enough food cooked up. The only true holiday I had that first year of housekeeping for the village was in the winter. Most others had left for a while. Some went to some of those early logging camps north and south of us. Some went to work their own land they had settled on," she added.

"We got paid pretty good though. Anyway, enough for me to get my homestead and buy the necessary tools and equipment to set up my own place. That all took place by the time you quit, Abigail, to marry Mr. Porter here, that next year."

"Ma, how'd you feel with all those men around? You've told me a few stories."

"Well, 'HANDS OFF' is what Simon shouted out to the crew that first night when he introduced me. We had men coming and going constantly. Some stayed a night and moved on. Others a week. Most others hung around a while and we became fast friends. We barely learned their names. Simon Stevens and John Farwell helped a lot and kept their eyes on the hotel, but until we were a bit more settled, I felt safer and had more company. But when your aunt

Mary and Cassius came, I felt I had more freedom. Between the two of them, they could work around the hotel and watch Little Mary in case she should get too close the dangers of fire and water. I remember I took some time to start walking in the woods for some wild onions and garlic, anything to add some flavor to the food besides salt and pepper."

"You ran into your own dangers, though." Thomas crossed his legs and looked like he was having a hard time keeping straight on the horsehair divan. "Do you remember who you met up there?"

Abigail thought, but she could not recollect what had transpired. "You might have to freshen my old, soft noggin' now, Thomas."

"Ma, are you getting tired? Is this all too much for you?" Maude asked eagerly.

"Oh, no. I'm just trying to think here. I remember taking walks but my favorite path took me to the overlook by the river, like you are saying, Thomas. I went there often. I just can't think clearly. Give me more clues."

Thomas shoved his spectacles to the top of his pink, bald head. He rubbed his face and massaged his eyes as if they itched. "Okay, let me think a bit as well."

Abigail looked at her husband as he looked at her. *What am I reading as I try to look into your soul, Thomas? I feel we know each other so well, but I've forgotten and unlearned so much.*

Like the calling of deep unto deep, the husband-and-wife half called, half shouted, "Pal!"

Thomas slapped his leg as Abigail clapped her hands.

Maude joined in, "Ah! Pally!" with tenderness and sadness in her voice.

"Why of course, Pal, that swell dog of yours," Tarrant replied. "Abby, she protected you like only T. C. could."

"You know the reason for that, don't you?" Thomas asked, looking at Abigail.

"Not sure I remember. Why?" Abigail stared into the deep unknown to picture her bodyguard. Pally, as Maude called her, had black and golden-brown fur, from head to scruffy tale that wagged wildly when he was around her. Although she loved Maude and protected her as well, Pal shielded Abigail from danger on all their journeys together.

~~~~~

"Abby!" Jared hollered as Abigail headed out the door. "Where are you going?"

First, Abigail did not recognize the voice and the question because of the saw's annoying buzz and the flume's near-constant roar. She stomped her feet. *Why can't I have a moment's peace without someone needing something?* She had worked hard the last few weeks, on call for every man's so-called need. Abigail had to admit to herself, cooking, cleaning, and washing clothes were not her forte. She needed more, something exciting; she needed a break.

She turned around to see who was calling. "Oh! Jared," she answered in surprise. "I'm just going for a walk. Thought I'd look for berries or grapes to make a jelly or dessert for the men tonight."

Abigail didn't want to tell him her feelings about being fed up with her job. This morning's request to add another customer to her laundry duty brought it all on her shoulders. *Maybe, she would have to admit she had failed this job and needed to head home. Of course, Cassius was here and helping with the hauling of water and bringing in wood. And with Tarrant and Mary helping me, I feel some relief, but I hate doing all that laundry. On the other hand, I don't want to sound ungrateful for everything he's done for me either.*

Trying to sound more cheerful and batting away the ever-present clouds of gnats, Abigail added, "Now that I've got some help around the hotel, I thought I'd reconnect with nature—specifically the Mississippi River. Why?"

Jared pointed toward the back of the hotel building. "Let's talk over by the bushes," he said grabbing her elbow and guiding her around the campfires and the rugged ground.

"You must have something important you have to talk about, Jared." She knew she sounded sarcastic as she asked, "Am I not doing a good enough job for the townsite hotel?"
~~~~~

"Who are you trying to kid, Abby? I have had only compliments as you have. The men are happy to have you here. The food's great. You're agreeable, maybe too agreeable to their requests. Now that you have your brother and sister, and even Cassius's help, you have some time to do things to satisfy your own gifts and to help me."

Abigail let him lead her around the campfires, over some above-ground tree roots, and toward the edge of the hill. She felt grumpy and stewed about how the men were so needy, wanting her time more and more, like this morning's request from a filthy worker who was the dirtiest man she had ever seen or smelled. He stared at her, wiped his mouth with his shirt, asked her to do his laundry and get him cleaned up, insinuating he wanted more from her than most of the men. This old man and his requests got to her. *What was I thinking of taking on a job with all these men?*

Jared really can't read me. He has had no clue to my emotions and frustrations with my job here at the hotel. He's just like George in a way. No matter how much I begged or pleaded against any decision he'd made, like going back to California, he assumed I'd change my mind eventually. Now that I think of it, maybe my own mother had the same problem with my father, my wonderful father. Maybe she didn't want the life exactly the way Pa provided. Men don't seem to get women. I'll have to spell it out for Jared.

Abigail thought a moment before she said another word. *I will just tell him how I feel about the job.* "... and so, I've been mulling the idea over about taking Cassius back to Stowe. I'm afraid I've failed myself by not understanding my full capabilities. I just can't do this anymore."

Jared threw his hands up in the air and asked. "What're you talking about, Abigail? You've only just gotten here. Besides, Tarrant could be talked into working a bit more. Cassius is eager to earn some money. Give them both more responsibility. Our crowd really likes you, maybe a couple are a bit infatuated with you. Besides, you're the one who sets the limits. You're the one who told them you'd wash their dishes. As far as that new man goes, I'll try watching out for you a bit more, and I'll tell Stevens and Webster to keep an eye out for him too..."

Abigail stared at her brother-in-law. She felt as though she had been slapped in the face, not by Jared, but by herself and a reminder of what she had wanted for her future. She had left Vermont with hopes and wishes about not being taken care of anymore. Yet, she had no clue how challenging her life had become.

After the encounter with the vagabond this morning and his presumptions, she realized that she needed to take measures to protect herself from people who could assist her, or she had to buck up and take care of them herself. For now, she had to realize she needed some help from others, and at times this wasn't a bad thing.

"Thanks, Jared. But as far as me offering to do the dishes and silverware, it was only because the men weren't washing them, merely wiping them on their dirty shirts and pants or swishing them in river water. I don't want my serving spoons going from one man's plate to another."

"I realize that, but sometimes, Abby, you gotta look away. You don't have enough time to change them and their habits. They mostly don't know much better or even care. They're men of the wild. And, if you don't want to do their laundry, tell them. You set the standards. So now, set a new one. Tell them you don't have any more time to do their laundry. Just do what you're paid to do. And when someone wants something extra, say no. If you want, see if Cassius or Tarrant wants the job. Remember, like I said, Tarrant's been looking for ways of making money for the land he's buying."

"You've given me lots to mull over. Now, I forgot what you came to talk to me about."

"Well, Abby, I've got a new patient I could use your help with. She's having a baby—and soon. The couple and their three other children arrived late last week by wagon from Northern Virginia. She's in a bad way. I don't know how she made it this far. She wants a woman not me to help her with her delivery. Her husband made it more than clear, and I'm quoting: 'We don't want your'n help with Ma.'"

Abigail looked at Jared as if she had just noticed his presence. She felt awakened from self-pity and her doldrums.

"Oh, dear! How old did you say she is? Where do they live? How'd you find about her?"

Jared laughed, and said, "Abigail Camp, I see you again! Slow down, already. I was nervous bringing the topic to your attention and now you're packing a horse to go out there."

"This woman needs help as soon as possible, Jared. Don't tell me to slow down. Can you take me out there now? If I get some of my supper ready to cook, I think Mary, Tarrant, and of course, Cassius, can pull it all together for tonight."

"First, I just left the family an hour ago. They live down around the Big Bend in a covered wagon. They go by the name McJoad. The man's gotta' be in his fifties. Not sure about the woman. She looks ancient without teeth in her mouth. Leathery wrinkles cover her face. I've never seen 'anything like it. She's way too old and thin to be carrying a baby. The children look half-starved as well."

"How'd you learn about them? Sounds like they need help."

"Simon Stevens told me yesterday that the family pulled up close to Markham's place. Asked if any land was still free to claim. Simon's not sure they'll make it. They've nothing to get started with except a set of tools."

"Don't forget, Jared, some of Vermont's countryside was civilized just with a set of tools. Maybe they'll make it if everyone gives them a hand."

"Not sure if they're smart enough or have enough wherewithal to get by in the covered wagon."

"You're telling me her husband carted her all the way to Minnesota Territory from Virginia in a wagon, and she is in the family way? What was he thinking? What was she thinking?"

"He wanted to get settled in before winter. I doubt she got carted much. I think she walked a lot of the way. Her legs and feet are swollen and bruised."

"Simon's staying in the village for a couple nights. He gave him the run of the house to rest in and his food and fresh milk from his cow to nourish themselves with."

"Simon's a good man and very generous. So, when should we go out there?

"I told them I'd try to bring you out tomorrow."

Wondering if the McJoad woman could wait that long, Abigail decided not to argue with her brother-in-law, for he was the doctor and should know best. "How about, after I get breakfast going in the morning, you and I can leave? Say, about seven?"

Jared nodded and turned to leave, but then hollered, "Wait!" He picked up a small, but long branch from the ground, pulled off the smaller branches, smacked it against his leg, and handed it to Abigail.

Ah! Jared had found and recreated a nice, perfect-sized walking stick for her.

"Thank you, Jared. This stick may come in handy!" *Odd looking! Almost like a large spindle, thick in the middle and pointed at the ends. Very sturdy, though.* Abigail leaned on it, jiggled it, pointed it ahead, and began her upward stride. She aimed to get behind the trees and wander up to the overlook of the Mississippi, which she hadn't seen since she arrived over a month ago.

Feeling more cheerful and relieved of some of her duties for now, Abigail took a deep breath and began her ascension. Nothing compared to her Vermont mountains; the hill entered a steep climb immediately, unlike Mount Mansfield's slow, lingering hike. By the time she brushed through some greenery and took one more step to reach the top, she stopped to catch her breath.

Surprised to see golden prairie grasses baking in the sun and smelling of fresh bread, Abigail delighted in recognizing fruit-promising bushes. With only a few conifers and small cotton woods circling this flatland, she witnessed a paradise. Butterflies of all colors spun in circles of orange and black, gray with flecks of blue, red and black, and yellow and brown. She identified a few monarchs, but their fairy wings flit when she got close to the wildflowers they were foraging. Berries of all kinds, some red and pink plums, some black and purple chokecherries, and some she did not recognize were an almost translucent red. She unfolded her burlap bag; its smell and scratchy touch reminded her of earth and the potatoes that were carried in it.

Carefully, Abigail examined each bush to make sure she recognized her edibles. What she didn't know, she left for another day until she learned what they were.

She had filled about a quarter of the bag with wild onions when she looked above the green leaves and branches, shielded her eyes from the strength of the overhead sun, and saw three eagles orbiting high above her. Oh, she felt their power, their rhythm, yet she knew they may be scavenging just the same. A few snaps and a few dead-leaf crunches alerted Abigail to some other wildlife creeping around behind her.

She stepped out into the open to get away from the black fog of mosquitoes. Somewhere behind her, an owl cried its "*Who! Who! Who*!"

Her staff helped her stretch and bend to limber her joints. *I had forgotten how back-breaking picking berries can be*. She poked her way forward to the edge of the hill.

The closer she got, the more of the river she saw as the water split around an island. Its sparkle and diamonds winked, going forward in some areas and backwards in others. It curved south on its lazy stretch toward St. Anthony, St. Paul's landing, and beyond to where she boarded in Dunleith, Illinois.

Up here, away from the green thickness of trees, the heavens displayed a whole new atmosphere. Wide, puffy billows floated over the sun's brightness, cooling the air and brushing a new hue over the gray-feathered clouds heading west. Her wooden stick turned into a strange and strong force as she stood at this overlook. With staff in hand, Abigail sat down on a granite boulder as if it were her throne.

She relaxed and lifted her face to the sun, letting its warmth cover her. Squirrel chatter, bird song, the ever-rushing water over the dam, and the river chatting from bank to shore nearly put her to sleep. She accepted the peace and let her mind relax. At least for now, Abigail had a place of retreat, her own crow's nest, so to speak, to provide her a clearer vision place to search for own types of whales. Yet, this river, sound, strong, and always moving, contained no such awesome creatures. Here she could search for menacing renegades or steamboats bringing new life and goods onto the village shores.

Abigail mulled over leaving or staying in Minnesota Territory. If she returned to Stowe, she acceded defeat, and would have to live with the consequences, the Lucys of the world. *But wait! Hold on! I have changed so much just in the short time I've been here. I could never hide back there. So going back is not an option.*

Now left with another decision. If she resigned herself to her exhausting and boring tasks feeding the townsite hotel's occupants and other crewmen until she had enough money, she might be here for years. Yet, Jared had laid it out for her back when she stepped off the steamboat. She had just forgotten. If she stayed to help him in his medical practice, she would make money and be able to relieve herself from some of the tedious duties at the hotel. Jared knew her strengths. She felt his sway.

Behind her, Abigail heard more crunching and crawling in the tall grasses. *Nature! Always in movement.* The eagles flew closer and nearly landed on her shoulders. She heard their screeching. She shook her hair and looked up. *What? Am I your next meal?*

Just as she stood up, Abigail heard barking and saw a wolf barreling on all fours toward her. Her heart sank into her stomach and her breathing narrowed in fright. When she looked closer, she realized it was not her the animal literally flew toward. Startled! She intuitively raised her walking staff and held back someone or something crawling in the grass toward her. To do what? She was not sure.

"Pal! Pal! Stop!" Another male voice hollered from back toward the trees where Abigail had been picking wild berries. He came running as the dog started growling, showing its teeth, and biting at whatever was crawling in the grass. Abigail felt the air spinning as the eagles soared around her diverse group.

As the dog's master came closer, Abigail recognized him from that morning. He had come to the camp on occasion to eat supper. Taller than Abigail, yet shorter than others around the camp, he had a shiny bald head and wore spectacles. He carried a rifle. *Porter, I think his name is … Porter.*

"Pal, I've got him." The dog stepped back and tiptoed toward Abigail. "Now, Mister, stand up."

She pet the top of the dog's head to show she had no fear.

The grass-crawling fellow pulled himself up while the dog growled at him to show who was boss. To her surprise, it was the same man who wanted her to do his laundry that very morning. Dirtier than ever now, he wiped stray grass from his beard and clothes, but he couldn't wipe away his odor.

"What are you doing here?" Abigail asked, trying to sound angry instead of afraid. "Why are you following me?"

Pal showed the tramp a mouthful of teeth as he sang his warning tune as well.

"I think you need to move on, Mister, and find a new location," the man Abigail thought was Porter said. "Let's get you down to the camp, and we will see what the rest of the crew want to do with you." He aimed the gun at the man's feet to indicate he wanted him to get moving.

"Thank you, Pal. Thank you, Mr., uh, Mr. Porter." Abigail felt embarrassed looking right at him so she lowered her eyes and looked at the river.

"No problem, Ma'am." He hinted again, aiming his gun at the ground creeper to get him moving. The tramp started limping away as if he wanted sympathy because he was hurting. "Come along, Pal. Let's leave Mrs. Camp to herself."

The dog stood close to Abigail. As he stood contented, Pal smiled as he panted, intently, tongue hanging out.

"Mrs. Camp, I think you have a new friend. He wants to stick by you. I'll check with you later to see if you're tired of him."

"Thanks, Mr. Porter. He doesn't seem to want to go back with you right now."

"Just call me Tom, Thomas, or T. C., and you're welcome."

The men hiked back to the hotel. Tom, Thomas, or T. C. (*Thomas Charles*?) taking up the rear, disappeared into the trees and shrubs that encircled the spot where she stood.

Abigail turned around toward the now western leaning sun. Pal turned with her. The sun's brightness reminded her it was time to leave. Besides being shaken because of the incident, Abigail struggled to understand her feelings. She mused over whether she needed all this attention. Surely, she could have handled him herself and made him understand she had no interest in him; or was the drifter wanting something she would have to fight to keep?

As the eagles backed off, pulling themselves upward and flying away, Abigail felt as though a cyclone had exploded over her head. Preying or protecting, she wasn't sure. However, today, she conceded she needed the help offered by Pal, Tom, Thomas, or T. C., and the majestic raptors to shield her from danger. She knew her small fright would not hold her back from coming up here again, though. She felt her courage had been tested. For here on this incline overlooking the new village and the mightiest of rivers in Minnesota Territory, Abigail felt the strength to stay awhile.

Chapter 9

Taut Threads

Jared knocked on the door before opening it. "Afternoon, Maude. How's your mother this afternoon? Your uncle Tarrant stopped over and told us he was going to stay with you folks on his visit."

"Ma's doing better, catnapping right now though. Pa's outside helping Mr. Wilks with some of the fencing. We had that, what does Pa call it? Something like Shinook ... Chinook winds? Remember last week when it got so warm the snow and ice melted? Some fence lines popped out of the ground. They're fixing them so the cows and pigs don't get out."

"I thought I'd check on your ma before I head out to the country to check on a patient."

Abigail woke up. She had heard her name being mentioned and Maude's voice talking to someone. Then she realized it was Jared, her doctor, mentor, and friend. She felt drowsy. She tried to come so he would not leave. Yet, she could not fully awake.

A cold blast of air blew into the parlor when the kitchen door opened. She saw the fire in the fireplace had burned down to sparks. Getting a bit chilled, Abigail knew it was time to change positions or move back to the bedroom. "Brr!"

She heard her husband talking to Jared. "I figured it was you driving into the yard," Thomas closed the door behind him. He looked at his brother-in-law and then at Maude. "You tell him your mother fell asleep in the middle of our conversation? She wanted to sit and talk to all of us by the fireplace, so she's still in the parlor."

"I was just going to. I think her brain really gets tired out from all the remembering," Maude said as she wiped a large tray and placed it on the table.

"If she is still sleeping, I can come back on my way home. I don't want to be gone too long. Mary's under the weather again."

"Sorry to hear that, Jared. Tell her we're thinking about her. Let me peek in on Abby. It'll just take a second," Thomas said as he kicked off his boots, and hung his coat around the chair.

Abigail stretched wide as she opened her eyes. Thomas gently laid his hand on her shoulder.

"Hello, again." She looked around the room and saw empty spots on the divan where he and her brother Tarrant had been sitting and the chair where Maude had sat as well. "I'm sorry. I sure know how to empty a room fast."

"Abby, you don't need to apologize. You need your sleep. I just came in to see if you were awake. Jared stopped to check on you too."

Wrapping her robe around tightly and straightening in the chair, Abigail nodded, and said, "Of course, and I hope he can tell me what ails my sister."

"Jared?" Thomas called. "Come on in." He picked up the poker and stirred the ashes. Then getting a fire going again, he laid a couple logs on top to start warming the parlor.

Walking in with a light step, Jared looked down at Abigail. To her, he looked depressed and tired. The dark circles under his eyes were proof of her concern.

"Hey, Abby. How are you doing? It's good you felt well enough to sit up a while. Are you tired enough to go back to your bed?"

"I'm fine for now as long as the room keeps warm. Can't wait to have more conversation with the family again. You know Tarrant is here? Thought you and Mary should come over for a good visit while he is around."

"Yes, in fact, Tarrant's over visiting with Mary now. She's sick. ... stomach ... again. You know how it goes, one day good and then the next two are not."

Abigail pulled herself up in her chair, shifting around so the blanket covered her toes. "What have you given her so far?" she asked excitedly. "I could make her something."

"She won't take anything with laudanum in it, like you. Most of my medicines have some in it, whether I'm treating gout or an ulcer. All I could get down in St. Paul. Been stirring up my own teas, but nothing seems to work. I have chamomile. I've some ginger."

Abigail thought a bit, "Seems like I have rhubarb that dried last year. Out on the top shelf in the pantry. Ask Maude. She'll know where it is."

"Great! I'll grab some for her. Thanks. Amazing how you remembered your work concocting, Abby."

"I was thinking the same thing. I must be getting better. I was recalling the day I met Thomas. Before that you told me about an old woman carrying a baby. Remember?" Abigail looked into Jared's eyes. Would he remember this woman who was her first patient?

"I remember, Abby. From then on, you and I have been a team, especially with the women who'd rather have you help them in their deliveries."

"Sad, she and the wee one didn't make it. I remember what she looked like, my first look at a real struggling pioneer woman. She was like you described, Jared, only to me she looked like a shriveled prune on spindly legs. Some men give no more thought about their wives than to haul them hither and yon. On top of that, she was in her forties and with child. She looked like she had been beaten with twigs, starved to death, and given nothing to drink for days."

"Struggling is right." Jared pushed himself back to get more comfortable on the sofa. Abigail knew he enjoyed a good debate on health and the human condition. "Mr. McJoad told me he gave up everything for a chance to own his own land. After his wife died, I asked him if he thought he had sacrificed enough. I'm not sure he understood what or who I was referring to."

Abigail nodded in agreement. "We've had a few of these types of people, haven't we? No one knows how rough traveling can be. At its best—train, riverboat, stage, it's tiring. However, riding horse or walking has got to be challenging for anyone not used to such a hard life."

"True," Jared said. "Clearwater's been a stop for many. Sometimes, they stayed awhile. They've tried farming or working at our local businesses. Unfortunately, the harsh winters, dry summers, and plagues of grasshoppers just caused them to move on, leaving only stories for us to tell."

"Do you recall when you asked if I'd check on that one very young woman? Oh, what was her name?" Abigail asked. "Last name was Hogan or something. Husband and wife were so young. They'd left their homes and parents in Kentucky and remember "lit out to find land in western Minnesota Territory'."

"She was Julia and he was Evan. Evan and Julia. I'll never forget. They symbolized new love to me, Abby, love, ignorance, and youth. The only time in one's life ignorance is forgiven."

"Oh, Jared. Are you feeling down today? Low?"

"Somewhat, Abby. I have a couple women who need you. I told them you were sick yourself. They don't want me, that's obvious, but they're putting up with me. You've got to get better soon. You've got to. I'm overwhelmed, and all I think about is Mary. I'm failing her, Abby."

"Oh, I'm sorry, Jared. I'll come help as soon as you let me out of here. But you aren't failing Mary. I'll help by researching. I'll ask Thomas or Maude to find Father's medical books."

"I keep researching as well. I've found a doctor who has recently moved to Minnesota, Doctor A. W. Abbott. He specializes in women's anatomies and diseases, basically, the whole abdominal area. Since she was so sick after her last bad spell, I think she needs a complete going over. I've sent a telegram to him already, asking for his advice. I'm not sure he can see her, but I'm going to try to get him here or I'll take her there."

"Jared," Abigail said as she leaned over to cup his hand. "You're not that concerned about her, are you? I know she hasn't enjoyed good health for quite a while, but you don't think it's that serious?"

Jared swiped his hair backward. Abigail saw wild fear in her friend and doctor's eyes when he asked crossly, "Have you not seen the weight she has dropped lately?"

Abigail thought a minute. His terror barked out at her. She lowered her head. She believed in the power of silence and solemn thought for such times as these.

Finally, she spoke as calmly as she could. “Yes, I’ve seen her growing thinner and thinner. I’ve asked her questions about her health, and of course, Mary-like, she poo-pooed how bad it was. I’m sure you’re frustrated. Of course, if you believe (Abigail almost said ‘think’ but, knowing Jared’s current disposition, changed her word to believe), she needs a more in-depth look, then I agree. Nothing we’re doing is helping her much or for long.”

Her calm answer brought about a change in Jared’s temperament.

“I’m sorry, Abby. I didn’t mean to sound so harsh. I just don’t know what to do. Mary needs to have her stomach examined as soon as possible, and we may need to talk her into this.”

“By all means, Jared, get her the help you think she needs. I had not considered her sickness one for alarm until now. I agree with your diagnosis. There comes a time when the homemade methods will no longer work. I will do what I can but you and your daughters may need to do some persuading by adding a bit guilt.” Abigail saw the confusion in Jared’s face. “You know how Mary Isabella wants to head to the cities to work”

“Yes, my daughter feels it is past time for her to be on her own. The world isn’t keeping many young women down anymore. She wants to find her own way in the world. She’s an excellent seamstress. She could make it that way.” Jared stood up to leave, “I’m glad you’re up and feeling better. Don’t, I say, don’t, overdo it. Thank you for your support, though. I suppose I’m admitting failure as a doctor for not knowing what else I can do for Mary, but my pride can take it as long as we can make her better.”

“I promise I won’t over do anything. Now, don’t forget to take the rhubarb and anything else you need. We need to make Mary better,” she hollered after him.

Abigail rested her head against the side of the chair. She had a feeling she now had to try to force her recovery. Her sister needed her. Jared needed her. Of course, she knew Thomas and Maude also needed her. Thomas and she were getting to know each other better, and she felt more comfortable around him.

Over the years, Abigail remembered with the help of her father and her brother-in-law she had developed more mature and intelligent skills at the end of the woman's bed. She had to. Some women might be able to deal with the toughness of pioneering, but they needed extra tender care, understanding, and encouragement in their deliveries and their other health issues. Here in the new west, a wilderness, men did not always behave properly, nor did they always take care of their wives or families.

"I dreamed about when I first met you and Pal, Thomas. It felt so real, so good, and so comforting," Abigail told Thomas. "I remember feeling stubborn too though. I would not let myself feel vulnerable being the only woman and all those men hanging around the river."

Thomas reached over and patted her hand as if to say: "I'm relieved, happy, that you're remembering me and our life together, Abby!"

Abigail realized that her husband was trying to hold back tears, because she recognized a sniffle before he wiped his eyes.

She patted the top of his hand. Then she repeated, "I'm so sorry, Thomas, Tom, T. C." She squeezed his hand. He was familiar, he was gentle, he was her devoted husband.

"I remember telling you my name, a long time ago." Thomas wiped his eyes again, laughed, and stood up. "Well, dear wife, I can't stay in too long. I've gotta help the hired hand. It's birthing time in the pig shed."

"I remember I love this time of the season. I'll wish I were out there, bringing you hot coffee, hearing the squeals, and seeing the pink babies."

"We may be going at this for a while though. Maybe Jared will let you come out for a few minutes soon."

Abigail felt hopeful because she felt stronger. She knew she had a lot to be thankful for. She had a strong and close family, brother Tarrant and sisters Annette and Mary, and her closest allies, her Thomas and brother-in-law and doctor, Jared, as well as children, Maude and Cassius.

"I'll talk to Jared if he stops by or when he comes tomorrow. I know he's preoccupied with Mary's health too. He took some dried rhubarb to make into a tea or something."

"I know. He told me. Hope she can get over this before it goes on any longer." Thomas started to stand up and then sat down fast. "Before I head outside, I wanted to tell you ... or remind you ... I'll be heading out Sunday night or early Monday morning for St. Paul."

Abigail thought hard. Something about this was familiar … him heading to St. Paul. She finally asked, "Thomas, I can't remember. Why are you going?"

"That's okay. Don't hurt that noggin' of yours trying to remember. Can you imagine me being a state legislator?"

Still in a reclining position, Abigail tried hard to open the hazy, circling orbs in her mind. Nothing familiar came to her.

"A state representative? It sounds familiar but give me another hint."

She watched her husband as he slid his glasses to the top of his head again and rubbed his face, a habit she recalled he had when he struggled to explain something or think something through. Then she saw Thomas jump up and make for their bedroom. Abigail heard wood scraping on wood like he had opened and closed doors. *What is he doing in there?* Soon he walked out, carrying a dress by its hanger. The blaze in the fireplace illuminated the gown's golden threads and sequins. The dress sparkled with yellows and golds.

The golden aura that her husband held in front of her woke her as if from a deep sleep. Abigail's vision cleared. "I remember, Thomas." Excitedly, she pushed her blankets onto the floor and stood up on her own. "I remember Maude and me shopping for the material in Minneapolis. I remember the fittings, and that tight corset that stifled my breath when you and I were dancing so fast."

Clearly, Abigail visualized where she had worn this impressive dress and soon knew where Thomas was going. She pictured herself sitting around a large round table with her whole family at Clearwater's Morrison House. Red, white, and blue bunting added to the chair molding circling the large dining and dancing hall. Like stalwart soldiers, two flags stood on each side of the stage between the band members. On the left, the United States flag stood with its thirty-eight white stars on red backdrop and thirteen red and white stripes for its original colonies. The Minnesota Regimental dark blue flag displayed its thirty-four stars and an eagle carrying a banner with the saying, "E Pluribus Unum," meaning out of many, one.

Their Clearwater friends and family had thrown a party for Thomas and "his better half" for his election to the Minnesota House of Representatives. Someone had lured him to the floor to do his famous Irish jig. The next thing she knew, her husband had her swinging through the air. Her corset had become so tight she could not breathe or keep up with Thomas. He was swinging so fast, she slid under him and hit her head. For a while, that was the last she remembered.

"Thomas! I remember our celebration. My dress! All the applause for you. I remember the pride I felt that you had been voted in as a state representative from this district. What a glorious night with all our friends and family!"

The town's, the county's, the state's T.C. Porter, her Thomas, had come a long way from being a shoemaker, fur trader, lumberman, and pioneer to farmer. After she met him and Pal on top of the hill behind the hotel that one day, she came to accept the fact he would show up sometime during the day, before, during, or after supper most of the time. Sometimes, he grabbed a scrub brush and started scouring the heavy pots, found a wet rag and wiped down the dirty tables, or made a large pot of coffee for anyone who wanted to sit around the campfire before bed and gab. During these cozy, dark nights of crackling fires and soothing conversation, Abigail learned about this storyteller and his years before becoming a settler in Minnesota.

Raised on stories of Indians, frontiersmen Davy Crockett and Daniel Boone, and explorers like Lewis and Clark, young Thomas desired to go to the Wisconsin Territory at the time to forge his own adventures. Spurred on by the letters his fur-trading cousin, James Green, sent from Fort Garry, Winnipeg, he knew there was hard cash to be made trading with the Indians.

"My uncle knew a master shoemaker in Philadelphia. He suggested I apprentice under him to learn the trade so at least if my dream faded out west, I'd have something to fall back on to avoid starvation," he said with a snicker. "Once I became a journeyman, he and I knew I'd make it on my own. As a generous severance and wink of his eye, my uncle let me have the pick of any of his horses, minus the racers, that I helped raise. He knew which I'd take, though. I had helped bring into the world a handsome buckskin quarter horse. His ma had a hard time delivering, so I got in there and helped pull him out.

"As soon as I saw him with his golden body and black mane and black boot-like-legs, I knew I had to buy him from my uncle. We made a deal. If I'd put in a couple more hours on one Saturday a month, he'd take out the remaining balance from my severance when I turned twenty-one.

"Because he looked like our family's and country's hero all suited up in his uniform, the famous Gilbert du Motier, Marquis de Lafayette, I named the colt in honor of him, as well as his namesake and god-son, my cousin Lafe."

Abigail never knew which trail Thomas's tales might take. Sometimes, he talked about his Porter family in Pennsylvania, the governors, the generals, corporals, and privates and the wars they fought to gain America's freedom. Often, he talked about how he started in the fur trading business.

"Lafayette and I rode off to St. Louis, Missouri, leaving Pennsylvania behind us. We rode close to the Ohio River and villages where if I needed I could stop for supplies, avoiding as much as possible the hostile environments, so to speak." Here Thomas always rolled his eyes but said little else because he knew everyone understood exactly what he meant. "Once I got to Saint Louie, I made moccasins for the trading posts in the area. Besides keeping busy with moccasins, I repaired many-a soldier's boot sole so I could pay for passage on a steamboat heading to St. Paul in Minnesota Territory."

Sitting on a tree stump by the hotel, he would puff on his pipe as he spun his tales. By that first late fall Abigail spent down by the river, she could recite them from all the different times he was asked to tell a newcomer his story. He might talk about his cousin Lafe Porter's wish that he could join him on his journeys. Unfortunately, he was beholden to his brother Captain Alexander Porter to go to Oregon Territory to help open the land and protect the pioneers by surveying where they wanted to settle.

Since Lafe still wished to be part of Thomas's endeavors, he invested in some of the equipment and supplies. He encouraged him to make his way to Fort Snelling and pick up his ox cart, a six-foot wooden box structure from top to bottom of the wheel, made of rawhide and wood. Lafe also suggested he pick up a yoke of oxen so he could haul more than the normal thousand pounds of supplies like blankets, all types of awls, beads, kettles, and all sizes of awls.

His other cousin James Green, a fur trader already settled in Winnipeg, suggested he take the Woods trail for his own safety. "He told me you'll never know when you'll run into a renegade Sioux as you head north to Fort Garry."

Thomas was a captivating storyteller. Whether he began his campfire talk with his discussions about the Red River Trail, his experience being nearly scalped, or maneuvering a yoke of oxen away from Fort Snelling with one of the team being nearly blind, everyone sat entranced in his lore. However, it was when he began reminiscing about his trips to Dakota Territory and up to Fort Garry in Canada that Abigail knew his adventurous tales had begun. These stories were not only entertaining but also provided a glimpse into the history of the territory and the forming of the state.

Yet, Abigail knew Thomas's desire to settle down began when the two of them married in Clearwater. They worked together to form a successful farming operation. From raising some of the largest hogs around the area, Thomas also worked determinedly to manage and support Clearwater, Clearwater Township, and Wright County. Now, after being asked many times to enter state politics-but declining, he finally agreed it was his time to help Minnesota in its early statehood. He already knew he would be working on a few committees he was interested in, one being involved in the construction of bridges, dams, and waterways. And this was no surprise to Abigail. Thomas was all about building connections.

~~~~~

As if petting Tansy her favorite house cat, Abigail smoothed her hand over the beautiful gown and was taken back a few months to when she and Maude went to St. Paul to look for fabric for a nice gown. Once she and Maude touched the material at Mannheimers' Department Store in St. Paul, they agreed Abigail had to have it made into a fancy ballgown to celebrate Thomas's political success.

She could not believe she had anything so luxurious. This dress, made from beautiful, but expensive cream-colored silk-velvet, belonged to her. A very light color, lighter than wheat waving in late summer, Abigail's dress symbolized to her more than success or luxury. This gown, "shown like the brightest sun in the darkest night." Abigail knew there were richer and more successful people in Minnesota, even richer than her old nemesis Lucy Webber-Koerner in Vermont. *Oh, my mind must be coming back for me to remember her.* Yet, this ballgown had little to do with their acquisition of money. For in fact, she and Thomas were quite frugal in their lives, making the most of what they had created from their work around their farm. She still wove, her favorite activity when she had free time.

In the leaner years, while Thomas built their first home and all its contents including their furniture, Abigail showed him how to build a loom like her grandmother's that she had used when she lived at home. He created wood bars and fluted dowels, ratcheted wheels, and heddle blocks. He measured, drew, sawed, and drilled some more until he created a machine for her to weave almost everything, including material for clothing, curtains, rugs, and bed coverings. They took pride in their home and in each other's creations. She crafted so many of their belongings that covered the floors, windows, and even some of the walls. People who visited often said her home was so tight and artistic with the delight of colorful weave, it left no room for spiders. In fact, once inside, many said they could not believe the Porters lived in a log cabin. Nonetheless, here, overlooking her own section of the Mississippi River, they built their lives together.
~~~~~

In fact, sitting in back of her loom on the bench Thomas also built for her, looking out the large bay window, Abigail felt free to observe her new world. Whether painted in a winter blue and white or a spring and summer blue and green, her changing scenery helped her recite some of her favorite Elizabeth Barrett Browning or memorize what she would write in her journal later that night. Whether she wrote, knitted, sewed, or wove, Thomas sat in his easy chair smoking his pipe and reading his papers.

Thomas raised and sold hogs, and when it was butchering time, they used everything "but the squeal." Roasts, chops, hams, sausages, headcheese, and Thomas's beloved scrapple or what his mother called *pannhaa*s. He, alone, took charge in creating his favorite breakfast food, a mixture of leftover parts of the hog, his own special seasonings of herbs, salt, and pepper, and flour and cornmeal. Sliced and fried, the scrapple was no ordinary fare. His father always said when they started off their days with his mother's delicacy, "We aren't hardscrabble if we start our day with eggs and scrapple."

I wonder if Lucy ever scrimped and saved. Had she ever touched anything recently killed, worked like a dog, or took chances like I had to do to start again. Heavens! Why am I thinking of her so much lately?

When Thomas told her to "spend some loot, on a fancy dress," Abigail knew he had no clue what clothes or material cost nowadays in a department store. She had almost always made her own clothing. But she had often purchased bolts of various fabrics and used them down to the wooden bolt they had been rolled on. H. Z. Mitchell's, the best supplied clothing and dress good store in St. Cloud, offered good value. However, she knew their prices could not compare to the new department stores in Minneapolis and St. Paul.

She had worked for Jared for over twenty-five years and had rarely spent a cent. So, added to what she figured Thomas meant by "spend some loot," Abigail had the confidence she had enough money to buy the fabric.

"Have you made an appointment for a fitting yet, Mrs. Porter?" Mannheimers's clerk, a young woman of Irish descent asked. Dressed in a green gown that set off her green eyes and red hair dolloped on the top of her head, she waved to the male clerk for help.

A young man, probably a teenager, walked fast to receive orders on which bolt to carry. Abigail noticed he wore white gloves. He picked up the large bolt and followed them, carrying and gently laying it onto the glass counter.

"A fitting? Abigail asked as they walked behind the clerk.

Maude looked at her mother. Abigail returned a quizzical stare.

The clerk answered, "I ask because usually our customers want to work directly with Madame Worley. She's the best for sure, but so busy. She often has one of her other dressmakers-in-training first work with the client."

Again, Abigail and Maude stared at each other, Maude with one eyebrow raised and Abigail with her mouth gaping.

"Ma'am," I'm sorry, but I thought I could buy the material and have someone else sew my gown," Abigail felt really embarrassed, as if she were a country bumpkin. "You see I'm, we are," she directed her hand to include Maude, "from Clearwater and only in the city for the day. I need this gown made for a very important event in January."

"Oh, my! Well, I'm sure this can be done, but I think you'll want to talk to someone before you purchase this type of fabric. I know it takes skill to work with it."

Abigail knew that Maude felt as confused as she. Her own mother Hannah, such a beautiful seamstress, never really spelled out the rules to follow or that she could not work with a type of fabric. All her sewing knowledge had been handed down to her and her sisters. Annette and Mary both wanted to help her design and create a dress for the Porters's special occasion.

"Let me find someone who you could talk with. Please, wait right here. I'll be right back," and she left with Abigail and Maude both standing against the counter.

Abigail turned and pulled up her stool. So beautiful, a purple velvet back and cushioned seat that felt as comfortable as it was beautiful.

Maude followed her mother's lead and sat down. She looked around before whispering, "Mother. I've heard about these young women clerks. They have to dress well. They have to pay for their own clothes to work here, and they have to stand in line each morning to be approved by the store managers."

Abigail leaned toward Maude to hear better.

Maude continued, "They receive a starving-woman's wage, pay for rent and food. They are often just poor farm girls or immigrants. They want a step up in life. Unfortunately, they are paid a pittance and work ten to twelve hours a day, six days a week. At least, according to *Godey's Lady's Book,* they feel as though they are receiving some respect as they learn a bit of culture."

Abigail removed both gloves and unfastened the neck clasp of her winter cape. She dabbed at her throat and her forehead with her white hanky. "I can't help but feel this young woman thinks we are really backwoods. I know how to sew, and I know you and my sisters have even more experience in the art."

Maude shook her head in agreement and added, "I bet she is told to say and do what she is doing, so let's just see who our helper is."

Compared to the St. Cloud stores that are little more than general mercantile or dry goods businesses, Mannheimer Brothers stood tall, sophisticated, and glitzy. So clean, she could find nay a whisper of dust on the glass counters or rich, dark mahogany counter bases, walls and woodwork. The windows that spanned this side of the building shined.

"I suppose," Abigail whispered agreement back at Maude. "Sad, that the young woman's job is all for show."

"Apparently, they come to learn a trade like sewing and then hope for a better life."

The two looked behind the counter to their left as the purple curtain was held open by a white glove. Then the hand went down and the curtain closed. Then the curtain was held open again. This went on for five minutes before a woman, a lady, dressed in dark blue walked out. She wore this gown as if she were royalty. Her dainty shoes, more like velvet pink and blue flowered slippers glided across the hardwood floors, making the faintest swishing noise. Her tiny waist, stand up collar with open neck, gave the woman an air importance.

"Mrs. Porter, I presume," the woman greeted, looking first at Maude and then at Abigail.

"My mother is Mrs. Porter," Maude answered as she turned and touched her mother's arm.

"Welcome, welcome to my floor. I am Mrs. Worley. What can I do to help you?"

Abigail and Maude exchanged glances again. Abigail hoped her daughter heard the "my floor," before she spoke. "I'd like to purchase this fabric for a dress, in fact, a ballgown. I had planned on taking it to my sister's house in Clearwater where we live." Turning to the young woman who had helped them earlier, Abigail added, "Your clerk suggested I speak with you first."

"Oh, a special event, I assume?" Mrs. Worley questioned.

"Ah ... yes, my husband has been elected to the Minnesota House of Representatives. Our town will be hosting a celebration for him, and I want to look my very best."

"Oh, congratulations, Mrs. Porter. Of course, you have so much to be proud of with your husband." Mrs. Worley turned her attention to the fabric laid out on the counter. The male clerk who had accompanied her, held up the bolt for her to examine it. "Oh, you have chosen a beautiful fabric. Let's see what we have here." I know it is our finest velvet silk from Paris. Do you have a specific style you'd be interested in?"

"Somewhat," Abigail answered.

"Do you have any idea how many yards you'll need?" Mrs. Worley asked.

"Oh, dear. I think about ten yards or so."

"You'll want more because it is velvet," Mrs. Worley answered. "When is your celebration? We could try to squeeze you in for an initial appointment at the end of December. Each morning, you will have to come for a fitting. This may take two to three hours each day."

Obviously frustrated and overwhelmed like Abigail, Maude lowered her hand gently to the counter before speaking up. "Each day? We are from Clearwater, Mrs. Worley, a village north of here.

We were hoping to take the material home today and get started sewing as soon as possible."

Mrs. Worley acted is if the sky had fallen. Her calm voice turned to a stammering shriek. "Without a plan, without a design, without a fitting to know how much fabric you need to buy?" Calming down slightly, she added, "Ma'am, pardon me but this fabric is our most expensive and the most delicate. Beautiful, yes, but it is tricky to work with. If you were to oh, my. ... ruin any part of the process, you'd not have a dress."

Abigail saw the late afternoon sun lowering in the sky. Thomas would be coming up the steps very soon to deliver them to the train in time to go home. Deciding she had no intention of causing anymore frustration to this woman and her department, she sighed and realized she had no alternative but to leave the material. All this fuss was not worth it.

Abigail picked up her gloves from the counter and stepped off the stool. "I think we have burdened you enough for one day. We will come again soon and make our decisions after we have chosen a pattern and such."

"Hello, how's it going?" Thomas Porter asked.

Startled but not shocked, Abigail answered, "Thomas! We're just finishing up."

"I asked a clerk downstairs what floor to go to. I thought I'd surprise you."

"You did, Pa. You did." Maude pulled her gloves on and started to turn her back to the salespeople at Mannheimer Brothers.

Abigail stepped off the stool and closed the clasp of her cape. "Thomas, we must make some changes. That is all. No problem. Maybe next week we will come back, or maybe I'll check in St. Cloud for a different kind of material." She did not want to bother Thomas with her problems.

That last statement must have shocked Mrs. Worley back into her business sense. "I know you are in a hurry, but maybe we could figure a way to get this dress made on time for your celebration." She turned to Thomas and said, "Oh, Mr. Porter, congratulations on becoming a Minnesota legislator."

Abigail heard the change in the seamstress's voice. *Was it her desire to make a sale? Was it because a male customer with strings to the family pocketbook had come on the scene?*

"Now," Mrs. Worley said as she looked directly at Abigail, "let's see. Could you come back as soon as possible, Mrs. Porter, say in a day or two?" This time she looked at both Maude and Abigail. We will get you measured. We will choose a pattern, and then we'll know exactly how many yards of cloth you need. We can do some updos as well. We will concentrate on you that day so you can get back on the train and head home with one of our senior seamstresses."

"Updos?" Maude asked.

"Senior seamstress?" Abigail asked.

"Oh! Just my words for altering or changes. We can add ribbons or different materials to your dress to make it even more spectacular. Yes, you would need to house one of our seamstresses for a few weeks. She will be hand sewing and basting you in your home every day. When she finishes with one part of the project, she'll bring it back to me for approval and sewing together on the sewing machine."

Abigail looked at Thomas and Maude who in turn gave her the impression it was feasible. "But Mrs. Worley, will this not cost a lot more?"

"Very easy to work out," Mrs. Worley stated. "She's still paid her salary from Mannheimer Brothers. You will need to board her, and maybe pay for her train trips back and forth, but otherwise, I think we will have her covered on all sides."

The Porters looked at each other back and forth.

Maude raised her eyebrows in surprise. "You know, we haven't had any real company since Grandpa Robison left to go back to Vermont and Annette married and moved to Lake Minnetonka. This might be a lot of fun," Maude said.

"Thomas, what do you think?

Thomas shrugged. "I have no problem with it. Make it easier for you, Abby, to have someone on our premises to get this dress made in time. I have to be back in a two days for another meeting. We can come together and see how it goes."

"Do you have any idea who this seamstress could be?" Abigail asked Mrs. Worley.

"All of our girls have been trained in deportment and professionalism, not to mention improving and building their skills sewing and working with the latest fabrics. They're all capable of living in your home and doing an excellent job. We will pick the best though for you."

"Mrs. Worley, do you have any Irish seamstresses?" Maude asked.

Abigail saw the surprise in her husband's eyes. Thomas was proud of his Irish heritage, so was Maude. They had had many of the Robinson relatives stay with them, but no one from the Porter side, since many had already died.

"Why, yes, we do. Would you like us to pick one of the Irish girls? All are personable and capable. One is like the other. We train them to be qualified in all our types of sewing."

Abigail heard a hint of bigotry when Mrs. Worley stated all the Irish women were alike. But now was not the time to bring it up to her. She felt she was winning a battle and did not want to upset the opposing team. She slid her arm through her husband's arm before saying, "Well, I think Thomas would enjoy news and talking with anyone from the British Isles."

"Well, then this is settled. We'll see you in two days to take your measurements, choose your pattern, of course, introduce you to your tenant, and get you all started."

While Mrs. Worley aimed her hand at Thomas to shake it, Abigail intervened and shook it instead. Abigail thought the look of bafflement on the seamstress's face was hard not to notice. Soon her royal-like entourage followed behind her as she walked back behind the purple curtain.

In two short days, Abigail returned to Mannheimer Brothers. As fast as Abigail unwrapped herself from her woolen cape, scarf, mittens, and bonnet, the man grabbed her winter attire to hang it up for the day. He led her behind the purple curtain, but only to "WOMEN'S WAITING ROOM."

"Mrs. Worley or her attendants will come to get you soon. Please, wait. You'll find several magazines to look through on the table."

Abigail walked around the small, but elegantly displayed parlor. The marble-topped table had a pile of magazines, including *The Ladies' Treasury* and *Godey's Lady's' Book.* She found an enticing French magazine *Moniteur de la Mode.* When she picked it up, an insert of designs and patterns fell into her hands.

Just as she began to sit down on one of the armchairs, Abigail's attention was drawn to a hushed but an understandable conversation.

She heard a stern female voice say, "And I remind you, Miss Murphy, if you do not abide by our rules of etiquette and deportment, you will not be allowed to stay at Mannheimers."

Abigail heard a sniffle and a sob—then a very quiet "Yes, Madame." *What in the world?* Within a few seconds, two women, Mrs. Worley and a tiny young woman whooshed their ways into the parlor. Abigail stood up to see who entered.

This time with her hand positioned to shake Abigail's, Mrs. Worley said, "Mrs. Porter. It's so good to see you again. I'm pleased this all worked out for you."

With as much graciousness as she could muster after hearing the threatening conversation, Abigail accepted the hand.

The Grande Dame turned around with an arrogant air about her. She pulled up her *Pince Nez* spectacles from the chain hanging around her neck and balanced them in place on her nose. As if to size up the young woman, she looked down at her employee, before introducing the two. "Mrs. Porter, this is Miss Murphy, Maeve Murphy. Maeve, may I introduce you to Mrs. Porter?"

Abigail could not help but notice a red nose and puffy cheeks, but this Maeve Murphy had the most cherub-looking face. Her dark brown hair curled around her face and stood piled on her head with a few ringlets like ponytails hanging down. She might have stood four-feet and a half, but she wasn't sure. Abigail could see she stood taller than the young woman.

"It's nice to meet you, Miss Murphy."

With a slight bow, the young woman looked up at Abigail and smiled, "Thank you, and likewise," only a few words, but Abigail heard her brogue.

Without much more ado, another attendant ushered Abigail into a changing room. A lush, white robe lay over a chair for her to change into. A pair of flat, white slippers lay on the seat of the chair. When she returned to the main hall, seamstresses of all sizes and shapes scurried around her. One helped her step up on a foot tall and three-foot round stool. Another gently helped her arm by arm remove her robe. With mirrors all around her, Abigail saw what others would see as she stood only in her chemise, drawers, and stockings. She had little time to be embarrassed as a small party of women whirled and spun the measuring tapes around her body parts, softly telling the "recorder" her measurements, Abigail felt like Cinderella being undressed and redressed by her fairy godmother.

When all the measurements had been taken, Abigail stepped backwards into the arms of her robe as she saw two young women carry in her precious fabric and lay it on a table. As if on cue, Mrs. Worley and Maeve came back with another few women, walking behind them and carrying large books. They stacked them up on the same table as the fabric, leaving with nary a sound but the swish of their petticoats. Abigail felt like a whirling dervish as she was cast from one person to another, it was all in the tap, tap, tap of time.

"Please, Mrs. Porter, sit down and be comfortable. Our next steps will be accomplished while we relax."

Again, as if on cue, two women appeared, one carried a Lazy Susan adorned with colorful finger-sized nibbles. The other carried a tray with two pots and cream and sugar containers. They laid the trays on the table, backing off until Mrs. Worley gave them their next command. With a "Thank you, ladies," and a small wave of her hand, they walked backwards until they turned around in unison to retreat. Maeve set the table, while Mrs. Worley became hostess.

Abigail wanted to see Maeve's smile again, to get to know her a bit. She would be living with her family for a few weeks.

She simply said, "Thank you, Maeve. I wanted to tell you I think you'll be a great addition to our family."

Maeve began to say, “Thank you, Ma’am,” when her mistress interrupted and commanded, “Sit down, Miss Murphy,” in a non-compromising manner. Apparently, this was too soon for such familiarity between the women.

Maeve’s face turned red. Abigail sat astonished with Mrs. Worley’s imposed guilt directed at Maeve. “I’m sorry if I’m not allowed to speak to this young woman. As far as I’m concerned, you need to blame me.”

Mrs. Worley paid little attention to what Abigail said, and asked her whether she wanted “Tea or coffee, Mrs. Porter?”

Abigail had had a workout, especially in exasperation, so she said, “Coffee please.”

As if sparring with Abigail, Mrs. Worley asked immediately, “One lump or two?”

Abigail understood the message loud and clear. Apparently, this commander and chief accepted no passing conversation between the two. Abigail became concerned for Maeve’s future livelihood when she returned to the store after her job was finished in Clearwater. She decided she would keep her mouth shut.

“None, thank you. I take my coffee black.”

Another woman knocked so quietly on the door, Abigail barely heard it. Mrs. Worley said, “Enter!”

A small curtsey followed from the young woman dressed in black. “Mrs. Porter has company. The woman says she’s her daughter, Maude.”

“Oh, I forgot. My daughter’s meeting me here after she did some shopping. I’m sorry, I should have told you earlier.” Abigail felt the coffee glide down her throat like acid. It was strong, black coffee, but her real thoughts circled around having Maude experience all that was said and done here. Her daughter had a way of jumping to conclusions before asking questions.

“Please, Miss Hampton, escort Miss Porter in, and bring us another cup, saucer, and luncheon plate.” She turned her attention to Abigail, and with the sweetest face, Mrs. Worley handed her the Lazy Susan filled with mid-morning treats.

Maude entered the room, Miss Hampton placed the plates and cup on the table, and then helped Maude remove her outerwear.

She pulled out a chair. Maude sat down. She looked at her mother with eyes wide open in speculation.

"Thank you for joining us, Miss Porter."

Abigail wished she had time to explain to Maude about the strange circle of communication that had transpired already before another suspicious incident occurred. She tried catching Maude's eye occasionally, but the tea and coffee time went quickly and smoothly. The only conversation was between three women, mostly chit chat, a little bit about Thomas Porter's career and his commitment to the Minnesota State House of Representatives. With Mrs. Worley's exclusive seamstress presence, order prevailed in the Mannheim Brothers Department Store.

Mrs. Morley also shared how Mr. and Mrs. James Hill, "You know, the railroad tycoon," had used their services for a live-in seamstress a couple of times. The latest was to design a wardrobe for Mrs. Hill's maternity period.

Before long, the table was cleared again with precision and timing. Maeve and Mrs. Worley each grabbed one of the pattern books, McCall's *Ladies Quarterly of Broadway Fashions* and *The Delineator.* Mrs. Worley pulled up a chair by Abigail, and Maeve pulled hers over to Maude's side of the table. The search for the perfect pattern for Abigail's dress began.

Whenever Maude asked Maeve anything, she replied with a "Yes, Ma'am" or a "No, Ma'am," and ended with a glancing look at her employer. Maude shared a few pictures to try to get her mother's mind narrowed down to a specific style. Abigail shared the same with Maude and the others.

Abigail's legs fell asleep. She rarely sat this long. She twisted and turned, trying to get comfortable. Every part of her woke up though when Maude and Maeve showed Mrs. Worley and Abigail a dress they thought would work. *My goodness! This is exactly what I was looking for. Except for the bustle. What do I need with the bustle?*

"Even though this dress shown in the magazine is burgundy, I think it will be beautiful in your creamy velvet-silk. Mother, you 'll be stunning in the stand-up color and oh, that bustle. Look at those pearls from the bodice swirling down to the hem of the skirt."

"Mrs. Porter, I could see a different design tucked into the middle of the dress in front like this one. A complimentary color that is. Like maybe, simply a silk design of contrasting colors. Oh, so elegant!"

"Well, I believe we have decided. This sounds wonderful," Abigail gushed. "You're so right. It looks elegant." Never in her thoughts and dreams had she thought she would have a need to wear such a dress.

"Mrs. Porter, we don't want to forget we also need to pick out a lining for the dress. This will support and protect your delicate fabric. Your present chemisette will not do because we need to build and protect the velvet silk inside and out."

Abigail could almost feel her pennies being stretched, but she agreed. This was not going to be a cheap dress. She could almost hear her mother saying, Penny wise, pound foolish."

Luncheon was served. Triangles of chicken salad sandwiches, a fruit salad served in small dessert glasses filled with pineapple, little orange slices, and topped with a cherry. After two young women cleared their dishes, they brought back a tray of delicate desserts and a sterling silver bowl filled with assorted nuts, some Abigail did not recognize. They also served the most luxurious, smooth, and dark roasted coffee poured into gold and pink flowered demitasse cups.

"Please, stay and help yourselves to another cup of coffee and another dessert. Miss Murphy and I will finalize our plans and gather the supplies she needs to take with her. We must take some time to make sure our measurements for each single step are spelled out clearly."

Taking longer than Abigail wanted to finalize the notes, Maeve Murphy and Mrs. Worley reentered Mannheimers' parlor with what looked like enough baggage to sew for an army. Abigail, Maude, and their guest Maeve Murphy boarded the train in the nick of time and headed home to Clearwater. From here on, at least until her ballgown was sewn, Abigail felt sure that over the next few weeks, the three women would be taking all types of measurements.

Chapter 10

Gathering, basting, binding

Maude and Abigail pointed to the Mississippi River often as they travelled north to Clearwater past many of the hamlets along the way, Anoka, Otsego, Monticello, even tinier settlements like Enfield and Hasty. The river turned white in spots where it had frozen, but it lapped clear in others. "Still not hardened enough to walk on," Abigail could hear Thomas say.

Abigail looked out the train window as they pulled into Clearwater. Reassured, her Thomas sat in their sleigh, waiting as usual. "Rather early than late," she could hear him say. Snow fell in white puffs and coated tree branches. Winter fell upon them.

After Maude introduced her father to Maeve Murphy and vice versa, Thomas loaded up Maeve's baggage and helped the women board. Thomas circled the depot and started to head home.

"This is Main Street, Maeve," Maude said. "Across the street is our newly built drugstore. Our neighbors and friends the Phillips's own it. Their children are young yet, but they come visit often because Maryetta, the mother, used to help clean our house and take care of me."

In her musical Irish accent, she said simply, "Oh ... I see. It's all so lovely here," she said as she looked up and down the sleepy street, "Quiet and pretty, especially compared to St. Paul."

Abigail listened to the two women. *They've connected already.* Bundled in snow, the charming business buildings, homes, and the Methodist Church resembled her hometown of Stowe, Vermont, in winter. The wind had picked up, and the street-lined elm trees, heavy laden with snow, swayed like dancers in a winter ballet. Abigail felt happy to get home and get cozy by the fire. Even though they were all wrapped up in fur blankets, she knew everyone felt the freezing gusts of wind as the sleigh slid them to the south end of town.

"Ma, I've been thinking."

"Oh, about what?" Abigail asked from under the robe and through chattering teeth.

"Remember the proclamation President Arthur announced in the newspaper?"

Abigail thought a bit. *Proclamation, proclamation? Hmmm. My brain has frozen. All I can think about is my coldness. President Arthur took over for Garfield, after a long, slow death after he'd been shot ... I remember that...a couple months ago.*

Maude answered for her mother. "Thanksgiving? He proclaimed a new United States holiday. Thanksgiving, a time for reflection about our history in forming our country and celebrating our country's united stand after all its wars for independence."

"Of course, of course," Abigail shivered. "So, what were you thinking?"

"Maeve will be here to help us celebrate."

"I forgot! Maeve, what do you think? Are you free to stay at our house to help celebrate Thanksgiving?" Abigail laughed. "We've been so busy with all the campaigning, none of us have talked about what we will do. I haven't even talked about how we're going to celebrate. You have any ideas, Thomas?"

Her husband steered the horses into their broad roadway that angled close to the lean-to in the back side of the house. After a little grunting, he coaxed the horses to a stop.

Thomas hollered over the sleigh to Abigail, "It's been celebrated for years. I don't know. Maybe keep it simple and invite others to share our bounty? I could butcher a hog or do some hunting."

"That's my pa, Maeve, always thinking of sharing what we have with others," Maude said, accepting her father's hand to help her step down safely. She grabbed a satchel to carry into the house.

He worked his way around the sleigh to help Maeve Murphy, who thanked him as if she had never been helped down from a carriage before. "You're very welcome, Maeve. We're glad to have you here to take care of Mrs. Porter's dress." He slid his feet to help his wife. "You can carry the small bag, if you wish, but don't try carrying that large bag. I'll bring it in after I bed down the horses." He helped his wife step out.

"So, what do you think, Thomas? She seems quite sweet, at least her voice is. I will tell you later how the mistress of Mannheiemers' treats her seamstresses. I was shocked, but I suppose she must have some control over them too."

"This should be an interesting bedtime story," Thomas said. "Watch your step close to the door. The eaves have been dripping all day but now it's freezing and slippery."

Abigail slid her feet over the icy path so as not to fall. She opened the door to the little entry, wiped her feet, and opened the regular kitchen door and stepped in. She stopped to listen. Maude had taken their house guest upstairs to unpack some of her things. She heard her talking to Maeve who occasionally said, "Yes'm." Maude's voice seemed even and smooth, a good sign. Abigail wondered how long her daughter would listen to Maeve speaking so subserviently before she gave the young woman "a talking to." She hoped Maude would be patient and understand Maeve's circumstance and background, a recent immigrant in their home country and now their town. For now, Abigail's biggest concern was making Maeve feel at home and feeding everyone a good nutritious supper.

~~~~~

What in the world?

If Abigail thought Maeve Murphy had come to sluff off, she soon realized differently. She woke before the sun rose to what sounded like a sharp knife or something dragging across the floor above. Thomas stirred, but he did not wake. Abigail grabbed her robe, and closing the bedroom door behind her, she went to the top of the steps. From there, she saw a soft light under the door. She tip-toed to the door and knocked lightly before opening.

"Is everything all right, Maeve?" Abigail whispered and noticed two lamps lit and sitting on chairs so that they'd be closer to her work.
~~~~~

"Oh, you startled me," she answered quietly, looking up from her kneeling position on the floor with large scissors in her hands. "I couldn't sleep so I figured I'd start with this pattern, Ma'am. Sorry if I disturbed you."

"You didn't really. I just wondered if something was wrong. If you're up, I'll put on some coffee, or are you a tea drinker, dear?"

"I'm both. But coffee would be good to give me a good start. Thank you, Ma'am."

"Come down when you're ready." Abigail whispered.

"Thank ye, Ma'am."

Abigail stepped downstairs, stirred up the fire in the cookstove and added some small wood chips to get it roaring. *Cold, cold, cold, down here*. She shivered and shook until the embers caught. Then, she added a small log. She pulled the coffee pot closer to the lid and picked at the ice in the bucket. Must not have been too cold last night; ice broke up easily. She added another log to the fire. After grinding her beans, Abigail filled the pot with the cold water, added the water and stirred the pot before setting it on the stove lid. The fire roared. The room soon warmed.

About fifteen minutes later, Abigail had set the table with bread, butter, cups, and saucers. She looked out the kitchen window. The snow had ended. The sun rose over the evergreens on the eastern riverbanks in pink and yellow flashes.

"Morning, again, Ma'am," Maeve whispered so softly, Abigail hardly heard her.

"Do sit down, and we'll have a cup of coffee, Maeve. Please help yourself to some bread and butter as well. It's bit early for real breakfast, but this'll give you a good start."

Both pulled out chairs quietly so as not to wake up Maude or Thomas. Abigail poured them cups of steaming black coffee. She passed the cream and sugar to Maeve.

Abigail liked her coffee black. Steaming her face, she eagerly took her first sip, letting it roll over her tongue and around the insides of her mouth before she swallowed. The first gulp ... it awakened her a bit, but a few more slower sips helped her face her day.

No food for her yet; she needed a refill, but now she could speak. She asked, "Maeve, so how long do you think this dress will take? I also wonder how many times we'll need to take the train back Mannheimer's in St. Paul."

Maeve blotted her lips and looked up from her cup and said, "Well, Mrs. Porter. I'll be wide about it. Maybe three weeks, or a bit more. Mrs. Worley'll probably wish you to ride down three or four times. Hard telling, my experience at Mannheimers ain't been that long."

"Oh ... well ... I guess we'll take it one step at a time. I know Mrs. Worley said you had to return by Friday so she could approve of your first steps."

"That's right, Ma'am. So, I'd best get started. Thank ye for the good breakfast."

As Maeve stood up, Thomas announced, "Good morning," from the doorway, snugging up his dark suspenders over his red flannel shirt. "Someone's up early."

"Gracious, Mr. Porter. Did I wake you?"

"No, not at all. I smelled coffee. Abby makes a good cup, doesn't she, Maeve. Good and strong. I can smell it in the pig barn."

Abigail started laughing about Thomas's and her inside joke as she recalled how long she endured the smell of hog after they married. He had moved the corral farther and farther away from the house until he finally said, "If I must set the fence back any farther, it'll be like Jesus when he sent the demons from two men into the herd of swine. Remember, those pigs ran straight down the hill into the sea and drowned. I have the same thing going on. As it is, mine are enjoying the most beautiful view of the Mississippi. One more move, though, and they too will roll into the river. Thank God, I can still smell your brew in the barn."

Not knowing how long she had been sitting in her dream world, Abigail stirred, stretching her legs, and moving her arms and neck. Thomas no longer stood by her side, yet the dress still swaddled her lap.

"Maude?" No one answered. "Thomas?" Still quietness. Then she remembered her brother Tarrant had come to visit with them. "Tarrant?" No answer. The house hardly made a noise. Abigail knew she had not been conked out for long this time. *Oh, I forgot. I bet they're probably out in the barn with the newborn piggies.*

Abigail pushed off the blanket. She stood up, holding the dress by the hanger. Taking a step to her left, she carefully laid it on the sofa. *I feel good. I can go to the kitchen and help myself to some coffee.*

For the first time in a long time, Abigail stepped by herself. She looked down at her feet. Moccasins? Light, nearly white, leather, blue and white beaded stars sewn on the tops and ties to pull around the ankle—. Like a flickering candle ... of course, Thomas made them so many years ago, patching occasionally, adding new draw strings, and even re-beading. He knew how to do almost anything and do it well, but his trade as a shoemaker provided him with extra cash when he arrived in Minnesota Territory so many years ago.

Her mind sparked as shhe recalled Thomas's tales of being a fur trader and his team of oxen pulling his creaking wagon from St. Anthony to Fort Garry in Canada. He would load his cart with various goods such as cast iron and brass pots, colorful woolen blankets, tobacco, and multi-colored beads that he could trade with the Indians for beaver and other types of furs to sell in the European markets.

Abigail wondered how long the slippers had been on her feet. So comfortable, she felt stable enough to walk but took it slowly, grabbing hold of the side chairs and the door frame. She walked into the kitchen—neat, organized, and sparkling! A large pot steamed on the back of the stove. The family could not be far off.

Walking from Thomas's corner where he worked on his leather goods to the kitchen table, Abigail made it to the stove. She lifted the lid on the pot. Steam blew in clouds toward her face. So hot, she could not really see what was cooking, but she sniffed, New England boiled dinner. Then she saw the large baking bowl pushed to the back of the stove, heaving with dough. *Ah, this is Tarrant's doings, but where is he?*

Tired from her short trek, Abigail grabbed a coffee cup from the cupboard and poured herself a cup of what was now old, thickened but still hot coffee. She sat down at the table. She sipped and stared out the window. Soon she heard the door open and lots of stomping in the lean-to. Then the kitchen door opened.

"Abigail, what are you doing up?" Covered from hat to feet with snow, including his thick, paint brush-like mustache, Tarrant started taking off his outerwear, shaking snow off like old Pal.

"Just wanted some coffee," she answered. "I wish I knew how long I was out this time. Where've you been?"

"Maude and T. C. told me to come out to see the new pigs after I visited Mary and the girls again this afternoon. I couldn't have been gone long. When I left, you were like a flickering candle blown out from the wind."

"I wonder when I'll no longer need these catnaps. I must admit, though, they often enlighten my past. The other day, I remember dreaming about George again."

"I hope you didn't say anything to T. C." Looking at her, Tarrant hung his coat on the peg. "He's been uncomfortable and upset since you lost so much of your memory."

"No, I don't tell anyone much about what I am dreaming. I know how sensitive Thomas is, so unless I remember something about him, I say nothing. For some reason, most of my dreams awaken my past. I dreamed I was sick and crying for George to come home. You know, Tarrant, he was never there when I needed him. He wasn't around when I gave birth to Cassius, or even when I miscarried those times. I took care of everything myself. I had to. Our folks, bless them, helped as much as they could."

Abigail shook her head and blinked twice after taking her last sip of coffee now turned cold.

"Here, let me make a fresh pot." Tarrant grabbed the coffee pot. "Yeah, T. C. has been walking around like a lost puppy since you went down. No need to cause hard feelings over a corpse."

"Tarrant!" As Abigail scolded, she remembered another time she hollered at him in alarm. *What had he been doing? Had he mishandled Cassius? They were only seven years apart. No, Tarrant knew how to hold a baby.*

Suddenly, Abigail saw a little blonde haired three-year-old boy. It was not Cassius. It was another child, and he had caught a cold. She heard him coughing and watched him put his head on the cold floor after one of his bouts. One time he fell asleep for a short minute. When he woke, he stood up and wobbled a bit, ready to hang on to the stove for balance. *Tarrant, NO! Don't touch the stove.* She and Thomas raced to the child, but it was too late. He had burned his hand. Thomas grabbed him and raced him to the cold-water bucket, plunging his little hand in it. The child, sick, in pain, and now scared, screamed louder.

"After I rub some salve on his palm and tie a rag around his hand, I'm going for Jared. I don't like the looks of his burn, and he is no better after taking the syrup he provided."

In a few minutes, Abigail sat rocking and soothing her little boy while he coughed and cried.

"Thomas, hurry," Abigail cried out. "Hurry, bring Jared." Her tears fell onto little Tarrant's soft hair and mixed into his own tears as she cuddled the child, trying to soothe everything that ailed him. She had felt alone before, but this was different.

Thomas ran into the house without stomping the snow off his feet, but Abigail said nothing. She needed him now like she had never needed him before. He put his arms around her and tried shushing her fears.

"Abby, it's okay. It's okay, shush, shush."

She began to relax, opened her eyes, and saw Thomas but she held no baby in her arms. Her brother Tarrant stared at Abigail as he punched down the bowl heaped with dough.

Abigail sobbed again.

"Our Tarrant died, didn't he, Thomas?" They had named their baby for her own dear brother because he looked so much like him.

"Yes, quite a while ago, Abby. Remember how he got so sick? Jared figured it to be a cold. We tried soothing him with warm bottles and ice to suck on. One night, we thought he was sleeping quietly in his bed. We got up to look for something to soothe his fever in the kitchen just in case he woke crying again. He had crawled out of bed and followed us. He didn't want to be picked up, and he cried harder if we tried. He was burning up with fever, so I suppose the cold floor felt good to him. Then he burned his hand. By the time, I got home with Jared, his ending was close."

"I remember our son, yours and mine. Cassius was still living with us. You proved to be a good father to him as well, Thomas. Our two sons." Abigail took a deep breath and sighed. "Jared told us there was nothing we could have done to save him. His throat just closed. Poor little thing. After we buried him, our house was quiet again."

Maude stood against the wall. Abigail noticed her wiping her eyes.

"Jessie Maude, come here." Abigail waved her daughter to her outstretched arms. "Then when I thought I was too old to have another child, God blessed me with you."

The three stood hugging each other in a dreamlike moment.

Laughing and wiping her eyes, Maude asked, "I suppose you want to add the house was never quiet again?"

Abigail laughed. "Brother! Come on over here. I think you should gather into our fold too," Abigail urged.

"Of course. We aren't a family without you, Uncle Tarrant." Maude pulled her uncle close to her and held tight to his neck.

The foursome hugged. *It feels good to have a close family.*

〰〰〰〰〰

Exhausted, Abigail walked to Thomas's chair again by herself. She felt her husband hovering behind her. But she was determined. "I will walk by myself from now on." She snuggled in the chair again by the fireplace and added, "Thomas, please hand me my dress." she held onto her beautiful gown. Massaging it like her children did their "blankies," she soothed herself to sleep.

After a short nap, Abigail saw Maeve Murphy working her magic in the preliminary stages of designing her dress. She cut and basted the top together. Abigail tried it on. Maeve fussed and poked more pins in place. Even though Abigail thought it felt fine, Maeve went back to snipping here and cutting there, adding a few more try-ons until she felt she had made headway. Once she was satisfied with her work, Maeve hopped an early train to St. Paul and was home on the night train with a good report from Mrs. Worley to give Maude when she picked her up.

"She seemed pleased with my work. I'm relieved," Maeve repeated the day's outcomes to Abigail.

"I'm glad. I knew you had nothing to worry about. By the way," Abigail said when the young women returned home, "did Maude tell you today she made headway with her plans for Thanksgiving? Thomas will oversee the hunting of a few turkeys and a few of us women will roast them. We have plenty of potatoes and turnips down cellar. We'll have a feast of friends and food. Don't know where we'll put everyone, but Maude's in charge so she'll figure this out."

"She told me. I'm excited to meet a few more of the town people, Mrs. Porter."

"Well, good. We should have a houseful."

Maude came into the house. "I saved a plate of corned beef and cabbage. It's at the back of the stove, keeping warm."

"Let me put me things upstairs and then I'll eat. Thank you, so much," she said lifting the bags she took in the morning.

Abigail loved her brogue—the softening of the vowels. Maeve dropped all "ing" sounds, turning them into a mere "in." If she said she were sewing, what a person heard was she were "sewin." Of course, Maeve had to learn English so when she learned to translate a word like *fuáil*, it came out sounding like foal, which meant baby horse and had nothing to do with what the real word meant.

Her words rolled off her tongue so fast, they tumbled to the ground like a heap of wool from a sheared sheep. Nearly unrecognizable until cleaned, dried, plucked, carded, and dyed, Abigail fed the fleece to the wheel until it spun into a string of yarn. Thus, somehow, Abigail had to gather and spin Maeve's mixed Irish and English words and phrases until she formed a American-English sentence she could understand.

Even though Thomas knew some Irish from his father who was born in Ireland, he, too, had a difficult time understanding her. Yet, Maeve was such an easy-going person, she was not offended by hers or their lack of understanding. It was a constant but fun struggle for all four of them.

Abigail set the table for Maeve, and then poured herself a cup of coffee. Thomas would be in from doing chores soon, so she set a dessert plate. Maude, to her credit, never stopped at simply baking a pie, she had to also bake a cake. "Pie goes too quickly around here." She had made both apple pie with the apples she had found on the ground before snow came, and a lemon pound cake.

When Maeve came back downstairs, Maude said, "Pa told us that our favorite supper, cabbage and corned beef, didn't originate in Ireland."

"That's so. At least, I'd never heard of it until I came here. Besides, my family seldom ate much beef. We sold our cattle for cash to live on."

"Oh, I understand. It was quite the celebration when I served it for those at the hotel." Abigail saw the confusion in Maeve's eyes, so she explained. "I moved here to join the crew at the hotel. I was the housekeeper. The owners brought me a list of meats for me to cook during the week, fresh fish, salt pork, occasionally a turtle or two for soup, just about anything. Some of the pork they bought from Thomas. One morning, I woke to a smell something unlike wood smoke or pine dust. I dressed and stepped outside to find Thomas stirring something in the copper kettle over the fire. Come to find out, he had exchanged his hams and salt pork for a good-sized chunk of beef. He said he was making corned-beef and cabbage for 'a shake up in flavor.'"

"Yeah, that's her story, but I always said it was to get Ma to notice him. She sort of had her eye on another fellow."

"Oh, Maude, stop that!" Abigail said, chuckling. "That's not true, and you know it," she scolded, laughing, and shaking her finger at her daughter because of their inside joke. "But Mr. Farwell, the man we are speaking of, did make a good impression. Tall, dark, and handsome, so we say around here, and I sort of felt sorry for him. He lost his wife and baby back in Canada East. He told me he ran away to clear his head. He headed west."

Maeve seemed to pick up the joke between mother and daughter and chuckled along with them. Abigail realized her own personal seamstress felt comfortable at the Porter home.

"Uncle John had so much heart," Maude admitted. "He often gave it away until he ran away again."

"I agree with Maude about John Farwell, and she said it well. Yet, he had such charisma," Abigail could picture her friend on recall. "I suppose I thought of him as a gentle but wounded puppy. The love of his life died with the baby they had prayed would live. His wife, I think her name was Sarah, but he called her Sally, had lost a few babies like I did early in my child-bearing years. Then, he told me they had such hope for having a family when his wife went into labor. Such hope, but her labor went on and on until she plum tuckered out. Neither she nor the child lived."

"Back home in Ireland we call that the *frowns an fhortúin."*

Abigail and Maude gave each other blank stares. Maeve's brogue proved difficult to understand even though Abigail could detect the word frowns.

"Ah, you do not understand *frowns an fhortúin*. Let's see, I'm trying to say, frowns," here she made her face look sad and turned her lips downwards. "Un is of, and *fhortúin* is fortune."

Maeve's attempt at pronunciation, her dialect so pronounced, still perplexed Abigail. She repeated the phrase over and over, as if she were spinning wool into yarn until her words came out "frowns of fortune," loudly and clearly. "If ever a phrase was a perfect definition of a man, it is fit for John Farwell, especially in love and happiness."

"Ma, don't forget to tell her about his marriage to Nancy Allen."

"I agree, Maude. He had that beautiful farm out in Maine Prairie, lovely farmhouse, with no one to live with him. But when he met Nancy, POW!" Abigail looked at Maeve to emphasize with her eyes and hands how their sad ending began with a mighty force of passion. "The two fell in love immediately. In America, we call that falling head over heels. I became entangled into their affair like a lot of those who loved them did." Abigail looked at Maeve and figured she and Maude had bored her with details about people she did not know. "Let's change the subject. I'm sure Maeve doesn't understand what we are talking about."

"I do, Mrs. Porter, I do. You see, I too, have felt the *splanc sa phluc.*"

Now Abigail felt confused. She looked at Maude whose one eyebrow arched in confusion and misunderstanding too.

Maeve covered her mouth while laughing. "Oh, you two. It means ... something like ... a flash in the pan and scorching hot."

After all the giggling had been accomplished, Maude, who never tied her tongue, asked, "So who was your flash in the pan, Maeve?"

Abigail saw the young girl's face blush a deep pink. "Maybe I should leave so you can talk to Maude," she directed her comment to Maeve.

Maude brought the coffee pot to the table and poured three cups of her black brew.

Looking at her feet and then the cup, Maeve thanked Maude for the coffee and sat down. Maude returned the pot and pulled the supper plate off the back of the stove, and with a dishtowel, carried it to where Maeve sat.

"Thank you, Maude," Maeve said as she took a sip of her coffee. "The other day, Mrs. Worley scolded me because my beau and me were talking by the building."

Ah, so that is why her cheeks were pink and her eyes were swollen that first day we met.

"It is the rule of Mannheimer Brothers that no one is to be seen or heard in a romance-type situation close to the store. He caught up with me before I entered work that morning. I told him the night before I'd been asked if I were interested in going to Clearwater for few weeks. He begged me not to go. Too far away he said. I told him I wanted to prove to myself I could do this work. You see, he and I, we had that *splanc sa phluc* or as you call it head to heels love after we met."

"So how is he doing now, with you here and he there in St. Paul?" Maude asked as she sat down to her own cup of coffee.

"We met, way out of the peeping eyes and listening ears of those at the store. He's still not happy I'm here and he's there. Yet, I insisted I come, for my career. You see, he don't make much money as it is so I'll have to continue to sew after I marry."

"Oh, marry?" Abigail asked. "It's that serious?"

"He thinks so. I'm not ready," Maeve said. "You see, I left a poor home in Dublin. My family put us all out to work when we were little. That's how I learned to sew. But I was so lonely for my ma and my sisters and brothers, I felt … oh, … how do you say … *croíthe briste*?" she asked outloud as she tapped her heart.

"Lonely? Broken-hearted?"

"Very good, Maude. You'll be understandin' me soon," Maeve said after she swallowed a mouthful. "But I do not want to be that poor again. In America, we are promised a better life if we work hard. I'm working hard and trying to get ahead. He hasn't had the same opportunities as me, and he is an awfully proud man. He won't have me working, he say."

"Oh, I'm sure," Maude answered. "We American women have some of the same problems. Men hear 'the richer and poorer part.' They want us to suffer with them. It's a lot easier to be poor than it is rich, and sometimes the men do their part to make their families even more poor by drinking up the wages."

Maeve stared at Maude. Abigail saw the conversation was heading in a different direction. When Maude started taking up her women's equal rights and temperance stands, which Abigail advocated as well, she often forgot where she was and to whom she was talking. Abigail wanted to tell Maude to tone it down, to distract her with "all in good time," but instead, she heard Thomas entering the yard whistling.

"Ah," she said interrupting Maude's loud mantra. "Here's Thomas."

The trio looked toward the door. A stomping of feet, a turn of the squeaky doorknob, and Thomas's fur-lined arm entered before the rest of his furry coat and hat. He carefully removed his outerwear and scarf before turning around to greet them.

"Hello!" He looked expectantly at each woman, and then with a more quizzical stare, he looked at his wife.

"Hello, back at you, Thomas. Everything go all right outside tonight?"

"Oh, fine. Everything going okay in here?" he asked, looking from Maude to Abigail.

"Of course. We have Maude's delicious pound cake and apple pie to go with your coffee, Thomas. Will you sit with us while Maeve eats her supper?"

"Let me wash my hands first," he said rolling up his blue flannel sleeves. He walked over to the dry sink and poured water from the hot kettle and then the cold pitcher into the wash pan. After he scrubbed his hands over and upward, he rinsed, and dried on the kitchen towel hanging from the rack.

"I'm glad you made it back, Maeve. It looks like we are in for a round of snow. Everything work out in St. Paul?"

"Yes sir," Maeve dabbed her napkin at her mouth. "Everything went fine."

"Glad to hear that. I'm sure it was a long day for you. The wind has really picked up. I hope it doesn't turn into a blizzard."

"We figured, Pa. Snow started coming down in huge splotches when we were riding back from the depot. Dark clouds banking up in the western sky."

"Good pie, Maude. Just like your ma's," Thomas said after he placed the fork on the plate.

"You know who taught me!" Maude laughed as she got up to refill the cups.

"Abigail always was a top-notch baker," Thomas said as he raised his coffee cup and toasted his wife.

Maude and Maeve raised their cups, and Abigail bowed to their cheers.

"If you don't mind, ladies," I'm going to my chair to finish reading the newspaper."

"Sounds like a good idea. You look tired. I'll be in shortly," Abigail said.

Maude sliced a small piece of pie and chunk of pound cake for Maeve.

"Thank you, Maude. The corned beef and cabbage was mighty good. Warmed my stomach, but I've gotta admit, I'm partial to sweets."

"Who isn't?" Abigail got up from the table to take Maeve's plate to the dry sink. "All of us want sweets so we usually have cakes or pies around here," she said as she sat down partially on bent leg. "Maeve, so tell us about your boyfriend. A re you two really this serious?"

"I think he has it worse now than me. When I'm here, I've gotta be, ummmm, let's see if you can understand me, *macánta*, which means honest, I guess. But I am so busy here. I don't think much except to get this dress done."

"I understand. It sounds like you feel guilty though." Abigail remarked.

Maude patted Maeve's arm. "See, Ma and I were talking about a few of the young unmarried men who might come to the Thanksgiving party. We don't want to cause a problem though, especially if you already have a beau."

"We've made no promises yet," Maeve said as she looked at both Maude and Abigail. "I will wait a bit for him to further himself. I'm serious, and he knows it, about not marrying until we have both feet settled on the ground. I'm not ready to become a Mrs. I want to see how my career goes. Working for you, Mrs. Porter, adds to my experience."

"Oh, and I can tell you, I'm impressed with your workmanship," Abigail responded. "Maude will go ahead with our plans and include you, too, for Thanksgiving."

"Will this John and his wife come to?" Maeve asked as she set her cup down on its saucer.

"Oh, I forgot. We never finished the story," Maude said. "Ma, you tell her."

"It's a long one for such a short marriage, Maeve. You sure you want to hear it?"

"Sure, Mrs. Porter. It's too late to do much sewin' tonight."

"I've told you about John. Over that first winter, I didn't see him so much. He, a brother, and a few other people settled another community halfway between here and St. Cloud. Maine Prairie became very successful and stayed linked to Clearwater, but it also connected with St. Cloud. They were not only farmers in their community, but many also became merchants, bankers, insurance brokers, schoolteachers, and even newspaper publishers.

"Lots of people are related to one another out there like the Atwoods, Farwells, Spauldings, Greeleys, Mitchells from Lynden Township, and Kirks. I could go on.

"Then some of them had relatives who weren't interested in land for farming as much as setting up businesses in St. Cloud. There's no wonder the two communities mingled. Anyway, John's out in Maine Prairie, and a sister to his neighbors, the Atwoods, arrives in both communities. Nancy Allen comes to set up a photography studio in St.Cloud.

Abigail added," Nancy called herself an artist right away. She trained under the famous Joel Emmons Whitney out of St. Paul. His photos have ended up in the state capitol and other national galleries. One portrait of Minnehaha Falls inspired Henry Wadsworth Longfellow to write 'The Song of Hiawatha.' Then when Jane Swisshelm, I'll save you from hearing about her tonight, but she was a journalist in St. Cloud. She defined Nancy, "Mrs. Allen is an artist" in her newspaper, *The St. Cloud Democrat*. You see Nancy was an ambrotypist." Again, Abigail read confusion in the seamstress's eyes. "You know, a photographer, an early photographer."

Maeve nodded her head, looking first at Abigail and then at Maude and saying, "Oh!" with understanding expression in her eyes.

"Nancy Allen took the most beautiful portraits and landscapes. She became very popular after Jane Swisshelm, newspaper editor and publisher, started advertising for her and writing short articles about her. One short article announced Mrs. Allen taking landscapes, which were unsurpassed in clearness and dependability. Mrs. Swisshelm had her take a picture of her home and Democrat office. She even urged her readers to quickly make appointments to have their homes counterfeited in black and white. Well, let me tell you, Mrs. Allen's business multiplied in just a few days after this announcement."

"We had our portraits taken as well," Maude said. "And she was a welcome visitor here in our home as well. She enjoyed coming down to Clearwater to visit us to take a few pictures of different buildings along the river. She always slept in your room, Maeve. She was a tiny, beautiful, and darling woman. I forgot to say she was smart and taught school too. She had to so she could take care of herself and her two sons."

"I believe you can tell how close a friend is going to be by inviting her into your kitchen. I was a little apprehensive at first when she asked if she could help me make supper. Efficient and tidy, Nancy glided around never getting in my way and knowing wat to do next just like Maude does now. Anyway, she and I confided in each other early on. You see, we were both widows, raising children on our own."

"You always told me you two were like sisters, Ma."

"That's true. I suppose we were soul sisters. Between my two real sisters, I'd rather work with Mary than Annette. Annette wants to get things done now. Mother always said if you want something done right, ask Mary or me. If you need something done fast, ask Annette."

Maude laughed, "So true, Ma. When she lived with us while Grandpa was here, her cakes often turned out too brown or underbaked. Oh, she tried hard to do better. But give her a skein of yarn or even just scraps, and she can create a masterpiece. Remember the jacket and matching cap she made for the Rothman baby? All those girls Mrs. Rothman had and finally a boy who needed different colors. Well, Maeve, I'm not sure how she did it, but Aunt Annette scraped together some pinks, yellows, even some blues and browns, and the infant products turned into a lovely shade of green."

"That's right, Annette's fingers and needles are magic, but she taught you how to create wonderful hats, Maude, and you both have plenty of customers for your millinery businesses."

"Annette, Nancy, and you have taught me how to take care of myself in case I never marry or become a widow. I will not be helpless. I can be independent and make my own way without a man."

"True enough, Maude. But time is getting late. So let's get back track as we were talking about John's and Nancy's head over heels kind of love. John spent a lot of time in St. Cloud with Nancy and her boys, so you'd think he'd have known what he would be up against with a woman who was so protective of her sons. Needless to say, the two got married. Jane Swisshelm announced their wedded bliss in the *St. Cloud Democrat* referencing John as having 'won a crown' when he married Mrs. Allen . But Nancy told me," Abigail said, placing her cup on the saucer, "they started fighting as soon as she and the children moved into his house out on Maine Prairie."

"Abby, I'm turning in," Thomas's voice broke through the night and the burgeoning story. "I don't know why I'm so tired, but you gals keep on socializing. I just can't keep my eyes open."

"I'll join you soon," Abigail said as she picked up a handful of dishes and carried them to the dry sink. "So where was I?"

"You were telling us about the problems this Nancy and John were having," Maeve answered, walking behind her with the rest of the dishes.

Maude washed the table before they reconnected their circle.

"Oh, of course. I didn't know they were having problems right away. She went about her marriage like she went at all her business. She taught in the Farwell School while she was out there. They often visited with their relatives. Nancy's brother was Edwin Atwood, Nancy was an Atwood, but maybe I said that already. His wife was an Allen, her first husband's sister. So, sister and brother Allen married sister and brother Atwood. Of course, John had family, his brothers Orlen and Gladden and families, and his own homestead out there as well. Many times, she had her women's groups travel out to their home in the summer or fall for soldier aid meetings, of course the Rebellion had just begun. Shortly afterwards, a scary time for all of us here in Minnesota when we started having Indian trouble. No one travelled much then."

"Ma, you always told me she kept her studio open on Saturdays. So, she was on the go, Maine Prairie and Lower Town St Cloud, where her home and studio was," Maude added.

"And dragging her children along with her and John in the beginning when life was good. He kept busy building additions on her town home while she took pictures. I must add, it seemed like sunshine and roses whenever she and I met up. Of course, she seldom got down to our place in Clearwater to visit anymore. She had way too much going on."

Maeve yawned and both Maude and Abigail followed suit.

"We could save the remainder of this for another night, Maeve," Abigail suggested.

"Let's continue with the story. I'll be fine for a while."

"The Indian skirmishes started shortly after they were married. John and others alerted neighbors all over the prairies. He even went after more rifles and ammunition down in St. Anthony, leaving Nancy alone to her own defenses. Her friend, neighbor, and sister-in-law Augusta Atwood said before John took off, the two hugged and kissed, making quite a spectacle of themselves before he and others took off. That was about 1862."

"Sounds like they had the fever all right," Maeve added.

The grandfather's clock chimed ten times. Morning came early in the Porter house. Abigail looked at both Maude and Maeve. "You two look exhausted. Maeve, you had a long day. Why don't we finish this another day?"

"I'm good thirty minutes or so. Let's speed up the story."

"Well, okay. You see the two got along all through the war and the Indian troubles. They were apart and then together."

"So, it's true, I guess, that the heart draws dearer when a couple is apart."

"Right, Maude. I know I told you they only lived as man and wife during the weekdays when they finally got back together. She went back to her house in south St. Cloud on weekends for her customers. So, there was always a homecoming. He kept busy building onto the farmhouse because Nancy's sister died, and they took in her sister's daughter Kathy who was a six-year-old. They had three children living with them out in Maine Prairie."

"When Captain Fisk organized his 1866 expedition to Montana, didn't they both want to go?" Maude asked.

Abigail smiled. No matter how many times Maude had heard the story, she enjoyed hearing it again.

"Of course, that was just like Nancy. She read in the newspaper Fisk was looking for a photographer to develop a visual record of the trip, showing the dangerous side of the trip as well as the beauty. So, she enlisted and sent a portfolio of pictures with her application. She got her brother Edwin and sister-in-law Augusta to take in the children. Nancy's rationale to go on this excursion was to gain experience and a broader reputation in her profession."

"Unfortunately, Uncle John decided he was going too. He wanted adventure all right and a chance to mine gold." Maude added.

Abigail could not help but relate to this story because of her first husband George's need to go off on adventure and to find gold.

Leaning on the table with her right arm and hand cupping her chin, Maeve interjected, "You don't say!" which she had been saying often during the more intense parts of the story.

Nodding affirmatively, Abigail said, "That became a problem. Not only did he say the trip was too dangerous for a woman, but he pulled the old 'wives have their place in the home' routine. Neither of them asked permission from each other for projects they wanted to do or events that were coming up. They had been used to living their own lives and going their own way for a long time before they met up. Nonetheless and without mentioning it, John mortgaged the farm to help finance his trip. Besides, he expected her to stay home with her children and take care of the farm so the crops could be harvested like usual to pay back his loan if he did not find enough gold. She could ask his nephew Quartus to help occasionally, though."

Maeve's eyes expressed alarm. She said, "I don't know about you, Maude, Mrs. Porter, but I'm not going to bed until I've heard how this mess turned out."

"Later, she told me although they'd had disagreements before, this was the first screaming, shouting, door-slamming, packing-up and-leaving-with-her-children fight they'd ever had. She called him a lot of words, she said, but she told him she wasn't raised to be some man's cow hand. She gathered the kids and moved back into her house in St. Cloud. Shortly after, she received a letter from the Miliary Headquarters District of Minnesota telling her the army did not hire women for such dangerous excursions. Of course, this had been John's rationale for her not going in the first place. Yet, I ask you, had none of these men in charge taken into consideration there were other women emigrants going with their husbands west to settle Montana Territory?"

"My guess is they had not thought this through, nor would they," Maude said. "And Uncle John simply wanted to get away from his responsibilities to go on an adventure."

How similar the stories are, Nancy's and John's and mine and George's. Man leaving expecting the woman, his woman, to keep the home fires burning. It makes me scared to think how close I'd come to choosing John over Thomas. John and I had nothing to help each other grow together. We would be borrowing mistakes from our past and repeating them.

Abigail thought a few moments before saying, "I have to admit, men can sometimes be blind and self-serving, and yet they own the keys to the world."

"Don't forget Ma, some of us believe our rights can be changed. We've brains to fix our problems when the majority of women have had enough. Susan B. Anthony says, "No man is good enough to govern any woman without her consent. That's what we have to change—the HER CONSENT!"

The Her-Consent! That is a good expression to help women to understand what we are up against in this male-dominated world. Some women are motivated, on fire, to change the world. Some are ***mildy interested*** *in women's rights, thinking nothing can be done about male superiority. Some believe the whole idea is wrong, almost religiously wrong. They're caught up in the man is the head of the house belief. I lived that way for a long time. It doesn't always work out for the woman and children's best. Oh, best get back to moving this yarn along so we can go to bed.*

"This isn't the end of the story, is it? I mean, he came home and they got back together I suppose," Maeve surmised.

"Yes, they did, for a while. The rest of this story is going to be abbreviated for time's sake. I'm sure sorrow for her behavior and womanly guilt played a part. Most women of my generation have been taught we are the guardians of the family hearth and the makers of peace in the home. Nancy met up with him and the others who were joining up with Captain Fisk out at camp at Lake George in St. Cloud. In fact, John said he was coming to see her too."

"Right, saving face," Maude said.

"A few friends of mine who were up there seeing loved ones off also saw them holding tight to each other. Each swore responsibility for the row they had caused. Then they made lovers' promises to never fight again. Nancy told John whatever money she made taking pictures, minus business and living expenses, she planned to put away for repayment of his loan against their home on the prairie. In their parting scenes, they created a lovely picture for a romance novel others told me. John mounted his steed, bending down to kiss his bride goodbye after which Captain Fisk shouted "HO!" and led the parties of men on mounted horses and all the covered wagons off to see the world."

"And that is the end of the story?" Maeve asked.

"On no," Abigail said. "When John got back home, many months later, they had a romantic reunion and a period of calmness before life became difficult again. Nancy had scrimped and saved to hold on to the house because his gold-mining had gained him little for his journey. If he could write his stories, fighting off the Sioux and trying to save Mrs. Fanny Kelly from a band that had kidnapped her a few years before, he might have become wealthy. After they helped the settlers stake their claims, they headed back home. Most of the men were broke but exhilarated and tired from their escapades."

"She just adapted to his ways? I can't believe this is how Nancy's story ends with John."

"You'd think so, but Nancy was a tough egg when her back was up against the wall. John promised he'd pay her back from his crops for the money he borrowed against his mortgage. This never happened. He started having problems with her children. They were disobedient or talked back and even reminded him that he wasn't their father. Little Kathy went back to living with her father in Wisconsin after he married again. More and more, Nancy stayed in St. Cloud to take pictures and teach at the Everett School that she and Rev. Phillips started up. John did not like this. He came up to insist on her coming home. He even insisted the boys come back to help with chores around the farm instead of studying all the time.

"They had another monster of a fight. This time John slammed out of her house, grabbed his horse, hopped on, and beat him to get out of town as fast as he could.

"Nancy was shocked when she received a letter from her sister-in-law Augusta Atwood out in Maine Prairie. John had joined Fisk's regiment again for another excursion to Montana. That next Monday, she filed for divorce on the grounds of desertion."

Maude asked, "Wasn't it a scandal, Ma? Divorce always is because the public sees it the woman's fault. She must have been talked about behind her back."

"It was quite a scandal for a while. John's friends and family took his side, and Nancy's took hers, which put her brother Edwin and sister-in-law Augusta right smack dab in the middle out there in Maine Prairie. She made changes so she could escape. She enrolled her oldest son, Ernest, in college out east earlier than she expected because the St. Cloud schools had little to help build his young mind without her help. He was only sixteen but ready. George, her youngest, who was still young enough to go to country school and really liked farm work, went to live with Edwin and Augusta. Nancy eventually took off to stay with her mother in Flint, Michigan, until everything settled down."

Maude spoke up, "I remember you telling me it was a nasty divorce, though."

"True," Abigail added. "Nancy accused John of stealing from her because he never paid her back the money had she paid on the bank loan against the house. Then he sold the house and farm, making a considerable profit and still never paid her back. Her lawyer posted a summons for him to appear in court to answer her complaint. Instead, he headed off with Captain Fisk again on another expedition."

"What a tragic story! Did John ever repay Nancy?" Maeve asked.

Maude pushed her chair back. Abigail watched her as she answered, "That's another long story. Maude, what are you doing?"

"I decided we needed some tea because the next chapter could be a long one. Anyone want more pie or pound cake?"

~~~~~

The clock struck midnight before Maude, Maeve, Abigail went to bed. They nibbled on cake and sipped tea while Abigail finished telling the tale of John and Nancy.

Abigail woke when the clock struck seven times. She stretched her arms and legs. Then she cuddled under the blankets, feeling like sleep could visit again. Soon wafts of coffee made their way to her bedroom.

Thomas must be making breakfast. I need to tell him I'm awake and can finish the job. But I feel like a lazy bug.

What was said to get me started telling John's and Nancy's story? Oh, I remember! That hot flash in the pan, Maeve called splanc sa phluc or something. The Farwell's love, their romance, almost passion, created nothing but chaos for Abigail's two good friends and those who cared for them.

What did Mother always say about George and me when we first married? "A day will come when your body changes, you're tired, you're sick, you have others to think of besides yourselves, and that ardor can't be lit for each other anymore. You'd better have friendship and true caring remaining or the marriage won't make it."

That sure held true in John's and Nancy's situation. George and I never got to live that section of our vows, the 'In sickness and in health' part together. He became ill in San Francisco and Marysville, California, and I couldn't help him from Vermont. He died way too young. Maybe he'd have settled down, helped build up a home for us, and been willing to let the younger generations go on the adventures.

On the other hand, Thomas had already sewed his oats and had landed with both feet on the ground. He liked excitement, but he wanted it closer to home now.

Mother, you were right. Passion can't stand on its own for long. A marriage is just that –a joining of two with different wants,
~~~~~

needs, desires. It must be built on more than the physical. Maybe that's all I was trying to share with Maeve, for her to understand her relationship with her beau.

Tansy jumped up on the bed. As if reminding Abigail morning had dawned a while ago and even if some roles had been reversed in the Porter household, she needed her nap even if the bed had not been made.

Abigail sat at the end of the bed, waiting to get some gumption to stand up. This would be a long day. She hadn't gotten her full night's sleep, something she had started after Thomas had come into her life. She usually lay in bed, slowly waking to reach her quarter day abed. She should be ashamed, but she never felt bad or guilty about not getting laundry on the line at six in the morning like her mother.

Wrapping her robe around her and slipping into her moccasins, Abigail emerged from the bedroom. The warmth of the parlor and the smell of bacon frying welcomed her into the kitchen.

No Thomas! What in the world?

"Mrs. Porter," Maeve said, coming out from the pantry. "You startled me. Mr. Porter told me you were still sleeping so I started coffee and breakfast. Maude's still sleeping too."

"Maeve! Goodness! This is nice of you when you are working so hard on my dress."

"Oh, Mr. Porter and I decided he'd go back and finish up his chores, while I made coffee. I'll be back up there in due time. I thought I'd whip up some pancakes to go with the bacon if that's okay."

"Oh, let me help. You're our guest."

"Not much of a guest right now. I feel part of the family."

"That's the nicest thing you could say, Maeve." Abigail went over to the girl and gave her a big hug. "You feel like you are part of our family too. As if you were born here." She took the ladle from Maeve's hands. "Now, I'll finish breakfast. As part of the family, I'm telling you to bring down something to work on and sit in Thomas's corner where he does some of his leather work. You'll have plenty of light."

Maude came down the steps as Maeve headed up. After their morning greetings, Maude stepped into the kitchen and gave another yawned greeting to her mother, scratching here and there.

"What's going on, Ma?" she asked, setting plates on the table.

Abigail flipped the cakes as she told Maude about Maeve's morning and their conversation. "She'll be back down with some handwork."

"I know. I can tell she likes it here." Maude grabbed silverware from the drawer and placed a knife and fork by each plate. "Ma, I was thinking about this when I went to bed. We should invite her boyfriend to come for Thanksgiving."

"Hmm, think that he'd fit in? I guess you could ask Maeve to see what she'd think." Abigail flipped another pancake onto the stack. "Might be good for him to get out of the St, Paul environment for a couple days."

Making her way back into the kitchen, Maeve said, "My! It smells good in here."

"We wouldn't be this far without you, Maeve. Before you get too comfortable there, why don't you sit down and start eating. Thomas should be in soon," Abigail said as she carried the platter to the table.

Maude followed behind with the coffee pot. "Wait until you try our very own maple syrup, Maeve. Here's the butter, too, from our very own cows."

Thomas came into the house, scrubbed up, and joined them. Eating their fill of the hearty breakfast, everyone's concern was on their upcoming Thanksgiving affair. Maeve agreed to ask her 'friend' to come up and join them for the potluck. She told them she hoped she'd have the dress bound together so she could enjoy her day before heading back to St. Paul the next morning. She and Mrs. Porter had lots to do before then.

Someone knocked on the kitchen door. They all looked at each other in surprise. The hired man never came up to the house for anything, but it could be him.

Thomas stood up and walked to the door and slowly opened it.

"Morning, T.C." Thomas opened the door wide for Maryetta Phillips. Always a bit "fleshy," she often said about herself, but after her last delivery she never lost much of the baby weight she had gained. Abigail, who oversaw all her babies, told her that if she had more children, she might think of losing a few pounds because each pregnancy would just become longer and more difficult.

"Maryetta, come in, come in." Abigail stood up and went to the cupboard for another plate and cup as Maude and Thomas sang a special greeting for their friend.

"Hello everyone, oh, and of course, a special hello to you, Miss Murphy," Maryetta said. "I didn't mean to startle everyone, and I know it's early, but thought I'd come up and talk about Thanksgiving. Jennie came home from school and told me the teachers are having a program the night before to celebrate the Pilgrims. She has a piece to memorize as do several children. Let's see! What else did she say would take place? Poetry reading, a few, will have parts in skits, and of course some singing. Everyone's invited. I thought maybe we should invite the teachers to our next day feast as well."

"That's a great idea. So, that's three more places, one for Mr. Bigford, one for Miss Bateman, and another for Mr. Howard," Abigail said as she looked around the kitchen.

"Ma, I was thinking, maybe we should hold the celebration somewhere else than our house."

"I'm all for that," Thomas spoke up as he forked another piece of bacon. "Except for the Whiting brothers, we have one of the larger homes in town, but as this event grows larger, I think we need to hold it elsewhere."

"With you already having company, Abigail, I sort of agree. The party is growing, and I don't have room for half the crowd you have. I was thinking maybe we could have it at the school or even at the Congregational Church."

"So, you think so, too?" Abigail asked, first looking at Thomas and then Maude. They both nodded their approval. "Then, I think agree. Did you all figure I'd be upset for not having the shindigs here? Not in the least. But where do you think we should have it?"

"Although the back rooms are not quite finished, I think Reverend Crawford would be fine with us using the rest of the church building, especially if we invited him and his wife."

"That's a great idea, if it's big enough," Maude answered.

"Should we just plan on a larger scale?" Abigail asked, filling her friend's cup to the brim with coffee and passing her the pancakes.

~~~~~

Maeve and Abigail moved from room to room throughout the Porter house to get the best lighting. Now it was noon, and the kitchen offered the brightest perspective on the dress. Here they were part of the action, and action and busyness was part of the Porter household due to the Thanksgiving Day preparation.

"I hope we have a few moments to eat our dinner in quiet," Maude said as she scooped chicken parts onto a platter.

The outer door to the entry opened. Someone stomped his or her feet. Then the door opened. All three women looked with bated breath to see who it was.

Thomas walked in. The women let out "woosh" sounds as they recognized him.

He must have recognized the strange looks on their faces. He asked, "What's up?"

Maude said, "Pa. We're happy it's only you. We'd like to sit down and eat a meal without another donation for the Thanksgiving celebration."

Since many did not know that the celebration would be held at the Congregational Church, they had stopped and donated some of their recently harvested crops like pumpkins, squash, potatoes, and rutabagas. One corner of the kitchen had been used to pile the vegetables.

"We'll get more if we continue to have Indian Summer. It's gorgeous outside right now. The sun's warm and a light wind is fanning the earth."
~~~~~

"Pa, can you wash up? Let's eat before anyone comes," Maude insisted. She scooped up mashed potatoes into a large ironstone bowl and poured gravy into its matching boat.

Soon the four sat around the table as Thomas led the family in grace:

Bless, O Lord, this food to our use
And us to thy service,
And keep us ever mindful
Of the needs of others.
In Jesus' Name, Amen.

As he picked up the platter of chicken to pass, he said, "This weather makes me think of building. I'm going to have the hired hand help me extend the hog barn another twenty feet. By the looks of things, we'll need more room soon for the piglets."

"Thomas, as long as the door faces the river or south, I'm fine with that," Abigail passed the potatoes to Maeve, who took a spoonful and passed the bowl to Maude.

"Pa, you want to talk a bit before the big dinner?" Maude asked, grabbing the gravy boat from Maeve.

"Not really. Do you think we need a speaker, Maude? Really? If you can't find anyone else, I suppose I could talk about what we are thankful for. But that doesn't take a speaker. What do you think, Abby?"

Abigail swallowed. "First, Maude, your baked chicken, fall-the-bone tender and delicious," she added as she swallowed and reached for her napkin. "As far as a speaker, I agree with your pa. Maybe you could just welcome everyone and suggest we think of sharing one thing we are thankful for."

Abigail saw the disappointment on her daughter's face. Maude's eyes, green-blue, said everything she was thinking. She knew her well. Right now, Maude needed assurance that all would turn out well since the whole shindig had been her idea.

Maeve must have felt the same. "Oh, Maude, I know how organized you've been. Everything will turn out all right. I agree with your mother. Just welcome everyone, tell them where they can sit and eat, and suggest each family tell what they are thankful for, like your mother suggests."

For a while, Maude picked at her meal. Abigail knew she would not leave this idea alone. In one form or another, Maude would have her way.

"Umm, this chicken really did turn out okay, Ma. We have enough left for supper too. Not sure about these biscuits. Not as tender as yours, that's for sure."

"Ah, just need more butter and honey," Thomas replied. "Everything is tasty, just tasty, Maude."

"You just stirred the dough a tad too much. They're fine. You'll get the knack."

The house turned quiet. They munched, and except for a few "yums," ate quietly, enjoying their dinner.

Dusty barked. Abigail hardly noticed until he barked again and again. Everyone looked up.

"Oh, well, we nearly finished our dinner this time," Maude said as she stood up to answer the door. "Always such a mystery who stands behind that door," Maude once said. "Could be bringing good news or bad."

Abigail heard someone using the boot scraper probably from walking through their muddy pathway. Then he or she opened the outer door, wiped his or her feet on the grassy mat again before knocking twice on the inner door.

Most close friends just knocked and walked in. "No need for ceremony here in Clearwater," she often heard town citizens say.

And so, it was. One loud knock, and the door opened, and a "Hello, Maude," followed as his voice and face identified who their guest was.

"Mr. Whiting, nice to see you, come on in."

Abigail knew it was Sam Whiting, store owner, attorney, and all-over dear friend. Thomas did too. He immediately wiped his mouth and stood up to welcome him.

"Sam, so good to see you. Come on in. Let me take your coat and hat."

"Oh, okay, but I can't stay long. Left Anna in charge of the store so I could run a few errands. Hello, everyone," he nodded to his hosts. "I'm sorry I'm interrupting your midday meal. I won't stay long."

"Welcome, Sam. You're not interrupting anything. We're just finishing up. We have plenty left. Won't you share some chicken?

"Or, better yet, share some coffee and apple dumplings," Maude suggested.

"I knew I smelled cinnamon and apples," Abigail exclaimed. "We've been so busy today, I forgot to ask what you were baking," Abigail said. "Welcome again to our table Sam. If you don't relax and share dessert, Anna will be mad at me. Please, sit down."

"With two strong women sharing how their husbands behave, I'd better take a seat."

Maeve had gotten up to help Maude clear the dishes and bring dessert plates and another cup and saucer for Sam Whiting. Maude laid the *pies de la resistance* in the center of the table. Gorgeous! Six golden apple dumplings with caramel glaze and a dusting of powdered sugar made her dinner and dessert partners say, "Wow!"

"I tell you what, Maude. I'd really be in trouble if I left this dessert and Anna found out about it."

"I brought an extra to wrap up and take one back to her, Mr. Whiting."

"Maude's our baker now. She loves it. I got tired of baking after I was housekeeper at the hotel. She surprises us often with her delicacies." As Maeve delivered the coffee, Abigail asked, "Sam, have you met Maeve Murphy. Maeve, please meet Sam Whiting. He owns a clothing store on the opposite side of town. Now that it's warm again, we could take a walk down there."

"Nice meeting you, Miss Murphy. I'd heard that you were in town sewing up a storm for Mrs. Porter for her hotshot husband's coronation."

"Sam, quit teasing. She hasn't been in this country long to understand your every conversational whim."

"It's nice to meet you, Mr. Whiting." Maeve smiled brightly as she took her seat, folded her napkin over her lap, and took her first bite. "Maude, I've never eaten anything so delicious."

"Maude, just wonderful. We have a few fallen apples. I might suggest one of my three daughters or my wife to baked them up like this."

"I agree, Maudie, this is a wonderful treat," her father commented before sipping his coffee. "By the way, Sam, what brings you down to our lonely part of town?"

"Oh, right. The older I get, the more forgetful. One of my customers stopped in to tell me he had a cow butchered. He gave me a quarter of beef to pay me back for a few items I ordered for him. I insist we use some of this for the dinner. Anna said she would bake it up and slice it before we come."

"That's mighty generous of you, Sam, mighty generous." Thomas placed his fork across his plate and laid his napkin over it. "It should be a nice get-together. Lots of people coming. So many offering foods, meats, desserts. Look what we have in the corner there. Harvest offerings from everyone around. Also a bunch of us are heading out a couple days before to hunt for what we can get. I hope for a deer and a turkey. You should join us, Sam. I know how you enjoy a good hunt."

"I'd like that. I'll see if I can leave for a bit. Since George died, well, it's been hard to take care of the place myself. Anna comes and gives me a rest when she can get away from the children. Oh, I forgot, my older sister will need a seat at the table. She got here last week. She's willing to help around the house so Anna can help me more at the store. We're glad to have her."

"The more the merrier," Abigail added. "Maude what do we have to wrap up this wonderful apple dumpling?"

"I think I'll wrap it in some butcher paper so it won't stick. Here let me take it."

"Speaking of butcher paper. Dave Pineo, the new butcher told me to tell you that he's offering up some pork and will have it ready to be eaten when he brings it."

"I hope we have enough people to eat it all," Maude said as she handed Sam Whiting the dessert. "I think it's going to be a good time.

"Your sister-in-law, Mrs. Adelia Whiting, and her daughters were at church last weekend. She said they'll be up here from

Minneapolis for a while. They volunteered to help cook and clean up for the dinner. I know they're busy right now. Her mother, your mother-in-law too, the Widow Walker will be moving in with them for a while."

"That has changed. She decided for a while, anyway, she wanted to stay put in her own home, "the home Deacon and I built," she says.

"Well, good for Maria. If she can care for herself, she may as well hold on to her independence," Abigail added.

Sam shook his head in agreement. "She feels better now after her bout of pleurisy. It's not like she lives far from any of us. Emma, Deacon's daughter, still lives at home as well. She takes good care of Maria. With all three daughters living within a small village block, Deacon's children all around us, along with all the grandchildren, someone is running in and out of the house constantly at all times of the day. The two are seldom alone."

"I'm glad she still has her 'can do attitude.' Make sure you tell her I'll be up to see her soon and say high to Anna and Adelia too," Abigail added.

"Right. I'd better be heading back. Thanks, Maude, for the delicious dessert. Nice meeting you, Miss Murphy. Abigail, T.C., we'll talk more about Thanksgiving soon."

The rest of the afternoon, Maeve and Abigail worked from window to window, finding the best light they could get.

"Right now," Maeve admitted, "it's crucial I have I see my very best. The bodice has to be exactly right But if I can get done what I need to get done today and tomorrow, I'm sure I can meet my deadline—the afternoon before the Thanksgiving event."

Abigail stood perfectly still many times during the afternoon, so she had plenty of time to recall the earlier days. Marie was a great companion once she and Deacon Walker arrived in town. She was a bit older than Abigail, but it made little difference. The two women had strong, independent mother figures who they both misunderstood for much of their younger years. Both women had been widowed, leaving them alone to tend to their children and homes, with little cash to do so. The two had endured struggle and survival. Both agreed it was important to encourage each of their daughters to be independent, to get some type of education that could help with the family income in case of the loss of crops, husband's disability, or even his death.

Abigail's knees buckled as Maeve pinned her hem.

"Oh, I felt that too. You've been standing too long," Maeve said. "Give me a second. Then I think you need to walk around for a while."

It felt good to get dressed in real clothes instead of her wool robe. She threw on her winter coat and told Maude and Maeve she intended to head to the river if it were not too soupy outside.

The sun hung low in the west as she closed the door behind her. The afternoon had turned chilly, not as warm now as Sam and Thomas had said. Abigail pulled her coat up around her neck, tugged it closer, and dug her hands deeper into her pockets. She intended to stretch her legs and get refreshed by the site of the Mississippi before it froze up solid for the season.

She followed the south pasture down to the riverbank. From where she stood above, Abigail heard water lapping loudly below. Up close, she saw frozen splotches of ice pushed onto the shore. Refreshing, but even colder close to the wate, Abigail knew she could not endure the temperature too long.

She looked across the river toward the marsh behind the small island. Ducks floated and bent their heads into the water. She only knew a few by their looks—the green-headed shovelers with their black shovel-like bills, the mallards, also green headed with rings around their necks, and the wigeons that looked a little like the other two. Yet these gorgeous birds were drakes. Just to show off, they flapped their wings, flew over their chosen bird to show how powerful they were, and bobbed their heads up and down to impress the females.

In less colorful hues, shades of browns and blacks, and mottled all over in various beige and white schemes dependent on the species, the females swam gracefully and played their part in their little mating game. Of course, Abigail reasoned, if humans followed this strategy, the whole male-dominated world would be tipped upside down. In fact, her dress bill at Mannheimers' would not have needed to be as expensive either.

~~~~~

Thanksgiving eve afternoon arrived. True to her beliefs, Maeve had met her deadline in time to enjoy the next couple of days celebration with the Porters. She received a letter from "Daniel," and he said he had planned to take the earliest train to Clearwater, which arrived around eleven in the morning.

"That'll work out fine. He can help us gather foods from our house to take up to the Congregational Church. I hope you know by now we don't stand on ceremonies long around here before everyone has to pitch in and help," Maude added and laughed. "We'll definitely need the help."

Abigail finished drying the dinner dishes. "You 're right about that, Maude. Maeve, we usually spend more time getting to know our guests. But this time because of his short stay and our busy holiday, it'll be the exception. In forgot to tell you that he can stay in the backroom where my father Doctor Robinson slept when he stayed with us. You've seen it. It's the room behind the pantry. We use it for a storage now, but it has a nice comfortable bed in there too. And it'll be toasty because it is behind the cookstove. Just have him put his things in that room."

"This is very nice of you, Mrs. Porter. I know he holds his money tight, so staying in a hotel would have been tough. Don't forget, we will both be on the early train going back to St. Paul the next morning. I'll be back that night though."

"I bet our three hotels in town will be full," Maude said.

"I'm sure. Did I tell you I heard from Cousin Hannah? She and the boys will join Francis here. You haven't met him yet, Maeve. He's one busy man. He built the Morrison House, and the first suspension bridge across the Mississippi down in St. Anthony. He's also an important lumberman. He's been working up in Crow Wing, north of here, on the Mississippi lately. His wife, my cousin, Hannah, keeps house down in Minneapolis. And let me tell you, she and her housekeeper create the best looking and tasting mincemeat pies! Of course, they will stay in their usual rooms at the Morrison House."
~~~~~

"Ma, Uncle Simon told me he and Aunt Katy are coming. He also heard Corinna Township plans on holding its own event at St. Mark's Episcopal by Clearwater Lake."

"Won't that be nice? Your pa said about the same after he ran into the Stevens's at the Masonic Hall last week. Apparently, Uncle Simon planned to meet up with the hunting group today. There will be lots to eat at this party."

"But this makes me wonder if the Congregational Church is large enough for everyone who's coming. Maybe we should move everything to the upstairs of the school."

"The room is large enough, Maude, but think of some of the older people trying to climb those steps with food. Of course, we 'll have lots of younger people and men around to help carry things. I guess it's up to you."

"How about as soon as I get up there tonight for the school children's play or after their program, we'll check it out and ask a few for advice?"

"This morning, while you two worked in the other room, Maryetta had Mr. Phillips come up and take all the squash and pumpkin. She told me she planned to cook it up today. She's bringing quite a few pumpkin pies too. Did you see our corner? Hardly anything but potatoes left, and I'll boil up them in the morning."

"Well, that's Stanley for you. Quiet as a mouse and all business. I bet he made quick time with all those heavy items?" Abigail said as untied her apron. "What time should we head up for the school program?"

"I'm sure around six. The program starts at six thirty. I want to get up earlier though and scan the rooms. Maybe downstairs would be better and the huge hallway. The only place to make coffee is in the church though. Each room has a different stove, but not enough space on top for even a pot to heat. Wonder what the schoolboard was thinking when they bought them."

"Oh, I'm sure they were looking for a bargain and didn't think of the teachers needing to cook or make tea or coffee. I forgot, Maeve, you can go with Maude or with Thomas and me, whichever you decide is fine."

"I'd like to look around the town, and Maude said we could go early enough before it gets too dark."

"Sounds good. I'll be lucky to get Thomas in early enough from chores to get up there by 6:30. Please hold two spots for us."

~~~~~

"Excuse me," Abigail said as she and Thomas crawled over neighbors and parents to get to the seats Maude and Maeve had saved for them.

Older and taller students stood solemnly at the back of the stage. Dressed in brown or black dresses with long white aprons and white caps on their heads, three girl pilgrims posed quietly, with shy eyes looking at each other instead of their audience. Four boys, three in shirts and black pants with black hats with buckles, and one boy dressed in brown pants and shirt and feathered headpieces stood waiting to do their parts.

Abigail sat forward and looked from girls to boys, trying to match up child to parents. It had been a long time since she had seen the families all together. How many of the children did she deliver into this world? While she stood by the end of the bed when a mother gave birth, Abigail followed up after delivery at least once or twice or more if called. However, here her work ended and Jared's began.

A young girl came from behind the curtains dressed in the traditional black and white like some of her classmates. Shyly and quietly, she attempted to welcome everyone to Clearwater Public School's Thanksgiving Celebration. A buzz of whispers as a few older folks cupped their ears and asked, "What's that she said?" Others in the audience murmured amongst their friends what family they thought the girl belonged to. Behind the curtain, an adult whispered to speak louder, welcome everyone, and summarize the program.

One by one, from the lower grades to the higher grades, children took their parts in the educational entertainment. The first and second grades recited the famous verses:

Over the river, and through the wood,
~~~~~

To grandfather's house we go;
The horse knows the way,
To carry the sleigh,
Through the white and drifted snow.

The young children left the stage in an organized fashion, front row from left to right, and the other two rows followed suit like one solid chord.

The middle graders gathered on the stage's back row. One of the girls stepped down to introduce Henry Wadsworth Longfellow's famous poem, "Thanksgiving at Plymouth"

It is the Harvest Moon!
On gilded vanes
And roofs of villages, on woodland crests
And their aerial neighborhoods of nests
Deserted, on the curtained window-panes
Of rooms where children sleep, on country lanes
And harvest-fields, its mystic splendor rests!
Gone are the birds that were our summer guests,
With the last sheaves return the laboring wains!
All things are symbols: the external shows
Of Nature have their image in the mind,
As flowers and fruits and falling of the leaves;
The song-birds leave us at the summer's close,
Only the empty nests are left behind,
And piping of the quail among the sheaves.

Abigail thought the poem might never end, but she remembered helping Maude recite the very words for her own Thanksgiving celebration quite a few years ago.

Then the upper grades performed their skit about the first Thanksgiving at Plymouth Colony. Abigail had a hard time recognizing any of the youngsters. But some looked like older brothers and sisters who had been friends with Maude when she was in this school.

One of the girls recited how they sailed on the Mayflower, a large ship that left England and set sail for America. Another girl described how once they arrived, they stepped down onto Pilgrim's Rock.

A boy spoke about meeting the Indians who gave them food to eat. "Yet, because we came too late to plant, we had a hard winter. Many pilgrims, men, women, and children, starved."

The young man who played the Indian spoke: "When spring arrived, we taught the pilgrims to fish, hunt, and plant."

Every time Abigail came to a public children's event, she visualized herself at the end of a mother's bed. In this room alone, she accounted for many of her deliveries. Although she knew the parents, the children became emblems of her work. Nearly all the babies were born healthy to healthy mothers because early in the mothers' pregnancies, Abigail educated them how to have safe deliveries, how to eat, and how to exercise without hurting themselves or their babies. In many cases, she identified the children by looking at their parents or siblings; this one was a Smith, another a Boyington, here a Webster, there a Ridley or a Johnson. Most families had quite a few babies, and their facial as well as body features became family imprints.

The tallest pilgrim announced, "And when autumn arrived, we harvested our fields and gardens. With grateful hearts, we invited the Indians to come to our table for our first Thanksgiving celebration."

The audience clapped while all the classes of children gathered on the stage. Mr. Howard, the principal and upper elementary teacher, led them in their final song while Miss Bateman accompanied them on the piano.

"Feel free to stand and join us if you know this song about the Pilgrims' thankfulness for their harvest," Mr. Howard said to the audience.

Come, ye thankful people, come,
Raise the song of harvest home;
All is safely gathered in,
Ere the winter storms begin;

God our Maker doth provide
For our wants to be supplied;
Come to God's own temple, come,
Raise the song of harvest home.

Abigail and Thomas both "ahhed" when they stood up. It felt good to stretch. After the song ended, the audience clapped again, long and loudly as the students bowed. Mr. Howard thanked everyone for coming to the school's Thanksgiving play. He said the children had provided coffee and cake across the hallway in the other room.

Abigail asked Maeve, "Wasn't that fun? Did your schools perform for the community to come to?"

"My, yes, lots of programs like singing is big back home."

"Singing and dancing, I imagine," Thomas pitched in to say. "My father told me the country is alive with music from street corners to pubs to churches."

"He was right, Mr. Porter. When I think of home, I see green grass covering the land and hear music and think of dancing."

"T.C., T.C." Abigail heard male voices above the buzz of everyone talking. She and Thomas turned in different directions to see who was calling his name. "You've always been popular in town, Thomas, but since you'll be adding a new address soon, everyone wants your attention."

"I guess I can't ignore them either. I'm going to aim for a cup of coffee, ladies, so I'll see you by the room across the hall. Maybe those looking for me will head that way too."

Abigail turned and waved at Katy Stevens. She gave her a little nod and turned back to her conversation with husband Simon. "That's fine, Thomas. We'll try to get there as soon as the crowd begins to move."

Two rows ahead of her, Abigail recognized Anna and Sam Whiting. To her left she saw the Phillips family, Stanley, Maryetta, and two of their three children. Abigail remembered seeing little Jennie in the play in the early recitation of poems. Hod and Miranda Webster, one of their closest neighbors and friends, sat ahead of them and to the right. Their children, Mary, Jemima, Fanny, and

George sat beside them as they all watched first grader Freddie say his part of the poem. No one turned around to see who was behind them. *Peculiar, I can't seem to get anyone's attention. I suppose they're focused on their children tonight.*

Soon sons and daughters found their parents, and the crowd began to move to the large hallway. In a few minutes, Abigail, Maude, and Maeve were looking around the near empty room.

"I see lots of older people made it upstairs for the program. I suppose it is a logical spot to hold tomorrow's dinner," Abigail said to Maude, as she scanned the room. The large portraits of Presidents George Washington and Abraham Lincoln loomed down from their lofty glass frames on the walls, role models of honor, patriotism, and service.

Maude turned around to inspect the site. "You know, the chairs are already set up. Now, I'm torn, Ma. I wish we knew for sure what to do. Oh, there's Reverend Crawford, standing next to Mrs. Adelia Whiting and her mother Maria Walker. You think we should get their opinions?"

Abigail waved at Adelia and Maria, but they must not have seen her. *Odd, no one else is looking around to see who to talk to.* "Why don't you and Maeve head that way. I'll be right behind you. The Laughtons are standing over in the corner. I haven't seen them for a long time. I want to know how Nathan's doing down in Stillwater."

Making her way through empty chairs to get to the back of the room was not easy. Some chairs had been pushed out of their rows and chairs had been turned back-to-back, causing a maze for her to make her way through.

"Julia! Josiah! Don't move away yet," Abigail said loudly. She could tell once she got their attention, they both looked like scared animals. They looked around them to see how to get out of their little jungle of chairs. She untangled one chair at a time. Finally, reaching the center of the maze, she moved sideways to get closer to the couple. "How are you and your family? We haven't seen you since your wedding this summer." She turned and patted Hattie and Bertha, she could not remember which was which, on their shoulders. "You did a wonderful job reciting your passages, girls."

"Thank you, Mrs. Porter," they girls said in unison after looking at their folks for approval to speak.

"Abigail," Julia answered bluntly. "It's so nice to see you. Wish we could stay talking but we have to get the girls home and into bed so we can get moving right after chores to make it back to town for the Thanksgiving dinner."

"Abby," Josiah said rather blandly. "I tried to get T. C.'s attention before, but I heard others calling his name too. I suppose he's been getting excited for his new job in St. Paul in a month or so?"

"Oh, he's put in time already down there, just getting to know everyone he will be working with and where everything's at. We've been down there a few times but came back each night. Once his sessions began, he may have to stay overnight. He'll either go to a hotel or to one of our cousins."

"I suppose," Josiah said.

Feeling colder because they were standing by the windows, Abigail felt as though they were leading her away from their corner. "By the way, I wanted to see how everything's been going, but I also wanted to see how Nathan's doing."

"I suppose you heard about the ruckus down in Stillwater." Josiah picked up a chair that got in his way and set it down with a bang.

Abigail wondered if this was how he always acted when his brothers' behaviors came into question. "Just what I read in the paper. Just wondering how he's doing now," Abigail said.

"Sad, very sad, Abby. Since he shot Orrin back in '74, and then Mother died right after Father, Nathan has been in an out of the hospital down there. It's like he lost his mind. He doesn't want to remember what he did and how he broke up the family. That sounds terrible; I know, but the family really did fade away since I am the only sibling alive. Unfortunately, when he remembers what happened, he can't live with himself. This time, he slit his wrists. You know, most of us understood his motive for trying to scare Orrin off the land, because he wasn't easy to get along with at times.

He'd get something in his head, like he thought Nathan was not taking good care of the folks, and no one could tell him anything different. I always said it were an accident, him shooting Orrin. He was just trying to scare him off until he calmed down."

"Of course, so is he out of danger?" Abigail asked.

"I think physically, but honestly, he seems better when he is lost in his fog. He often talks about how you and T. C. helped the folks, you for making sure Ma's health was taken care of, and T. C. for getting so many people to feed them and help them out around the farm."

Soon they were able to make their way to the hallway to imbibe in a cup of coffee. Abigail thanked and said goodbye to the Laughtons and tried to find her own family. Standing on her tip toes, she searched for Thomas, but she did not see him. As she made her way up the long line, she could not help but think about Nathan Laughton.

The newspaper article really caught everyone's attention, "Fratricide in Clearwater." It was a sad case. Nathan went to the Buffalo jail immediately. The case moved to Hennepin Country within a week. It didn't take long for the jury to come to a decision during the trial. He was guilty because he killed his brother. With Orrin dead and buried three days after the murder, there would be no winners in this case.

Sadly, Nathan was sent to Stillwater. His elderly parents had no fight left in them to stave off age-related sickness First, Luther died and then a few months later, Martha followed him to Acasia Cemetery.

Fate wasn't finished with the family yet. Josiah's first wife Nancy died as well as the twins she was carrying. Of course, Nathan had nothing to do with that. Six Laughtons gone, and Nathan's shoulders carried the guilt. Yet, Abigail reminded herself, although no one talks about it, Jared had told Nancy to have no more children. He had diagnosed her with consumption. Yet, she then gave birth to Bertha, but the next little boy and girl couldn't make it without their mother's final push. She had died because her own lungs gave out when the babies needed them the most. No, Nathan was not the only one who should feel guilt, but Abigail's judgement was lost in grief for this family.

~~~~~

With the decision to let people sit where they wanted, Maude told Abigail there would be no speaker. Reverend Crawford wanted to say a few words, though. Abigail thought it odd. She liked the pastor, but he was rather, well, what could she say, bland. She hoped their celebration would turn out better than that. Other than a welcome when everyone came to fill their plates, the day had been drastically simplified. *If I had been in charge…No use pondering that. I am not.*

Before half past ten Thanksgiving morning, Thomas drove Abigail up to the church. She knew she had arrived earlier than she should have, but Maude, Maeve, and the men needed the carriage. I know someone will put me to work. Nevertheless, she brought a bag of coffee Maeve had ground up for the large pot. At least, Abigail felt she could help even if all she did was make a good pot of coffee.

The late morning proved warm like the other days in the week, but Abigail's right knee hurt, her sign of weather change. She limped up the church steps while Thomas waited. Reverend Crawford surprised her by opening the left side of the double doors, nearly knocking her over.

"Welcome, ah, Mrs. Porter," he said somewhat nervously. "So glad to see you. How are you this bright Thanksgiving Day?"

"I'm fine. Are we meeting here? I thought that is what Maude told me last night. We're supposed to be using the big stove to make coffee and keep food warm."

"Why of course! Come on in and join the rest of us."

The rest of us? I thought I recognized Maria's voice as well as Adelia's or Anna's. Lots of rattling and scraping noises too. I guess I'm not so early then. What could they be doing?

She turned around and waved at Thomas, indicating he could take off and get the horse and carriage back home. Maeve's boyfriend should be on the eleven o'clock train. The plan was for all
~~~~~

of them, Thomas included, to turn around and bring everything Maude had cooked and be back by noon.

Now she heard whispering. She could not make out what was said. It took a while for her eyes to adjust to the dim light in the church. Even with a few candles, the sanctuary seemed dark and sometimes gloomy. The windows needed to be larger to let in the glory of God.

Walking toward the voices, Abigail said, "I can hear you, but I can't recognize you yet," and then she chuckled. "Is that you, Maria? Adelia? Anna?"

From the back of the church sanctuary, Abigail heard more whispering and faint giggling. She thought she heard, "Good, she can't see." Soon more shuffling around before the back door opened and let in a bit of light. Abigail turned around but saw nothing out of the ordinary.

"It's just you and me." Pastor sounded too happy and his voice sounded strained as if he held in a secret. "I'll bring some water for you though," he said as he grabbed the enamel pot.

"I'm going to take a little walk. I'll be back to get the coffee going."

I heard him say 'come in and join us.' Who were the "us" he was referring to?

Such a beautiful day, a good day to be thankful. Abigail headed to Whiting's Grove. She looked back at the two-floor school building that the whole community was so proud to have in their town. It stood for their hard work and core educational values—mostly New England values.

As Abigail scrunched the fallen leaves of orange, red, and yellow below her feet, she also looked at the newer homes and small backyard farms. Everyone had one, including chickens and ducks, rabbits, horses, and a cow or two. Also, each family worked hard to provide large gardens plumb full during the summertime with fresh, delicious produce like spring lettuce and radishes, summer cucumbers, onions, and later tomatoes. Oh, how she loved her juicy, red tomatoes, and the feel and smell of earthy potatoes. Now a harvest full of pumpkins and squash rounded out the season and filled the house with amazing smells while they baked in the oven.

For some reason, the changing seasons reminded Abigail of her father. *You'd throw on your red flannel shirt on the first chilly morning back home in Stowe. Then you'd fill the carriage with woolen blankets and the bear rug, the very bear your father had once shot, killed, and cleaned way back in 1700's. You use it to line the floors and sides of the buggy to keep our feet warm. On our way to a patient's house, you might even tell me the hair-raising story about Grandpa's adventure killing the dangerous animal.*

Pa, life is changing too fast. Your granddaughter has organized this whole Thanksgiving celebration. I had been helping Thomas with his campaign and now I'm getting fitted for a fancy dress, for the party the town is throwing for him after the new year. Imagine me! I remember when I had nothing to wear to church much less a nice party.

I've been so busy but not the way I'm usually busy and like to be busy. I need to get back to helping Jared because I feel, well, I feel useless, lonely, and a bit depressed. This time of year, I miss our mountain home, Ma, and you.

Abigail entered the hollow of the trees, a sanctuary she often came to when she felt sad and needed to look at the Clearwater River and how it reaches for the Mississippi.

"*Whoo! Whooo*!"

"Oh, my friend. It's late in the morning for you to be awake after guarding all night. Did you follow me here?"

"*Whoo! Whoo!*"

"I'm not sure. I'm a bit forlorn today."

I suppose I've neglected lots of people during Thomas's campaign, and now for nearly three weeks, I've been stuck in the house in my robe while Maeve is working on my dress. A few friends had come to the door, but Maude had to give them my excuses if I weren't near the kitchen. Occasionally, I could talk or shout from a room. All of this might have really made some upset, but they usually said they had nothing serious to talk to her about. Besides, everyone knows if it had been serious, I'd have undressed and donned my usual clothes to help where I needed to. At least, I hope they knows this.

The sun started to shine overhead between the near empty branches. But the sheen seemed too bright, too hopeful today at high noon. Her knee started to throb. Abigail knew she had to return to the church. Yet, she lingered. She had never been so uninvolved in the village, her village, before. What am I worried about? As soon as I get there, my family will be there to keep me company.

Walking out of the grove, Abigail felt a slight breeze from the flapping of wings above her. When she looked up, she recognized Eagle, flying to a tree branch to roost. Up there from its perch, the magnificent creature could see the whole area, the Clearwater River for sure. Its shrill squeal and chiding screech brought her back down to reality, easing her gloom and sensitivity.

Refreshed and much less sad, Abigail realized her knee hurt less too as she walked back to the church. From a distance, she saw Thomas waving as he walked by Sam and Anna Whiting's white house, a mansion in Clearwater's eyes. Below, she could make out the roof of his brother George's house as well. Sad to say, he is gone. Abigail thought of Adelia, his widow, and their children still in mourning. *I need to quit feeling sorry for myself. Others have it worse than I do. I have some family in town so I'll have someone to talk to.*

"Where have you been? I think they want to get the food started so I said I'd come out to look for you," Thomas said, grabbing her arm.

"I went for a walk to clear my head. It's beautiful out here. I haven't had much free time lately because of the dress making. I thought I'd be heading back sooner than this. The mind is willing to go faster, but the knee isn't … in for some weather I think."

"It's humid for sure. I agree. My hip hurts a bit too," Thomas added as he did a bit of a Do-si-do, twirling her around. "Oh, I should warn you. Someone else made the coffee."

Abigail couldn't read her husband's happiness. "Oh, well, I thought for sure I'd get a good cup sometime today. May have to wait for supper now," Abigail said before adding a chuckle. "I usually enjoy this kind of get-together with our friends in the village. This has been a challenge for me. I feel out of the loop, I suppose." Abigail knew she wasn't completely telling the truth to her husband.

"Well, all being said, we're here. Hopefully, you'll enjoy yourself," Thomas said as he opened the door to allow her to go in first.

As she entered the sanctuary, Abigail heard clapping to the right, clapping in the middle of the church, and clapping on the left. She wondered what all this fuss was. Not able to adjust her eyes to the light yet, she followed Thomas into the dark.

I don't know why they did not include wider windows when they built this Greek Revival church, supposedly a reflection of the churches we attended back east.

Abigail's eyes adjusted. She noticed everyone looking at her. *What's this all about? It's past my birthday.*

When she focused, she noticed her women friends and their husbands, the Whitings, Heatons, Laughtons, Tollingtons, Websters, Fullers, Lyons, Walkers, Johnsons, Markhams, Oaks, and so many more, clapping and smiling at her. On the steps of the altar, her good friend Maryetta Phillips stood. With her was her own dear sister Mary and little Mary who wanted to be called Isabella now, clapping and smiling. Thomas took her hand and pulled her so she was front and center in the sanctuary. Mary and Maryetta pulled her close as they each gave her a huge hug. Thomas went to sit down.

"Auntie," said Isabella, grabbing her around her waist.

Mary and Maryetta pinned a beautiful corsage on her left shoulder.

"What in the world? Why me? And where did you get roses in winter? What's this all about?" Abigail turned around shyly to see the audience that apparently came to see her. Right up front in the right pew, Abigail watched Thomas sit by Maude and Maeve and Maeve's boyfriend. A quick look at Daniel, and she approved. A very handsome young man, the dark hair of an Irishman. He smiled so wide and cheered her on as if he knew her. She looked straight at Maude, asking 'what?' with her eyes. Maude shrugged, smiled, and shook her head.

Then she moved her eyes around the pews to see who was here, Hannah and Francis Morrison, other friends from the community, many woman who she had helped as their midwife. She brought her eyes back to the left side. Abigail's hands flew to her mouth. There, in the front row, stood Cassius, his wife Martha, and their little ones. She held back a happy cry, but her eyes watered up.

Abigail walked over and grabbed the new baby, Orlo, who had been born a month before. She kissed his blond but nearly bald head. She gave grandchildren Annette and Riverius hugs and kisses. Oh, their innocent pink faces gave the church the sunshine she needed. Then she saw her recently married sister Annette and Mark Knowlton, her husband.

"When did you get here? Where have all of you been hiding?" Abigail asked as she hugged her and Mark.

"We'll talk later, but we stayed at Jared's and Mary's."

Of course, there stood her own baby brother Tarrant and his wife Sarah Louise with their children. *How'd all this come about without me knowing anything?*

Martha took the baby from Abigail as Maryetta and Mary, her sister, ushered her to one of the red velvet altar chairs sitting at the bottom of the center aisle. *What's this all about?*

First, her sister Mary said, "Welcome. Welcome!" She tried getting everyone to quit clapping so she could reveal the secret surprise. She spoke louder, "Welcome!" to no avail. She started fanning her hands for everyone to sit. Jared reacted first and sat. Slowly, the front row of guests lowered into the pews and the rest followed. She began again, "Thank you for coming to our special party within our Thanksgiving party."

Abigail heard the clapping fading away whe the pews started creaking as people sat down.

Mary went on, "A few of us women met and decided it was past time for you, Abigail, to be honored. You met me at the boat landing a little over a month after you came. I was the second woman to come with my first daughter, Little Mary, but you all know her as Isabella, and Abigail's son Cassius. You had already settled in at the hotel and had almost every one of the men in line and behaving." Mary waited again as the crowd laughed and clapped. "You'd already begun to weave a community, sister. I had little to do but follow in your steps and do what you told me, as we often did when we were children." Mary rolled her eyes and spoke sarcastically, exaggerating her voice by spreading out her words. Again, the Clearwater crowd laughed.

Then Simon Stevens stood up from his place and said, "Me and Hod here," he pointed to Horace Webster, another of the first settlers in Clearwater, "we had no idea what we were getting when Doc Wheelock said he had invited his sister-in-law here to become our housekeeper. One look at her and all the travel bags she brought with her made us both realize she had planned to settle in."

"Got that right," Hod Webster shouted. "We couldn't have made all the headway with the mills and developing this village without her."

Jared stood up and nodded to the crowd that returned a hand clapping. "I knew she was the one we could count on. She was the oldest in her family and knew how to take on responsibility. Like Mary said, she knew how to boss her siblings around."

Again, more laughter from the community. *I didn't think I was ever bossy. Maybe a bit headstrong.*

Jared continued. "I've seen her work with nothing, a few kernels of corn and a cup of flour. What she could create out of that surprised even her mother, my mother-in-law, who also had sleight of hand." More laughter from the crowd. "She and her mother had one thing in common, economy. I guess as part of her package as housekeeper, I knew she could help me with many of my patients like she had helped her father in his practice in Stowe. Many of our young ones wouldn't be here without the help of Abigail Camp Porter and her midwife skills."

A loud thunderous round of clapping followed by so many coming to their feet and clapping harder. Then four of her best friends, Maria Walker, Anna Whiting, Adelia Whiting, and Kate Stevens came up to the front. A couple hugs and a few shoulder pats and Maria began.

"I arrived here shortly before the Rebellion and the Indian scares. T.C. and Abigail were the first people to welcome me and my family off the boat saddled up to the banks of the Mississippi. She carried two loaves of homemade bread to eat with our first supper that night. You all knew Deacon before I came. He'd come here earlier to build a house large enough to hold our two families."

"I remember!" Abigail commented loudly while shaking her head. Her eyes misted over. She grabbed her hanky in her sleeve and wiped her eyes. "Mary gave you some of her wild strawberry jam. Later, you told us what a delight everyone had eating bread and jam. You had polished off the jar already."

Everyone laughed because they knew the Walker-Mayo household and how large it was.

"Yes, five nearly grown men to feed and all the daughters. We made it with lots of help from all of you and the guidance of people like Abigail."

Adelia interrupted, "Mother, don't forget, shortly after we had arrived, we planted our gardens. June, July, and early August, the vegetables stood tall and healthy. Corn was up, beans looked plentiful, and the wheat and rye were waving a great hello to all of us pioneers. My George had planted his first round of apple trees down in our grove. Little sticks only, but they too promised us a hint of riches to come. Then, as if we lived in the times of the Bible, the sky and sun blackened. A great wind of wings flew down on our heads, tangled in our hair, flew off to devour everything we had planted."

Someone shouted from the crowd. "Remember the chewing that went on for days? The talk of it afterwards and how the sound of it nearly drove us crazy."

"You got that right," Simon Stevens hollered as he stood up. Known locally as Uncle Simon, he seldom talked about his past. If a person knew Minnesota history, he or she knew he had worked long and hard before he helped found Clearwater. Along with his brother, John Stevens, the "Father and Founder of Minneapolis," he cleared land acquiesced land to the federal government from the Dakota Indians. He became an explorer too and helped found Lake Minnetonka, building its first sawmill at the end of its creek. Now, simply a local farmer, town officer, and carpenter, he is happy to live a quiet life, unlike his older brother John whose voice still rings out for the state.

Stevens recalled, "That gnawing and gnawing until all we had left was bare earth and holey clothes as they chewed them hanging on the clotheslines. The next year weren't no better. Before the wife went to bring in eggs from the coop, she covered up Little Henry with his blanket and then pulled netting over his cradle and set him under the window to nap. Before long, she heard his screaming. She put down her basket and ran to him. Those dirty devils had eaten through the netting and the blanket and had settled on his face. They'd even chewed up the curtains hanging from the windows."

"My poor Henry. He was bitten a few times. But I swatted at those creatures as if they were merely ants. Nothing like a mother's need to protect her young'un'," Katy Stevens said.

Adelia continued, "So many of us lived through this time. We all talked about going back home. Some did. But my George had a stubborn streak and said no darn creature like a grasshopper was going to scare him off his land. So, we struggled to find food to keep us going. Thomas led everyone on hunting trips, and the rest of us stayed back and fished with Abigail below the Porter farmland. She led us on to make up some of the greatest fish stories."

Everyone in the audience laughed. Abigail looked into Thomas's damp but glistening eyes.

"We took turns frying up what we caught and ate right down at the riverbanks because we didn't want to share our meal with the flying devils. Oh, Abigail kept us going all right. Without her spirit, many of us would've given up," Anna Whiting commented.

Her husband, Sam Whiting, the stalwart mercantile dealer that he was said, "Don't forget then the panic of '57. You'd hardly believe here in Clearwater, we'd be dealing with a panic because we had no money due to the grasshoppers eating us out of crops and home. Yet, when anyone of us tried to get a loan, we found that the cash they gave us was worthless. The banks that lent money to those needing to purchase tools and materials found their investment worthless."

Maria Walker cut in, "That's where Abigail, like she always did, showed us all how to find and dig ginseng."

"I'm sure you'd all have found someone else to help you find it, though," Abigail remarked.

"Not as easily as you found it, Abigail," Sam Whiting said. "Everyone dug it up all over the county. And at one point, Brother

George and I sent out on one shipment over ten thousand pounds of ginseng."

"Yes," Jared Wheelock spoke up, "she comes by it naturally, finding wild onions and all sorts of herbs all over in her walks, to season her food. That's the just one of the differences she made as the housekeeper and cook at the hotel.

Anna Whiting said, "She led by example, enthusiasm, and energetic enthusiasm, telling us women we had brains on our shoulders and didn't have to stay so close to our hearths. She reassured us we could do anything we wanted. Most of us wanted to stay here so she taught us how and where to dig ginseng, which kept us from starving to death. With everyone in the family chipping in, we earned enough to pay all our debts collected during the grasshopper raids back in '57 and '58 and got ahead for once."

More clapping began, but Hod Webster stood up and interrupted loudly, "Speaking of 'stock,' think of the stockade we constructed around the Congregational Church. We wouldn't have built it without T. C.'s and Abigail's crazy notion that we might have some Indian troubles way back in '62."

Abigail remembered that. She looked at Thomas, who looked at her as if he could read her thoughts as well. Only the two of them knew what the other was thinking and what had transpired. *Some called me loco, but I wonder what they'd say if they knew exactly how I came to realize that we settlers would have been vulnerable to attack and especially vulnerable because most of our men had gone off to help fight in the Rebellion.*

Tom Tollington, Captain of the Minnesota Eighth Infantry Division during the Indian troubles, shouted from where he sat next to his wife Sarah, "Without her instinct and T. C.'s insistence, we all may have been chased back to where we came from. She was right on target for us men to build the stockade, which she called 'a fortress in the wilderness,' and to fill it with daily necessities if we or our country neighbors needed to take shelter sometime."

Again, she appreciated the vote of confidence from the men; however, Abigail remembered the incident quite differently. She and Thomas had taken a couple days to visit with friends down in Corinna Township on Clearwater Lake. The Longworths and

Porters had become instant friends since 1859 when they unloaded their children and their baggage from New York onto Clearwater's Mississippi landing. Once they were settled, the Longworths had written to the Porters asking advice about building a new church. They invited them to come visit them and help them and the neighbors sort out a few of their ideas. Their experience before they left their home by the Clearwater River prompted Abigail to push her husband in turn tot insist on the building of a fortress for protection from attack.

Abigail looked all over the room. So many of her friends and neighbors had come to celebrate Thanksgiving. Then her eyes spotted one of her first friends, John Farwell. *He looks old and tired. His once broad and strong shoulders are now slumped. Apparently, the rumors of him heading back to Canada were simply rumors.*

"I don't think I have done anything more than any of you have done for me and my family," Abigail said as she wiped her eyes. "You all have given both Thomas and me as much as we have given you."

Cousin Hannah's husband Francis Morrison stood up. "You all know who I am."

Applause broke out. However, as Francis started waving, the sanctuary turned quiet. Francis stood nearly six feet tall and carried a lumberman's bulk in the shoulders and a gray head that symbolized respect and wisdom that comes from his engineering know-how. He had called himself a lumberman, but he made a name for himself because of his many railroad, bridge, sawmill, hotel, and business building projects all over the country. He stood tall beside the biggest names in Minnesota's early history like John Stevens, his brother Simon here, Sibley, Steele, Rice, and so many other territory to state boosters.

Francis said, "I can tell you from the moment she stepped off the plank of the steamboat, this raw village was a-stir. From above the landing, I watched as a lady of grace, intelligence, and ability had entered the community. You know I knew her when she was a child."

Doctor Jared Wheelock, one of Francis's best friends, had the daring nature to blurt out, "Oh, oh, Abby, now you're in trouble."

"Doc, you'd be the one to break my concentration," Francis said, laughing along with the rest of the audience. "Now, where was I? Oh, yes, and she came from a strong family, which includes my wife, myself, and our sons. Remember her father Doctor Joe who came from Stowe, Vermont, to Minnesota, after his dear wife Hannah died? He was a man of instinct, intelligence, and moral character. Abigail learned from him. He, Jared, and Abigail made a great team mending some of our wounded who fought during the Indian problems and those who came back home to recover during our national crisis. She was born with a knack of knowing what works to heal. Both Doctor Jared and his father-in-law who moved from Vermont from his medical duties there in Stowe to Clearwater to live close to his children said she was his right arm. She has instinct and responsibility built into her too because of her family roots in New England. I can tell you firsthand what the Perkins and Robinson families can do, but that would take all day."

More applause broke out and ended when a lone man, sitting in the dark shadows way in the back pew of the church, stood up. His voice vibrated deeply. The crowd quieted when he spoke. "I'd love to say I knew you when, Abby, but I do not remember when I didn't know you. You've always had the confidence and ability to help those afflicted with pain or sorrow. I heard tell you organized rag wrapping parties for the military as soon as the war started."

Abigail knew immediately who it was. Her dear cousin, companion, and friend, Ellet Perkins, Cousin Hannah's brother, had accompanied her to Minnesota Territory so many years ago. Later, he became a hero as Captain of the Color Guard of First Battalion of the Minnesota Volunteer Infantry after one of the battles at Gettysburg. There, he had been hit in the leg by the enemy. He spent time in an army hospital and then was discharged because of his wounds.

Ellet Perkins sat down after he received a round of applause. After a lull in the conversations, the women took back the program.

"Could you please stand up, Abigail?" Maria Walker asked.

Abigail followed their instructions. *Now what?*

Two of the younger daughters of the community, Jennie Phillips and Jennette Sanborn, each carried one end of a long ribbon up the aisle of the church.

"Mrs. Abigail Porter, Clearwater would not be the village it is today without you. You are, in fact, the heart of the village."

Adelia and Anna each took one end of the ribbon and slid it over Abigail's head, laying it crossways shoulder to hip.

"For those of you who can't see," Maria said, "it reads, 'Abigail Porter, First Woman of Clearwater.'"

The friends who had gathered stood up and applauded. Maude and Thomas walked up and put their arms around her.

"What did you two know about this?" Abigail asked.

"Mother, Maryetta caught me and filled me in last night. I knew nothing about it beforehand."

Thomas squeezed her and said, "Me neither until last evening up at the school."

"I'm amazed and grateful. I want to thank everyone before we are excused to eat."

Maude turned to Adelia who stood by her and said, "Mother wants to say a few words."

Anna Whiting told Samuel to whistle or something to get everyone's attention. His loud voice got the attention of the crowd.

"Please, please, may I have your attention? Anna reminded me to tell everyone there are a few chairs outside because it is so warm. But you may serve up and sit anywhere—the pews, outside, and even upstairs of the school. Just, please, clean up after yourselves. We have a trash barrel set up behind the church for food scraps. I know you will take all your left-over food, your dirty plates, cups, and silverware home as well." Anna whispered a reminder to him that Abigail wanted to thank everyone. "Oh, yes, now, Abigail Camp Porter, our first lady of the village, wants to say something."

The crowd quieted. Abigail choked back her first words and then started again. "I want to thank all of you for coming. I'm overwhelmed by your thoughtfulness and humbled by your kind words. You all are part of this tight-knit community and that's what makes it easy and wonderful to live here. When help is needed, everyone pitches in to get the job or jobs done. I hope to talk with each and everyone here, but if that proves impossible, come over for coffee. Thank you again for coming."

While Abigail, Thomas, Maude, Maeve and her Daniel visited with those who wanted to talk to all of them, the women-folk along with husbands, sons, and daughters, got to setting up the tables, sawhorses and old fencing that laid in the grass between the church and the schoolhouse—the very same fort fencing, now weathered, Abigail insisted on having built during the Indian scare and the Civil War.

Hugs, kind words, several apologies punctuated with laughter gave Abigail a bloom of pride in her true friendship in Clearwater. Although she wondered about the near snubbing the night before at the Thanksgiving program at the school, she soon realized few talked to her for fear "we'd spill the beans."

Brother Tarrant and his wife Sarah Louise came up next, followed closely by Francis Morrison, Cousin Hannah, their two sons, and of course, Ellet.

"Big Sis, so happy you were honored, and I have to say it's about time."

"I'm happy you four made it." Abigail received hugs from her nephew and niece, Freddie and Louisa. Wonderful children, she thought. "All of you taking time out of your busy schedules to come to old Auntie's party," she said as she gave them one huge hug.

After Abigail thanked Francis for his wonderful words and everyone headed to the line behind the sawhorses, Tarrant stepped out of the food line to say, "I received a letter from Nathaniel. He was hoping to come to T.C.'s party in January, but now he thinks not. He can't seem to get much help in the post office. He'll try, he said. Anyway, he included a small note for me to give to you. It is interesting. Sorry, I read it since it was still in the same letter." Just then Samuel Whiting again got the crowd's attention. "Everyone … everyone listen up. I promise I have only one more comment."

A few scattered voices finally "shushed" to attention.

"The reverend here would like to pray over out meal before we start gobbling up."

Maude squeezed through the crowd to bring her mother a cup of coffee. "Ma, I grabbed this quickly before Samuel required us to be quiet. I think you could use it.

Abigail whispered a thank you. She took a sip and bowed her head for prayer.

"Mrs. Porter," the minister said loudly, "there is one thing I've been asked to say before we pray."

Abigail looked up.

"The women asked me to say they were sorry about their uncourteous behavior last night. Each woman said she was afraid she'd let the cat out of the bag if she talked with you about today, yet they hated keeping it all a secret."

All eyes were on her. *What should I say?* She laughed, shook her head, and answered more enthusiastically than she had felt earlier, "Goodness, all's good."

I wish I weren't so sensitive all the time. Every time someone looks at me funny, I figure something is wrong. I wish I didn't feel like this at times.

"Let's bow our heads and thank our generous Lord for his abundance."

Abigail lowered her head. She tried to concentrate, but the letter from her brother Nathaniel back in Stowe burned in her hand. She browsed down to the part Tarrant thought was so interesting.

"Father, we want to bless You for You blessed us when You died on the cross."

"Sis, the saddest news today."

"We're grateful for this great country that our ancestors found for us to practice our individual faiths. Thank you to all those who fought for our freedoms as well.

"Friend or foe, remember Lucy Webber who married W. D. Koerner?"

How many years has it been since I really thought about Lucy, my former nemesis?

"Bless all our leaders in our country, state, and communities, especially now both T. C. Porter will be our representative at the state level and his wife Mrs. Porter, our first woman of Clearwater, who has helped so many who needed her strength, wisdom, and nursing ability."

"W. D. Koerner lost his banking job down in Waterbury during the Panic of 1873. It was a tough financial time for everyone back here, as I know you all faced it there too. Well, after a while, Koerner decided to follow a few friends out to Dakota Territory to try to get a homestead so he and the family could start over. He promised he'd send for Lucy and the children when he was able."

"Bless this beautiful meal and the hands that made it."

"After a while, without any money, Lucy lost the house and had to auction off her belongings to pay their debts. She and her son and daughter went to live with her folks. Yet, her parents had all they could handle to take care of themselves much less take in three more mouths to feed."

"On this Thanksgiving Day, bless those who gather around your table today, Lord."

"This is just the beginning of the story," Nathaniel went on to write.

Abigail agreed with her brother. This was just the beginning of the story for Lucy. Abigail knew what she faced, lonely days and years ahead of her without many people, family, or friends, to help support her—for without money, Lucy had no platform to stand on to be heard or noticed. She lost her place in society. Abigail hoped she would not waste time hanging around the area but move on and try to start over again.

No one deserved the trouble Lucy and her family had to bear. If Abigail remembered right, her mother never expected her to clean, cook, or take care of her siblings. Her husband William had not expected that either. She had live-in help, someone to cook, clean, and take care of her children. Even if it all had worked out, and her husband would write for her to come to Dakota, how would Lucy have managed out there? Abigail had read about so many people, unfit for the wide-open sky and the struggle to survive on such a vast prairie, who had been committed lately to the South Dakota Hospital for the Insane. She was a flower that needed to be admired or a doll who hung on her husband's arm so he could be admired, not a pioneer.

As Abigail recalled, Lucy was book smart. Unless she had changed, she had few skills besides working with her hands, spinning, weaving, even embroidering.

Abigail had little love, only empathy, for her former nemesis. Nor did she owe her anything. Yet she felt in her heart, if she met Lucy on a street, Abigail would offer her an olive branch in peace.

"In Jesus name, Amen."

When Samuel Whiting announced the committee wanted the guest of honor and her complete family to start the meal line, Abigail tucked the letter up her sleeve for later reading. Thomas swung his arm back to encourage Abigail to stand and take her place at the head of the line.

Before she stood up, she took the last swallow from her cup. What a day! Plus, now, she realized someone else in Clearwater could make a good pot of coffee.

Chapter 11

Finishing Touches

Abigail wondered how long she had been sitting in Thomas's chair, transported back in time again. Her soft dress still lay across her lap.

"Maude?" she choked out before she cleared her throat. "Maude?"

The house is quiet. I only hear the ticking of Thomas's grandfather clock.

Abigail thought she heard a light knock on the door followed by a quiet "Abigail?"

"Yes, come in. Who is it?"

"It's me, Mary."

"Oh, Sis, come in. Come in! I didn't recognize your voice. I'm in the parlor," Abigail said as she tried to stand, but the weight of the dress and the blanket held her down.

Mary's boots whacked the floor as she pulled them off. She walked into the room and patted her older sister's shoulder. She sat down on the divan but soon slumped. "Oh, I forgot about the sliding sofa." She dug her toes into the rug to steady herself.

"I know. Horsehair does that," Abigail responded.

"Oh, remember when Pa lived here? He hated the one chair in our parlor because of the same slippery cover. He nearly slid off once and said, 'Whoa, this one needs stirrups.' Remember how we all laughed? Oh, I miss him so much."

"I do too, Mary. I think of him so often. Such happy times."

"But it's so good to see you," Mary said. "It's been a while."

They both started asking "How are you feeling?" at the same time. Abigail said, "You go first."

"I'm fine. Stomach has been acting up. One day I'm fine. The next day, I'm sick. Jared's trying a few things."

"Yes, he said that. Where all does it hurt?"

"Inside, of course, here and here," Mary said, touching her esophagus and over-all stomach area. It hurts when he presses his finger into my belly-button area, too."

"Have you any other symptoms?"

"When the pain comes, it comes in spasms. I feel like I could throw-up, but it usually doesn't develop into that problem. Thank goodness, but I am exhausted after it all ends, and then I can't eat."

"Today, you're feeling better obviously. You're so pale, Mary, and you've lost some weight. I know Jared has tried everything. I've only given advice and offered some innocent herbs. I wish I could help more. I'll search in Pa's medical books though. Maybe Jared and I are missing something."

"Thanks. Today's a good day though. Now tell me. How're you doing? How's your head?"

"Today," *or was it yesterday?* Abigail quickly questioned how long she had been in deep thought and sleep this time. "I walked to the kitchen on my own. I sat at the table for a while as well. Head is doing better, so I know I must be careful. But I need my independence as well as I need to build up my strength. Hopefully, I'll come visit you soon."

"I know you'll be careful, and I understand your need for freedom. Just don't go far at first, or have someone go with you, okay?"

Stomping in the lean-to, then more stomping brought an end to the intimate conversation. Soon the kitchen door opened.

"We're back. Everyone ready for supper?"

Obviously, that loud voice belonged to her brother Tarrant. She heard him walk into the kitchen, kick off his boots with a thud while another person came behind him.

This voice, much softer, belonged to her brother-in-law Jared. "We stopped by the pig barn. Maude and T.C. are coming up now too." He walked into the parlor. "Hello, you two."

"Evening, Jared," Abigail returned.

Abigail watched Jared and Mary look at each other. Still after thirty-some years of marriage, they showed each other the tenderness and care of a couple still in love.

"How are my two patients this early evening?" he asked as he stroked his wife's shoulder.

"I'm hungry, and Tarrant's cooking's hard to turn down. My sister and I are making promises to each other. I'll take it slow as I start puttering around and she'll eat lightly."

Immediately, the cover came off the pot. Wafts of cooked onion, cabbage, ham, potatoes, and maybe rutabagas too drifted into the parlor.

The back doors opened as Maude and her father stomped their feet as they entered the house.

"Glory! I smell Uncle Tarrant's boiled dinner. The Porter household is going to feast tonight. He even made fresh bread. I'll wash up and set the table, Unc."

Mary lifted her nose and closed her eyes, breathing in the kitchen aromas deeply. "I feel like Blackie when we hold him back from his bowl until one of us finishes filling it. Once we let go, he tears into his food. I promise I'll stick to the broth and potatoes . Oh, maybe I'll take a small carrot and a chunk of ham. I know I must take it easy," Mary said.

"That sounds smart. Let's see how it goes." Abigail said. "Now, I will ask for a bit of help to get me started on recovery. Would someone unload me … like lift the heavy dress and the blankets off my lap?"

"Want me to hold the bowl, Abby?" Thomas said, holding the vegetables.

"Yes, please. It's heavy," Abigail said spooning out a nice chunk of rutabagas, a carrot, a fe circles of onion, some cabbage, and a potato.

Maude grabbed the bowl from her father, piled her plate and continued to pass it on. Everyone took their turn forking chunks of ham from the ironstone platter and followed up with a dowsing over the plates from the gravy boat fill with the brothy juices the meal had been cooked in.

"If it tastes as good it smells," Thomas said, "we'll be passing bi-carbonate tonight."

Everyone took his or her turn reaching for a thick slice of buttered bread, which was followed by quiet sounds of contentment. Abigail bit into the soft, yeasty bread smothered in butter. She could have made a meal of this as well.

While Maude and Mary cleared the dirty dishes, Abigail asked, "Does anyone know how long I was out this time? I know I was partly in thought while I slept."

Thomas spoke up. "I don't know what time you woke, but we left when we could no longer reach you," he added with a snicker. "I'm joking, Abby, but it seemed like you were caught up in a trance or something."

"I was thinking about the wonderful party the town surprised me with last fall. I had been feeling kind of sorry for myself, you know, earlier because no one talked to me the night before—then seeing all the people who came and your responsibility in all this, Mary."

"Nonsense! You've deserved this type of recognition for a long time."

"I haven't been doing much of anything lately, though." Abigail admitted, regretfully.

"Ma! Do we need to remind you how sick you've been?" Maude asked .

"Oh, I know," Abigail said as her regrets withered away. She couldn't help but feel guilty knowing Jared's caseload lately. She knew many had caught viruses over the last few months. He had been running for them as well as a few babies that had come down with diphtheria out in Lynden Township. On top of that, two mothers-to-be had already asked for her help out in the township too. *Oh, I need to recover faster.*

Mary joined in, "Do we have to remind you how many people you have helped in one way or another? Seriously, how many houses in town and in the outlying area have you run to clean and watch over when you heard the wife or mother was sick?"

Maude added, "Think of when you helped Mrs. Whiting when her husband was dying. You kept them in food. Afterwards, you had many women in the village taking turns helping them deal with their grief. You started and organized all that."

Jared, her doctor and mentor, followed up with, "Don't worry, Abby. You'll be on your feet and doing what you do so well soon. What's the old adage? You can't keep a good woman down."

"And," Thomas added, "Abby, don't forget. You'll be really free to help Jared and anyone else. I'll be gone for quite a while doing the state's business. You helped me so much these last few months. Now it's your turn to deal out your magic potion of goodness always at the exact time it is needed. The community and its welfare are in your hands."

"My goodness! You all have a voice in this. Thank you for your good thoughts and reminders. I just need to get better faster.

"Well, Big Sis," her baker, cook, and brother Tarrant started, "You have taken care of everyone all your life. Remember, how you wanted to be a doctor like Pa? Maybe you couldn't attain that, but you have been available to anyone who needs you. Pa and Jared have said many times how they couldn't have taken care of their patients without your help."

"That's right, Abby. Your father said it, and I've said it many times. If I haven't told you lately, I'm sorry. Many of my patients ask about you because they know about your fall. They are concerned, and many want you back up and, on your feet, where you are your happiest."

"That's so nice, Jared. Thank you, but you've thanked me many times."

"Good. I'd say the way you're feeling and gaining your strength, it will be only a couple weeks before you are totally on the mend. Each day, try to do a little more than the day before. You'll be ready for anything by spring."

"Ah, I remember what I wanted to ask you, though." Tarrant said as he quickly tilted his head backwards and drained his coffee cup.

Their family group stared at him, wondering who he wanted to question.

"I wasn't here at the time of the Dakota troubles. You know Sarah and I were back in Vermont when I enlisted to do my part in our other rebellion. What was it, Sis, what had you found out that persuaded you the town needed a fort around the Congregational Church? You know like Hod referred to last fall?"

The family faces turned to Abigail. She in turn looked at Thomas who also showed surprise by raising one of his eyebrows.

"Oh, my, I don't know how to explain what happened. You, dear Jessie Maude, were born back in January so that was way back in 1862," Abigail said, looking at her daughter. "It had been a sizzling summer, and when the Longworths, you know, in Corinna, invited us down for a few days in early August, Thomas said we could all use a break. He went to the barn and told the hired man he was in charge for a few days. I promised I'd be back before Sunday morning so he could go to church with the family in the morning. I came back up to the house, took a quick bath, and we loaded up the wagon and took off."

Abigail continued telling the story of how the lovely vacation gave them some relief. She also said that before they left to go home, she wanted to take a walk down to the lake through some of the woods. Thomas had joined her while Phoebe Longworth and her girls watched over their napping baby, Maude .

The late afternoon breeze in the cool dark forest could not compete with the black swarms of mosquitoes. She and Thomas tried to fend off the insects by waving their arms until they gave up and turned back.

"Now, what I am about to tell you, stays here around this table, all right?" Abigail lifted her hand and looked at everyone. "Everyone knows the basic story about how Thomas and I persuaded the town to build a fortress around the Congregational Church, but what I'm going to tell you truly needs to stay here. Promise?" Abigail looked at each of her family and waited for head nods. "Well, just as we turned to run out of the woods, we felt the earth trembling. Thomas grabbed my hand to pull me out faster, but I held him back. The quaking steadied to a rhythm. I told Thomas to stay where he was. I wanted to go up and around the path, and I'd be right back."

Thomas chuckled as he said, "I hung onto a tree and asked her if she'd lost her mind. I had no idea what was causing the earth to tremble like it was except for it being an earthquake."

"Are you sure it wasn't?" Tarrant asked.

"I knew it wasn't so I moved with the beat and followed my instincts. I didn't have any fear at that moment. I panicked afterwards," Abigail confessed. "Later, I laughed it off, but I knew it was strange and scary, let me tell you." she added. "Well, I came upon a rise in the earth. You know like many of the Indian mounds around the area, only larger—about five feet high and seventy-five to a hundred feet round. It rests right close to the edge of Clearwater Lake."

"Mother! I've heard about some of this, but not all of it. Pa felt safe where he was and let you wander away? I'm amazed," Maude stated, looking at her father.

Thomas laughed again and gave his daughter a wink before adding, "I wouldn't exactly say I felt safe where I was. But I've had to follow a few of your ma's hunches before, so I didn't question too much until she came back."

"I had a strong sense something would take place soon. I thought I felt drums beating and feet pounding all the way around the mound and on down to the lake. What was strange though was the river water wasn't affected. It lapped its way on in its east-northeasterly direction. I walked back to the hilly rise and stepped to the top. While I swayed to the beat, I thought I heard chatter."

Abigail looked at Thomas again. He bobbed his head in her direction, folded his napkin, laying it on the plate, and reached for the coffee pot. This told Abigail, he knew he was in for a long sit at the table.

"Alright, let me explain as best as I can. From little on, I've been able to … um … 'know,' well, to know, something was about to happen."

"You mean like when you were about ten, and you told Pa you knew Grandma Robinson was going to die? She did, the next morning, remember?" Mary said.

Surprised, Abigail looked at her sister. "How did you know? You were too little to realize she died."

"Oh, Abby, come on. We all know about your powers," Tarrant said.

"What? What do you mean about my 'powers'? I don't have any special powers. What do you mean, Tarrant?"

"He's teasing, Abby. Don't mind him." Thomas said.

"I'm sorry, Abby, and my choice of words, but seriously, you think we don't know you have a special gift."

"I don't understand? I've never proclaimed I had a gift if that is what it's called."

"Nathaniel told me," Mary interjected. "Mother and Pa never kept it a secret either, especially, when you knew ahead of time when someone died."

Abigail blurted out, "Of course, Nate would let it slip. I suppose he was sarcastic about it too."

Mary answered, "No, Abby, he wasn't. But I think you're making too much of this. You have something. You should be happy about it," Mary said. "I picked up on it all when I was little. I never had any insight. I tried though. When I was little, I pretended to be Cinderella's godmother. I remember trying hard to conjure up a doll I 'd seen down at Camp's Store. I'd squeeze my eyes shut tightly and then think hard about it," she laughed.

Everyone laughed, including Abigail, which calmed her edginess. She replied, "But I don't have it like that. I can't conjure up anything like with witchcraft. Out of the blue, I'll just know things. At other times I'd hear or 'see' things.' I can't explain it, and I can't ask for it. It just happens. I know Pa and I talked about it too. He said his mother, Grandma Robinson, had a special gift as well. She always said it was a gift of prophesy from God and expected to help others. But I'm not sure that's what I have."

Mary shook her head in agreement. "Abigail, no doubt you have a gift of some kind. You've always tempered it with wisdom …"

Jared interjected. "I'm sorry to cut in but all of us need to think back to a few years ago. If you, Abby, hadn't had such a need to get down to Corinna again to check on the Townsends, Jane might not have had a friend to trust in during her trials after she murdered the handyman who also raped her. You, too, T. C., you went with her because you and old John were friends. You'd lived close to each other over in Clear Lake before they moved down to Clearwater Lake."

"True, Jared. The whole Townsend family came from close to where I grew up in Pennsylvania. Before they got married, I saw how John treated Jane. I knew John had a crush on his young wife. Jane acted like she really enjoyed his company too even though she was so young. I figured their marriage would work out—that is until we got down to their farm minutes after Jane hacked Dunham nearly to death."

"Willian or Will Dunham was the name of the hired man, Thomas," Abigail said. As soon as we got close to our turn to go down their long driveway, I told Thomas to go faster. I felt something was terribly wrong."

"Right, right, Abby. Then we learned John told Jane to leave his house. He told me she hung onto his leg and begged him to believe her. He called himself an old fool for thinking she could love him an old man. If Abby hadn't had such a feeling to get down there as fast as we could, we'd never have known the problems they were having. We stayed until the Wright County sheriff took Jane away and the doctor got there to help Dunham," Thomas said.

"Don't forget you two told Mary and me that John Townsend was strangling his wife when you came around the corner of their yard."

Excitedly, Thomas replied, "Yes, we saw him with his hands around her neck just as we pulled into the yard. Abigail couldn't wait for the carriage to halt. She jumped down and ran to them."

"Jared, jumped and twisted my ankle but I wouldn't stop for the pain. As soon as I got close, I began hitting John on the shoulders and back. Thomas grabbed his arms and pulled them around to his back. I half-carried Jane to the porch steps . I told John's daughter Augusta, who was fussing over Dunham, to bring some water. Later, I thought about that. It was like Dunham wasn't there. I had ignored a bleeding man. It was like I was supposed to be there for Jane."

Thomas joined in, "It was an awful morning. I'd never manhandled anyone like I did John. He was a friend, almost like a father to me, and yet, he was out of control. And Dunham laid there in pools of blood and the ax by his side."

Both Abigail and Thomas quietly sat there for a few moments. The rest of the family respected their silence.

Abigail was the first to speak again. "Remember, Thomas, John told you Dunham and Jane were having a liaison and John believed it? I'm glad I got there when I did. You know her folks are out east. Except for her short marriage to John, she has had nothing but trouble since she came to Minnesota. John's children didn't cozy up to Jane much. They thought she was there for his money. I s tried to be a friend. I have felt that feeling of aloneness myself in the past."

"She weren't much older than me, Ma! When they came into town and stopped here, Pa would take John out to see the hogs. Jane seemed nervous when John wasn't around. He seemed to soothe her and make her feel protected."

"Poor thing," Mary said. "You said she and her first husband had divorced because he would beat her up when he came home drunk."

Abigail shook her head affirmatively. "Which she said was all the time. So, when she met John, the two seemed to need each other. John's first wife had died a few years before."

Thomas nodded as he puffed to get his pipe going. Soon he added, "After I saw them together, I had the same feeling. This whole situation was insane. I wish I had known sooner that they were having trouble, but we had been so busy on our own farm, we couldn't have taken any time off to go down on a visit until then and obviously, it was too late."

"After she had a couple sips of water, I asked her what happened. She didn't respond, just stared off," Abigail said, staring off into space like her younger friend.

"The sheriff arrived and a reporter came with him. He was a young kid without good sense. Thomas gave him a brief synopsis of who was lying on the ground and how the whole ordeal took place. Abruptly, he started asking Jane the same questions I was going to ask. She still wasn't talking. He walked over to John and asked how he could have let this whole act go on as long as it did. I thought that was a good question, but then he came back to Jane. After a while, she started crying, waves of tears and anger. We all watched in shock as she got up from the stoop, ran to the lake, and hopped into the boat. The sheriff ran after her, like we all did. She rowed and rowed until she tuckered out and came back to shore. The sheriff grabbed hold of her and slapped the handcuffs on her."

Abigail picked up where she left off. "Only then did we hear some of the rest of the story, though. That kid reporter had more courage than sense. As if he were an official from Wright County, he began questioning her again and the sheriff took notes. Apparently, Jane said the handyman had set his hopes on John's daughter Augusta. Being only fifteen, the young girl liked Will Dunham's attention too. Jane saw nothing but problems with this relationship and told Dunham to lay off or she'd tell John what was going on.

"By now, I took over asking most of the questions, although more soothingly. Slowly, got up to the part where John had told her to leave his house. I asked why. Jane said Dunham had told John they had had a tryst. She told John, "It were no tryst, John. He took advantage of me in the barn last week. I would have told you, God knows I wanted to, but you two were such good friends. So, John believed Will and told her so. She admitted Dunham wanted Augusta and vowed he'd do anything to get her. Why couldn't he see this? Jane said she fell to the ground, grabbing him around his lower legs and pleading with him. John kicked her away. She got up and walked ahead of him to the gate and grabbed the ax that was leaning against it. Jane hollered, 'Maybe now, Will Dunham, you'll get off our land.' She threw the ax at him, nicking his arm. He tried to pick it up in time, but she had it back in her hand. He pushed her to the ground, but Jane said she became angrier than ever. She looked at the reporter and said, 'Who wouldn't go mad if your husband had kicked you out of your own home and didn't believe that his own daughter were at risk of getting Dunham's attention? I had had enough. I went after him like a madwoman, nearly axed him to death by going for his neck.

"It sure is a tangled mess of bad memories," Abigail added, shaking her head. "Sadly, I can remember all that. Of course, it was only a couple years ago."

Jared replied, "Without your testimony, Abby, Jane would still be in jail for murder because Will Dunham died the next day. Because of your account of the incident, the judge pronounced her Temporarily Insane instead of guilty of murder."

"No one's a winner here. John could have been, and probably should have been arrested for attempting to murder Jane," Thomas rationalized. "Instead, most everyone believed him. They all assumed he had gone love crazy." He shook his head. "Now he's dead too. Jane will be out of the asylum soon, according to a letter Abby received. She has a sister living in Wisconsin whose husband said she could come live with them for a while."

Maude interjected, "That's so kind of him," she said sardonically. "The wife shouldn't need her husband's permission to invite someone into their home."

Abigail saw everyone stare at her daughter. "I understand what you are saying, Maude. I suppose she did. We women are still facing unfair treatment, like Jane. We have no rights but what our fathers and husbands give us. John was never accused of trying to kill his wife. Why? Because the sheriff didn't see him with his hands around her neck. We saw it and said so. But the sheriff held to his ways and didn't ask John about his own behavior. Yet, because Jane admitted to nearly killing Dunhan, and eventually he died, they might have thrown her in prison for the rest of her life. In the court's eyes, she got off easy."

"Again, Abby, you were there at the right time. This is what we started talking about earlier. Your special ability or gift, whatever anyone wants to call it, has empowered you," Mary replied. She added, "Think of the babies, you've saved, Abby. Sometimes, and again I say, in the nick of time."

"Exactly. You'd get a hunch a mother was suffering and off you'd go," Jared reminded her.

"True, but my patients or clients are always on my mind, and I know their conditions. So, when I follow a 'hunch,' I don't see it as something special. Maybe I am being sensitive to their needs."

Mary responded, "I'm glad we're family here so I can talk freely. Jared's always been open, honest, and plain speaking. So along with what I know and he tells me, I can say your patients appreciate everything you tell them to do. You know how to make a mother-to-be more comfortable. You give them sound medical advice—what to eat, what not to eat, the right herbs to calm their nerves and to help them feel better faster. I know you helped me throughout my period of melancholy. Abigail, you have to accept the fact you have been blessed with wisdom."

"I hope, as I'm nearing sixty-one, I have some wisdom." She had a quick ghostly vision of her youth, of her competing against Lucy Webbers and winning by cheating. *So many regrets. Maybe Lucy deserved it, but I was so immature. How many times I've asked God to forgive me for that! Now she is on her own tough journey.* "And, because we talked about it before, I don't see anything that tells me some person is dying, seriously." Abigail looked at Tarrant and then Mary. "Seriously, I have a whiff of flowers, a mixture of lilies, wild roses, even lilacs and I can tell someone is about to die. Except in Grandma Robinson's case, I most often don't know in advance who it is. But it's always someone we know very well. Remember George Spaniel, back home? I smelled sweet violets. That could have been because Pa and I were treating him with tincture of violet because of his cough and gout. Seriously, I seldom know beforehand when these little situations happen." Abigail looked around the table and finally rolled her eyes and said, "I guess I've proved myself wrong by talking long enough to prove you're right. I guess, maybe, I have a wee gift. Unfortunately, I'm only sometimes alert to why and what."

Tarrant clapped his hands as everyone laughed and joined in on the clapping. He spoke up, adding "And she's always had to think it through 'her way.'"

"Oh, that's not fair, Little Brother. You too were always trying to push Ma and Pa over the edge. You were the baby and a boy. You got away with a lot more than Mary or I did."

"That's right. I also had to watch over you while Mother sewed. Man, you were better than Nathaniel when digging up trouble. Oh, T. C. would you have loved to have seen him riding one of your beautiful, prize -winning hogs. That hog bucked him as if it were a mule. He lay in the um … what did he call that? Oh, I kinda' remember ... pud-mud. Unfortunately, Pa went after Tarrant with a broom because all the pigs got out of the fence in the yard. He went to swat him, and the broom just broke in half. No reason why either. Pa and you had a good laugh over that one."

"Okay, okay. Anyway, let's finish about the fortress around the Congregational Church." Tarrant insisted.

Mary added, "That's a good idea. I'm getting a little tired and need to go home soon. Nothing major, just tired."

"I'm sorry, Mary. We can finish this story another day," Abigail suggested.

A loud and in-unison, "NO!" surprised Abigail and made her husband reply, "Mrs. Porter, you have the floor."

"Well, then. Let's see, where did I leave off? I told you about the weird river water?"

Tarrant sat back. His arms wrapped around the back of his head and teetering or "riding" his chair, as Abigail often said. He then replied, "Affirmative. Keep this story moving."

"I got back from the looking at the lake and quickly on the beat hefted myself to the top of the mound. Once up there, I looked around, and although I saw nothing physical, I felt something dangerous was about to take place. As I stood on this ancient and hallowed tribal ground, I sensed those buried under my feet. The group made noise like their drums and feet were beating a war dance and warning me of something. Like pictures we have all seen of Indians in their war garb, I imagined seeing many gyrating to the music and songs, angrily and determinedly. Were they calling all their brothers and sisters to join in the fight against those who had pushed them too far like Big Chief in Washington and all his men who had broken so many promises and treated them so unfairly?"

Abigail looked around the table. Eyes were on her, as if everyone knew she had more to tell. She did, but she had to get to the hardest part. Knowing at the time she could not tell this story to anyone but Thomas. Nor could she tell Jared or Mary, not even her dear friend Nancy Farwell. For now, she could not tell even her father who came to stay with them for a while. Abigail felt relieved to confide in her husband because, he in part, experienced what she had.

"After I met up with Thomas, I showed him a white feather that landed on my head when I stood on the mound."

"Yeah, I showed Abigail one as well. Once the earth stopped shaking, I walked a ways down the path, but I remembered Abby told me to stay back. Now, I know you can't believe I listened to my wife," Thomas said as he winked. "But when I turned back, I saw the eagle feather lying on a bush and picked it up. I showed it to her once we got going."

"It was all so strange. The river lapped calmly, no sign of an earthquake down there. The ground beat as if in rhythm to the drums during a war dance. And then there were the two white feathers. Didn't know what to say to Longworths, and they never mentioned anything out of the ordinary had happened either. So, we made our rounds with thankyous, handshakes, and hugs. Then we left."

"From what I learned in my trading days with the Sioux near the border of Canada, Abby's warming was a sign of Wakan, messages from the Great Spirit that show up now and then." Thomas added, "We had a lot to ponder after we picked up Maudy and headed home."

"And ponder we did on that long ride home! I knew I couldn't tell anyone about the incident out in Corinna—none of the male leaders, nor the females no matter how they said they respected me. And I would be suspicious of anyone else who had a crazy experience like I had," Abigail said. "But something was up, and I was worried."

"All I thought about was what had happened out there," Thomas said. "You know there was lots of talk and suspicions in the area. John Farwell and I had met up in St. Cloud a couple weeks before all this. We talked prices of rye and wheat. Then he got around to telling how a few of the Dakotans were being blamed for taking things in Maine Prairie. Eggs were one thing, but whole chickens, cows, and a few horses were missing. Their housewives had learned to always bake another loaf of bread, another cake or pie, and always be prepared to barter. But lately, I'd heard some scuttle-butt from our local farmers who were having other troubles.

The women spoke of their fears of being left alone in their homes because more than a couple strangers showed themselves in the doorway after farmers left for the fields in the morning. Sometimes up to a half dozen Dakotan walked into their houses and took what they wanted."

"Well, you know we got home from Corinna after dark, safe and sound, but tired. Thomas hauled in everything while I took Maude in and put her to bed. He joined me soon and I only had to get up once during the night to change Maudy. It wasn't until the next morning, Jared, you brought us the news about a group of settlers being murdered by a band down in Acton."

"It weren't long after that, a day and a half later, we heard news about the Lower Sioux Agency being attacked," Jared stated.

"And the rest is history," Thomas added.

"By Tuesday, we read about the atrocities in the southwestern part of the state and about the skirmishes close by. Nothing too serious yet, but we knew only time could or would tell whether local attacks would take place." Abigail reflected. "All of a sudden, I knew the incident out at Longworths was a warning for me to act. I told Thomas the town had to build a fort or a fortress for those in the countryside and maybe even for us in town to take shelter."

Thomas shook his head as he remembered the situation. "I thought we might need to come up with a plan to persuade the village council to act when they had a meeting that afternoon. Everyone knew and respected Abby, but we both knew a few of the men would be hard pressed to do anything. They hate change but especially if the change costs money."

"I suspected a few wouldn't see a need, but I was determined to get it done. I took the buggy the next morning and stopped to pick you up, Mary. I know at first," Abigail looked at her sister, "you were startled and didn't want to acknowledge we might need a place of shelter such as a fort."

"Well, first, the word fort scared me," Mary interjected. "All we have read and talked about was our nationals crisis. Our own men like Fiske, Webster, Tollington, and your Cassius, they had need of forts. Not us! Plus, I wondered who would man these forts with most men serving our country in the South already. Yet, the more Abby talked the more convinced I was we would have trouble soon."

Abigail agreed and shook her head. "So, we went to talk with a few of our good friends. Husbands were gone to work, which is what I wanted. Without a word to anyone about what had transpired in Corinna Township, I explained my case that we needed a place of refuge just in case. Everyone agreed we all knew people living in the country who might need a place of safety. Their decision was they'd be there at the meeting if I'd do the talking."

"Yep," Thomas piped in, "and I drove her to the meeting, went in alone while she waited for the Clearwater women. I told the members we were going to have some town citizens join us. At the time, having town people join our meeting was a normal occasion so it didn't cause them any grief. But when five women walked in, Maria Walker, Adelia Whiting, Ann Whiting, Mary, and then Abigail, they knew something was up for discussion."

"I started to talk once the meeting was called to order and all the normal business was dealt with. I started with, 'Well, gentlemen, what are you going to do to about our current situation? How are you planning on keeping your families in the community safe if we are under attack? How about our neighbors? What responsibility do you feel towards them?"

Thomas sat nodding his head in agreement while Abigail explained what she said to the village council before adding, "She came out with both barrels. You should have seen Simon Stevens's mouth when his wife Katie walked into the room."

"I figured a few other ladies would join us if they could find babysitters. Many of the men were also at the meeting. I must admit I shocked myself with what tumbled out of my mouth."

"But she played on their common sense so they eventually came to her way of thinking."

"I'm glad Cousin Francis was there, though, as he said, 'Good idea, Abby,' and offered $5 to be invested in posts. Then Pastor Sterrett from the Methodist Church suggested we use the Congregational Church for the fort since it was sitting empty until it got a minister. I think when you offered up another $10, Thomas, we nearly had an auction going. Deacon Walker offered to do the cutting and sawing of the logs for the fortress."

Jared joined in on the conversation. "She was a browbeater, for sure. I didn't get there right away, but Mary's eye contact coerced me into coughing up another few dollars to help in building the fence and fort."

Thomas added, "I think we had more than enough money since we had free lumber stacked up drying from floating down the river earlier in the year, so money really wasn't the issue. Just persuading a few of the slow movers on the council was the problem. We all know Hod and a few others aren't swift in his decision making. Stevens, I knew, would come around, but the others I wasn't so sure about. If it's not their dime, they share little concern."

"I suppose I should've driven out to get Hod's wife Miranda, but I felt I could get enough rope from the town women. This might have gotten done a little faster."

"I think I got home about one in the morning," Thomas added. Lots of arguing back and forth as the meeting went on until after midnight. First on why I knew after the women left, Jared and I had to become the force that'd keep things going." Thomas said, nodding to his brother-in-law. "Finally, that concluded with an affirmative decision when you started quoting scripture on how we need to look out for our brothers and sisters, especially further out in the country. Everyone decided the church was a perfect site for shelter. It being so late, we adjourned until the morning to commence the building of the fort."

Abigail added, "And it was done in time. Within a couple weeks, quite a few country farmers, friends and strangers, found shelter in the Congregational Church. Town men had even planned an escape route in case of attack. They dug a hole through the dirt cellar that led to the bottom of the hill, which provided a means to escape to the river. Someone earlier had provided a boat for them to row to safety. Besides with so many of our state's men being called up to help with the rebellion in our nation over a year before, we were now faced with another type of rebellion. This time we were vulnerable with only a few young men to help guard our towns, farmlands, countryside, and state. However, Minnesota demanded more. They soon found others to help in this fight for our lives and livelihoods."

For a while, the family sat quietly, either in contemplation or meditation. Abigail noticed her brother grab the coffee pot and move from the table.

Mary said, almost too quietly, "Jared, I think it's time to go home. Thank you, Abby and T. C., for such a nice visit. Thank you, Tarrant, for such a wonderful supper, just as the doctor ordered," she added.

As if on cue, Maude had stood up to gather coats. She stood waiting while her aunt struggled to pull on her boots. Jared bent to help her, stepping closer to her so she could use his knee to push on one boot at a time.

Shocked over Mary's obvious weakness, Abigail asked, "Are you going to be warm enough during your ride home, or maybe you should sleep here tonight?"

"No, don't worry. We'll be fine. You forget, dear sister, we live next door," Mary said as she with her husband's help stood up to accept Maude's offering of her coat.

With another round of goodnights and Tarrant informing all of them he would stay with T.C and Abigail to clean up the kitchen, the doctor and his wife, Abigail's dear, younger sister, walked out the door.

Although Abigail stood up and started scraping plates, Maude suggested and Tarrant insisted she rest in the parlor. Thomas had piled on enough clothes and coats to go out to check on the livestock before settling in for the night.

She walked into her bedroom and opened the drawer of the small table by her bed and pulled out her diary. Abigail knew she had not written in it for some time. Like she promised, she also grabbed her father's medical book to search for something to help Mary.

After grabbing a pencil from her husband's little corner table in the kitchen, Abigail carried everything to his chair again to take up her own counsel, her writings, and her father's medical book.

Laying the book aside, promising to search in a few minutes, she browsed through the pages of her diary, the book she had woven together. From childhood to adulthood, how her writing changed! She recalled returning home with her father after joining him on one of his house calls. Pressing firmly and slowly, Abigail wrote what she remembered from the visit. Her handwriting exhibiting deep concentration and a struggle to spell correctly certain terms like *bilious attack* her father had used to explain a patient's stomach condition or *Angina Membranacea,* which was *diphtheria.* This disease had affected quite a few Stowe's little children's throats, often causing them to suffocate. As she grew older and became more confident, she could even abbreviate Latin terms.

Abigail perused a few of her journal entries. Some read like the dreams that had awakened her from her concussion into bits and pieces of reality. However, from her first to the last entry, she had penned honest accounts as she confronted them. She wrote about her childhood, teen years, and her work, from childhood, through her teen years, along her with her father. She documented her struggles in her marriage to George, raising Cassius mostly by herself while he chased butterflies in California, nearly committing suicide from want but dying soon after from dysentery. Abigail also wrote about starting a new life in Clearwater, giving birth to two more children, losing her second son, seeing her child Cassius go off to war, and finally, falling at Thomas's celebration.

With book in hand, Abigail weaved through the interlacing twists and turns of her life like a labyrinth, encountering both dark and bright moments. At times, she saw only one event at a time, like peering through the wide end of a spyglass and seeing moments, tiny moments, of deep pain or tremendous joy. But when she looked through the narrow end to the magnifying lens, she saw her life laid out before her so far. She discerned patterns that connected her past to her present. From her early days in Stowe to her eventual settlement in Clearwater, Abigail saw how each experience had shaped her and given her purpose—and maybe some wisdom.

As she thought about the family conversation the evening before, Abigail decided she wanted to be done with war, never to think of it again. She hoped Thomas could be part of the creation of that wish now that he was a state legislator.

"What's this, Thomas?" Abigail asked. She looked up at him in surprise because he seldom bought her presents unless it was her birthday, and this year he forgot with all the hubbub with the election. She untied the white bow wrapped around a small square box.

"Something I was going to give you Monday before I took off for St. Paul. I want you to enjoy it now and admire it before I go."

Abigail eagerly lifted the cover to the box. An exquisite cameo rested on a white silk puff. "Oh, Thomas! The detail, the white cameo built on pastel green background. Thank you, but why?"

"I never thought about it until you were sick. Your father and your husband George gave you one, but I never did."

Abigail looked at the cameo—no helmet head. The woman's hair was puffy with sweet waves and a few ringlets, like she wore the night of Clearwater's celebration for Thomas.

"We usually give each other practical presents. This is charming."

"I think it is time for a change. Besides, I wanted to give you something that keeps us connected because I may be gone more than usual."

"We don't need anything special to connect us. However, this present is very special. The colors are divine, Thomas, thank you," Abigail said as she patted his hand. Surprised and slightly embarrassed at his attention, she asked, "Would you attach it in the back?"

Thomas took the necklace and connected the two ends. He turned her around carefully and laid the cameo flat on her neck. He took her hands like the day they married, sweetly and tenderly. Thomas kissed her mouth and then her forehead before pulling her closely to him in a hug.

The two said nothing. They didn't have to.

Epilogue

Abigail waited for everyone to leave Acacia Cemetery after Mary's funeral. Thomas and Maude had hopped into Jared's carriage to get home. Thomas called a quick meeting with the Clearwater village council to discuss a road issue he needed to clear up before he went back to St. Paul Sunday evening. Maude wanted to visit with her cousins, Isabella, and Fanny who had just lost their mother. Abigail wanted to stay out here for a while yet.

"Mary, Mary," Abigail choked. Her tears falling again, she wiped them away with her gloves. "I wish we could have found out sooner what was causing all your stomach problems It was too late by the time the specialist diagnosed you with cancer. I'm so sorry."

Abigail stared at the coffin. *You were my best friend. You knew me the best.* More tears spilled down her cheeks.

Abigail had spent the last few months nursing her sister. Whenever Thomas came home on a break, he knew where to find her and Maude. Their lives had changed; their families' lives had changed. They went from hope because they found a specialist, to some hope they caught the malady in time, then to no hope as Mary received no comfort from her medicine, no sign of healing, and the specialist's headshaking verdict of finality. When Jared got Mary to swallow a spoon of morphine, Abigail nodded her approval. In her last days, everyone, including Tarrant and Cassius and their families, gathered around her and shared blank stares with each other as they took turns sitting beside her.

When Mary breathed her last faint breath, Jared took his stethoscope and listened to her heart. Then he laid his head on her chest. Mary's girls moaned, "Oh, Mother."

Abigail sought solace on the Wheelock back porch. *How ironic the morning is so beautiful—so alive! Birds sing and flit from tree to tree. The Mississippi sparkles and laps its way south to*

Louisiana. Inside, the Wheelock house, though, it is black with pain and death.

There at the cemetery, often dark and as Maude said, "kind of spooky out there at times," looked different this afternoon. Autumn leaves fell gently all around, and the sun burned bright between the nearly empty branches, giving Abigail's little scene a golden glow.

It was as if Mary, her little sister was saying, "You've spent enough time caring for me."

A retired English instructor, Cynthia Frank-Stupnik holds a B.A. in English/Education and an M.A. in English. She has authored *Steppes to Neu-Odessa,* a historical biography of Yankton County, South Dakota; *Postcards from the Old Man,* her memoir about growing up near the Mississippi River; *Passages,* a book of faith-based poetry; *Around Clearwater*, a pictorial history and biography about her hometown, Clearwater, Minnesota; Scr*uples & Drams*, *Pins & Needles*, and now, *Where Two Rivers Meet*, a prequel and the third in her Minnesota Main Street Women series. The recipient of numerous literary awards, Stupnik's writing reflects her faith, family, women's rights, and the varied landscapes that tug at her heart.

www.ingramcontent.com/pod-product-compliance
Lightning Source LLC
LaVergne TN
LVHW050626100826
845148LV00011B/1751

9780788428210